SHAKESPEARE'S
DON QUIXOTE

ISBN 978-0-9506715-1-2

First published in Great Britain in 2011 by Book Now Publishing

ROBIN CHAPMAN

SHAKESPEARE'S DON QUIXOTE

a novel in dialogue

BOOK NOW

For Boo

Note

The first part of Don Quixote appeared in English in 1612. A year later a play called Cardenio was played at court by Shakespeare's theatre company, the King's Men. This play was then registered for publication as by William Shakespeare and John Fletcher but the text is lost.

The story of Cardenio triggers much of the action of Don Quixote, Part One and reads like a ready-made Renaissance comedy in which a quartet of star-crossed lovers encounters a lunatic would-be knight-errant and his sceptical squire.

John Fletcher is known to have borrowed at least seven plots from Cervantes and my belief is that, as dramaturge-designate to the King's Men, he presented Cardenio's story as a plot on a plate to Shakespeare and that they worked on it together as they did on Henry VIII and The Two Noble Kinsmen.

Shakespeare's Don Quixote is a novel in dialogue creating what might have been. Within it the lost play of Cardenio is reconstructed and played out in front of the reader while subject to the scrutiny of Shakespeare, Fletcher and Cervantes. Appropriately they soon become involved in the action - on stage and on the page.

Prologue

Welcome to the theatre of my mind. Think of it as I do. As a black box. A space in which the past can become the present at the turn of a phrase or the drop of a hat.

You could, if you wish, envisage it as a fringe venue set up in a redundant pumping station perhaps. Or in an obsolete bus depot if you prefer. I certainly see it as somewhere on the edge of somewhere else. The only bright thing about it could be the flyers that have led you here, and the posters outside announcing the show: *Shakespeare's Don Quixote.*

So, welcome to this off-beat but expectant place with its creaky old seats ramped up in front of the flat floor stage, second-hand lighting equipment and matt black walls.

But before we begin, allow me to ask what's really brought you here? The show hasn't been reviewed as yet so was it the title caught your eye? I hope so. I meant it to intrigue, amuse. To get you to ask: how on earth did Shakespeare come to write *Don Quixote*? He didn't, did he? To which I can only reply, you're absolutely right. That work was indeed written by someone else but even so my title is accurate enough. And who better to explain why this should be than William Shakespeare? In person. After all he was there, and today he's as much alive as he ever was, so let's leave the stage to him.

Enter Shakespeare looking very much like himself - provided the pudding-faced portrait on the front page of the first collected edition of his plays is to be whole-heartedly believed. But the leather-patched tweeds he's wearing appear to be more of our age than his. Or should I say they have about them a timeless air? As do his lovingly preserved brown brogues. In other words he would seem, at first glance, to be a middle-aged country gentleman who never goes anywhere without his dog - an English setter, known as Jessop.

1

Two things qualify this conventional impression however. One, the gold earring in his left ear; the other, his favourite walking stick - the gift of an Irish admirer - a highly polished, grotesquely knobbly, blackthorn shillelagh. And the first thing he does before speaking to us is to stab this monstrosity in my direction. At where I've just gone off.

SHAKESPEARE
Who on earth was that? No one I know. (to Jessop) Sit, there's a good dog.

Jessop sits.

SHAKESPEARE
And what in heaven's name did he imagine he was talking about? Announcing my *Don Quixote*? As if I'd ever lay claim to that! I've got far too much respect for that lunatic gentleman and for his distinguished creator. For Michael Cervantes, as ambitious Jack Fletcher used to call him. More of whom later, by the way. But had I been tempted to write novels - not that I was - where was the money in those in my day? - you'd have seen me following faithfully in that Spaniard's footsteps. His book looked at the world very much as I had but talked about it quite differently. Here was another way to go, it seemed. Where was I? Oh, yes, still entranced by his knight and squire. What a double act! Pure theatre on the page crying out for adaptation. Jack Fletcher - we'd recently taken him on as company dramaturge - came up especially to Stratford to persuade me to put the pair of them on stage. He brought the novel with him - it had just come out in English. Read that! he said. You must! Especially where the knight and squire bump into four young lovers. It's plot perfect! Well, by that time I'd come to admire Jack's nose for dramatic potential if not his cocksure pushiness. But to be fair, back in 1612, he was still a young Turk on the make. As I had once been. Whilst I, at almost fifty, I was feeling much older and more uncertain than I cared to admit. Do I hear someone laughing? Now why should that be?

Shakespeare, knowing perfectly well why, turns to look down at his dog who has produced a large, pink erection.

SHAKESPEARE

I thought as much. Jessop always does that when I speak of Jack
Fletcher. Fancies him no end, despite Jack detesting him. Not a
dog man - Jack. Put it away, Jessop, there's a good boy.

Jessop obeys this command but hangs out his tongue suggestively
instead. If dogs could wink, he would.

SHAKESPEARE

To cut history short I read *Don Quixote* there and then. Straight
off, straight through. And I was charmed, almost rejuvenated.
Was there ever such a diverting mid-life crisis as the one
depicted there? By the time the old boy had decided various
windmills were forty giants I told Jack I'd work with him on
the dramatisation. And for thanks I got one of those smirks of
his which make you feel predictable, tolerated. The bumptious
have much to answer for, haven't they? Still my consolation is
that eventually they get asked, don't they? I knew you'd agree,
said Jack, still grinning. At which - pulling what rank I'd got
left - I made a proviso, telling him he'd have to do the spade
work. That is, construct the overall romance action of the play,
writing it all up in appropriate verse, naturally. Thereby leaving
me to do the comic subplot in prose, of course. What this meant
in practice was that Jack had to invent a whole new set of
variations on the eternal theme of carnal desire frustrated - or
not - by social propriety as experienced by the usual foursome of
sex mad teenagers in pastoral surroundings of a quasi-classical
nature. A literary and theatrical convention I felt I'd somewhat
worn out. Jack agreed, and I had a fine time turning Don Quixote
and Sancho Panza into parts to be played by Dick Burbage and
Bob Armin. By November of that year the play was ready for its
first performance at Blackfriars but unfortunately I wasn't able
to get down to London to hear it - or as we say nowadays, see it.
It went well apparently. So well that it was chosen, along with a
revival of *The Tempest*, to be presented at court that Christmas.
Where, Jack said, it went even better. So much so - and this gives
you some measure of the play's success - the King commanded
us to perform it yet again, early the following year, at his
daughter's wedding. Jack's romance action enlivened by my
comic subplot, was thought spot on for this high-powered state
event at Whitehall, scheduled for St Valentine's Day 1613, when
the Princess Elizabeth Stuart was to marry Prince Frederick, the

Elector Palatine. This time I *was* able to attend and I must admit Jack and the company had done a more than decent job. His Majesty the King was pleased to be pleased, and Her Majesty the Queen was pleased to pass out under the table well before the end of Act One Scene Four. Being a Dane she was a notorious soak, of course, as I'm sure you know.

Jessop yawns hugely, eloquently, musically.

SHAKESPEARE
Manners, Jessop, I've nearly finished. And Jack will be here soon if the programme's anything to go by. So just think how you can embarrass him rather than me, all right?

Jessop wags his tail then barks.

SHAKESPEARE
Shush! (Jessop subsides.) Perhaps I should add that the play was then known as *Cardenio* - taking its title from the name of the juvenile lead, a highly sensitive youth who goes mad when he's cheated of his childhood sweetheart, Lucinda - a nice supporting role for the freshest, prettiest lad in our company. Whether what we are now about to experience will bear any resemblance to our *Cardenio*, I can't say. I'm as much in the dark as you are. Still it may be Jack can enlighten us further. Don't be put off by his appearance. He always dressed to impress. And if I know Jack he won't have allowed the afterlife to dull his fashion-sense. Come on, Jessop, heel.

Shakespeare and Jessop go. Enter John Fletcher. Jessop looks back, whines, then barks eagerly.

FLETCHER
(at Jessop) You bugger off you! Go on!
SHAKESPEARE
(off) Jessop! Heel!

As we might expect, Shakespeare's evocation of John Fletcher has been exact. Here he is in an electric blue, shot-silk suit of in your face Savile Row casualness, 60s-nostalgia flowered shirt, designer shades worn across the top of his well-cropped, well-gelled head, and handmade speed boots. Don't ask me what they are - just gawp and admire the metropolitan athleticism they imply. In other words he looks like a very successful playwright. Which he was, with some fifty-five plays to his credit either by himself, or in collaboration with such London luminaries as Francis Beaumont, Ben Jonson and, of course, Shakespeare. All of this achieved by the age of forty six when he died of the plague and sheer vanity. I say vanity because that invaluable gossip John Aubrey records Fletcher's death in 1625 as the consequence of his preferring to stay in town for what proved to be an only too final fitting with his tailor, rather than leave for the relative health and safety of East Anglia.

Fletcher and Francis Beaumont lived together at the start of their careers but quarrelled when Beaumont gave up the theatre to marry an heiress. According to Aubrey they lived "on the Bankside not far from the Play-house, both bachelors; lay together; had one wench in the house between them, which they did so admire; the same cloathes and cloake &c; between them." This sounds fun but I'm not quite sure what, in fact, it suggests. Were the boys bisexual? Admiring each other *and* the wench between them? Or were they gay and admired each other and their house instead? And did they dress identically or simply borrow each other's clothes? Aubrey can be as opaque as he is informative but even so he does present us with a pair of believable young men - a seventeenth century metrosexual show-biz couple. And it is, of course, as Beaumont's collaborator that Fletcher is now chiefly remembered, despite huge success in his own right, and with others such as Shakespeare. This is unfair on Fletcher but then history often is - especially literary history. And it has led me to wonder if this might have bothered him? Dramatically it would be helpful if it had. It would give his character a nice, resentful edge. What author cares for second billing? Especially stretched across four hundred years or so? But that's enough from me.

FLETCHER

Trust William to give you his lovable country gent act. *And* to bring his horrible dog with him. Yuk oh yuk. Am I to understand he was banging on about *Cardenio*? That play of ours it would seem is about to be resurrected here? Though how that can be I've no idea. The script got lost, you know. And that's something that's always struck me as rather spooky - given the play was massively, stupendously popular. It got revived over and over. Boffo wasn't in it. It grossed far more than the other shows I

worked on with William - stuff like *Henry VIII* and *The Two Noble Kinsman*, for instance. *Cardenio* was a real must see, kill for a seat, a stonker to die for. Of course William took all the credit. You should've seen him strut his stuff after the show at Whitehall! Embraced by the royal bride, toasted by His Majesty - like it was gut-wrenching. The Swan of Avon's swan song the King called it. No mention of me, natch. But then I'm used to that. Always have been. Look at me and Frank Beaumont. Look at the posters for this show. I don't exactly get my name up in lights here either, do I? No. Not even here. Wherever this is? Jeez. But don't let's get bitter let's just stay paranoid, shall we? (he takes breath) Right then. How it really was. Actually. In fact. And this has got to be strictly hush-hush, confidential, like between you, me and the duvet, ok? Working with William was no joke. No. No joke at all, right? Don't get me wrong, I'm not saying he wasn't, at least for the most part, affability in person, honeyed charm itself. He always was, always will be, ask anybody. By that time he'd more or less retired to Stratford of course, but he still liked to keep his hand in. But, oh, dear, oh, shit, the stuff he turned out! What was happening? His verse, his prose, both had started to stick in our actors' throats. They couldn't get his words out they were so impacted. His first thoughts couldn't move for his second thoughts. Context was forever losing out to subtext. We were getting garbage like, I quote:
   'As I belong to worship and affect
   In honour honesty the tract of everything
   Would by a good discourser lose some life
   Which action's self was tongue to.'
Sort *that* if you can! And then try getting its meaning across to an already gob-smacked audience on a hot afternoon at the Globe. So when Richard Burbage - only William ever called him Dick - when Richard insisted I take *Don Quixote* down to Warwickshire to persuade him we could make a play out of it together I said yes, sir, no, sir, three bags full, sir, *but. But, but, but!* But what? says our supreme actor-manager. And I say, this time I do all the verse, okay? That'll be the entire romance action - and William can just do the prose add ons - that'll be the comic relief - all right? Why? asks Richard. Because, sir, say I, because his prose will be easier to make sense of than his verse - if and when its head gets stuck up it own backside as tends to happen only too often these days, doesn't it? With William? Correct? Long pause for managerial reflection. And while Richard cogitates allow me

to ask you a question. Did William, by any perverse chance, tell you it was he who chose to do the subplot, leaving what he called the major romance action to me? If he did that's what he's always said. That's his official line on how it was with *Cardenio*. And it's totally untrue. Utter bollocks. What in fact happened was that William's initial reaction was to do the whole job himself. The lot! Oh yes! All of it! With me just as dogsbody script editor! Or scribe! Well, as you can imagine, we had quite a ding-dong about that. Like I hit the roof, right? Metaphorically speaking, I mean. You don't shout and scream with William. He doesn't do drama off stage. No, it was all iron fists in velvet gloves - the pair of us. And in the end I won, thank you very much, because Richard - after his pause for thought - had said to me as follows: Yes, Jack, he said, yes, on mature reflection I think it would be best, Jack, if you were to take overall charge on this one. Yes, you tell William - from me - he mustn't overdo things. Tell him I'd like him to apply himself purely and simply to the knight and squire. Since in my view they match his genius perfectly. Coming from me that should do it, especially if you indicate that I'm thinking I might play the knight. Provided I can lose some weight, of course. That should clinch it with him. We laughed and he was right. Richard's diplomacy won the day. I got total script control with William just doing the funnies. So you can put his version of the play's genesis down to old man's pride, poetical face-saving and history revamped to keep him on top as king of the literary castle. Or should I say queen? Don't laugh. But back to the finished farticle as played at court for that royal wedding. *Cardenio* was one of fourteen shows the King commanded us to present. Yes! Fourteen! The lads were stretched to the limit. Richard was like a ghost by the time he played Don Quixote on the 14th Feb. But that only made his performance all the more amazing. Awesome! I've never seen him better - never sadder, never funnier. And all thanks to me sorting out William's contribution which had been just as mind-bendingly inaccessible to your ordinary punter as I'd predicted it would be. After that - as said - the play did well, though the text wasn't licensed for publication for another forty years, would you believe? And even then never got into print apparently . So it's still just a one-off title with our names attached to it in the Stationers' Register as of 1653. By which time William and I were - how shall I say? - elsewhere. It could be the Cromwell thing had something to do with its non-publication possibly. Or not, who knows?

Dog barking off.

FLETCHER
  Hear that? Can't even keep his pooch in order, can he?

Jessop stops barking off.

FLETCHER
  Well, maybe. Sometimes. Where was I? Oh, yes, *Cardenio*. Latter-
  day miniscule history of. Hearsay has it the odd prompt copy
  survived in manuscript but that could be eighteenth century
  tittle-tattle. A character called Lewis Theobald claimed he had
  a copy which he adapted under the title *Double Falsehood*. It ran
  for ten nights at Drury Lane, I'm told. A decent run for those
  days. Theobald got duffed up by Alexander Pope for being a
  real dunce but this could be because Theobald proved to be a
  better editor of William's works than Pope was. Bitch Lit at its
  best. But that's all by the way. Mind you I love digressions -
  what writer doesn't? Anyway back to *Cardenio* as was. To our
  version, which, I flatter myself, did stay faithful to the original.
  Well, to that sequence which begins when Don Quixote - already
  deeply doolally - decides to go mad for love of Dulcinea, his
  oh so platonic non-squeeze. In imitation of such idiotic role
  models as Sir Amadis of Gaul and Don Orlando the Furious.
  What this meant in real terms was that he had to find a quiet
  spot where he could take his knickers off and do cartwheels -
  thus demonstrating that he was head over heels in love with
  his so-called Princess Dulcinea. At which crucial juncture who
  runs into him doing just this? You're right! Our hero, young
  Cardenio. But - dramatic irony - Don Quixote is only pretending
  he's disappointed in love whereas Cardenio actually is. And
  how! So much so that latent schizophrenia's been triggered in
  him by real betrayal, real deception. The interaction between
  them - and between others involved and similarly exercised
  - enabled me to flesh out the thrust of the drama - true love
  versus false love, sex versus sentiment. So our version or, let's
  hit the nitty-gritty, *my* version, dealt faithfully with the original
  material. I just hope that what we're about to sit through will do
  the same. See you later - in the bar if there is one.

Fletcher goes before Jessop re-enters at speed. He hurtles across
the stage barking, wagging, in hot pursuit of Fletcher.

SHAKESPEARE
(off) Jessop! Bad boy! Come back here!

Shakespeare enters in pursuit of Jessop. He's a bit puffed.

SHAKESPEARE
(hurriedly, to us) Jessop's a perfect gentleman except when it comes to Jack Fletcher. Jessop! I know what you're up to so stop it! This instant, sir! D'you hear?

Shakespeare has gone.

SHAKESPEARE
(off) Jack, I do apologise. Sit, Jessop! Sit, sir! That's quite enough from you!

Pause. Then a gentle guitar chord heralds a change of light.

Enter Miguel de Cervantes. He's considerably older than Shakespeare or Fletcher since he was sixty nine when he died. I think it would be helpful if he were provided with a chair to sit on. Oh, look, my thought's become the deed. Here's the stage manager with not just a chair but a glass of iced water for Cervantes to sip. How kind and how appropriate. It's as if Cervantes is now sitting in a public place you might still find somewhere in the heart of Spain. Somehow he seems to have brought the best of the Iberian peninsular with him.

Is it that crumpled linen suit - black, of course - that creates this impression? Together with that old cream shirt, black tie, black socks, black shoes? And that Panama hat which has known better days? He's surely in mourning? Most persons of a certain age in Spain used to be. Who for? His wife outlived him. His sister perhaps? He was very fond of Magdalena.

He sits very straight in a military sort of way. Hardly surprising - he's a grizzled veteran of many wars, real and literary. That's why he keeps his left hand discreetly tucked down at his side. Because it's not so much a hand as a lump. He lost most of it and much use of it in a battle long ago. If you like old soldiers' tales do ask him about that battle. If you don't, don't.

Cervantes sips his iced water then looks directly at us and smiles. What a smile! It warms us all.

CERVANTES

(in fluent, lightly accented English) I must say this present experience strikes me as a trifle unusual. For me to be making my appearance in what I'm obliged to describe as someone else's imagination. In the mind-set of an English person quite unknown to me. And then - or rather now - to find myself cast as a kind of additional chorus to a play based on a work of mine previously exploited by two other writers - one of whom I have heard of, but not the other. Most odd. Especially as it seems their particular play no longer exists. The whole affair strikes me as what literary souls call a layered concept but that isn't to say I dislike it. Quite the reverse. I like complexity provided its expressed simply. That said, I'm not sure I care to hear *Don Quixote* referred to as 'the original material.' A phrase as sharp as a media lawyer's pen. As a definition it seems to me to diminish what I did. I accept that the writing of a novel can be compared with designing and weaving a tapestry at one and the same time and that therefore *material* as a description could be said to be accurate enough. But only, to my mind, in a very limited way. And *original* is even trickier to cope with since it's a double meaning in itself. First defining something that already exists and next something unlike anything else - something quite new. Never seen or heard before: as in such phrases as "this novel is truly original." Of course authors in my day weren't expected to be original, no, we were expected to be good. As good as Homer, Virgil, Ovid. A challenge we had to accept. And so, in the hope of joining such elevated company, we imitated them. And now and again one or two of us succeeded. So, you see, in principle, I've no objection to others reworking my work - especially for the stage. I loved the theatre all my life but my love was not requited. Chiefly because I wasn't a born poet. Oh, I could versify readily enough. Who couldn't, in those days? But my verses never took flight. And verse in my time was as essential to the theatre as electricity is today. However, I did get some plays produced. And they weren't booed off the stage either. Nobody threw aubergines or other suggestive vegetables at the actors. No. I enjoyed what the French call a *succès d'estime*. That's to say some praise, no real money. Certainly not enough to feed me, my wife, my parents, my sisters, and Isabel, my natural daughter with a would-be actress. At least in that sense my love for the theatre was returned. So I had to find alternative employment - anything that brought in something - and got a job as a travelling taxman. But I continued writing whenever I could and eventually became what's now called a novelist. So you could say I wrote *Don Quixote* on the hoof. Well, the first half of it anyway. And that brings me back to here and now. And to what I've heard so far - much of it news to me. Of course I've known for a long time - four hundred years or so - that my knight and squire rode straight into folklore. They featured on stage and in carnivals there and then. The moment they appeared in print people impersonated them. But I'd no idea England's national poet had put them on the stage. In collaboration with his successor in the royal theatre company. I'm flattered to hear it. But I'm sorry their script got lost. I'd have liked to see how they treated my book. As for what's now about to occur I can only assume it's some sort of reconstruction of what they might have done. I do think however, along with your Mr Shakespeare, that calling it his *Don Quixote* is perhaps mildly opportunistic on the part of whoever's done it. And as for Mr Fletcher's reference to me as the author of the original material - well, you've already heard me on that, haven't you? After all, I like to think that my experience in the theatre, although as nothing compared with that of Mr Shakespeare, nevertheless influenced my work as a novelist. Thus making his and Mr Fletcher's job of dramatisation that much easier.

Drum roll off.

CERVANTES
What's that? Thunder? (he listens) No, drums. Drumming. I think someone must have decided -

The stage lights start to fade.

CERVANTES
I should make myself scarce. Vanish as it were.

Blackout in which we discern the shade of Cervantes leave the stage. A creak of a seat in the front row could indicate he's joined us in the audience.

Act One - Scene One

Let me conjure up a few properties to set the scene. To indicate a private chapel in a rich businessman's mansion in southern Spain at the start of the seventeenth century. These effects need to suggest (both for the sake of the action and historical verisimilitude) that this chapel is in fact an alcove adjoining a spacious reception hall. Here is a small, sacred theatre set within a larger, profane theatre.

In the alcove a heavy wooden crucifix hangs above a gilded altar. Both the Christ and the altar are tortuously carved. Four tall silver candlesticks stand along the ornately embroidered altar cloth. The candles in them are yet to be lit. Stage left of the altar a doll-like Virgin Mary, richly dressed in silks, lace and pearls, stands on a plinth. Stage right, also on a plinth, stands the family's patron saint, St Michael, killing a dragon.

A cherubic altar boy now appears with a lighted taper. He genuflects before lighting the candles on the altar. Then he steps back, extinguishes his taper - practised pinch between finger and thumb - and stands devotedly to one side.

A bridal couple enters. The groom grips the bride by the wrist. She is not yet fifteen years old and she is terrified. Her cheeks are wet with tears; she's trembling from head to foot. Her name is Lucinda.

The bridegroom is Lord Fernando. He's just seventeen. The second son of a duke. He can be charming but he's also sexually rapacious and arrogantly self-regarding.

Lucinda and Fernando genuflect and then kneel in front of the altar as Lucinda's parents appear. Her father is fat, her mother fatter. They cannot, and do not, conceal their satisfaction at this socially advantageous union of their only child with this young aristocrat. Both are smiling outwardly and inwardly as they too genuflect and then kneel.

After a moment the chaplain of the household makes his entrance. He is a gaunt man of God, demandingly severe. His genuflection before the altar is as profound as it is professional. Next he turns to face the bridal couple. He blesses them. But almost immediately the Latin benediction becomes a background murmur, a soundtrack to a more urgent action. Because this is theatre. And theatre is the verb not the adjective, isn't it?

So we bring on Cardenio in a headlong rush, brandishing his sword. To claim our exclusive attention. The wedding group don't register him at all, of course.

Physically, mentally, sartorially he's all over the place. Though well-dressed (he's a rich man's son) he's coming apart at the seams. He's not yet sixteen and, like the trembling bride, he's convulsed in mind, body and soul at the thought of what is about to occur. And it is not, repeat not, what the chaplain, Lord Fernando or Lucinda's parents expect. For you, as a playgoer, the outcome will, I hope, come as an agreeable theatrical surprise - what else have you obligingly suspended your disbelief for? But, as a reader, I've little doubt you already know only too well that in any decent novel nothing is ever quite so simple as it is on stage.

Thanks to this digression Cardenio has now got some of his breath back and also managed by swallowing and gulping frenetically to produce enough saliva to moisten his tongue. He's still trembling violently but he's just about recovered enough presence of mind to articulate his desperation; to tell us what's brought him here uninvited; and why his childhood sweetheart, Lucinda, is being married against her will, to Lord Fernando. In other words here's an explosive, plot-establishing Renaissance soliloquy or formalised stream of consciousness such as even John Fletcher would have recognised as an efficient, if conventional, dramatic device.

CARDENIO
My friend is proved my foe! False, false Fernando!
Let Heaven witness! Here's my place usurped!
To plead my suit was his declared intent
But not his aim! He spoke himself for her
And won his prize, against her will and mine.
Such vaunting power does high-born blood possess!
False friend, but true, forever true Lucinda,
Who, knowing his deceit and falsity
To halt this enforced match has brought the means.
A knife she has concealed within her gown,
And she will sooner sheathe it in her heart
Than she shall say 'I will'. So has she sworn.
But to prevent this issue I am come!
And with this sword I've pledged to kill the groom
To spare Lucinda death at her own hand
And hellish pain thereafter.

As the chaplain concludes the benediction with a sonorous *amen* Cardenio steps aside into shadow. The bridal couple rise. Lucinda still shakes visibly. The chaplain takes their right hands and places Fernando's over hers. He grips it fiercely. She gasps - ah!

CHAPLAIN
  (in scrupulous prose) Will you, Lord Fernando, take this lady, Lucinda, here present, for your lawful spouse, in accordance with the laws of our Holy Mother, the Church?
FERNANDO
  (without any scruples whatsoever) I will! Yes! I will!
CHAPLAIN
  Will you, Lady Lucinda, take Lord Fernando, here present, for your lawful spouse, in accordance with the laws of our Holy Mother, the Church?

Pause in which all wait for Lucinda to speak but she can't.

CHAPLAIN
  Will you?

Lucinda still has no voice. So Cardenio addresses us instead.

CARDENIO
  Say no, Lucinda! Speak as you have sworn!
  Did we not vow to be each other's own?

Again, there is no reply. The chaplain clears his throat - with menace.

CHAPLAIN
  Answer, lady. Will you take Lord Fernando, here present, for your lawful spouse?

This time Lucinda does respond, but only with a wordless outcry - the inchoate protest of an innocent who knows she's about to be sacrificed on the altar of social expedience.

FATHER
  Reflect, my child, what glory shines upon you;
  What honour is bestowed upon our house.

14

MOTHER
  Say yea, my child! Do your father's bidding.
  Such vantage never falls from Heaven twice!

Lucinda sways. The chaplain swells.

FERNANDO
  (angry hiss) Speak!

Silence.

CARDENIO
  Still no word? Denounce him for a traitor!
CHAPLAIN
  Speak! Will you take Lord Fernando for your spouse?
CARDENIO
  Deny him now but never harm yourself! Since I shall kill him
  straight.

All now urge Lucinda to speak. The only person she cannot hear
is Cardenio. Consequentially she shudders violently and then her
body clenches in upon itself. When, eventually, she does manage
to speak, her words contradict her true feelings.

LUCINDA
  I will.
CARDENIO
  (horrified) Lucinda! No! You swore otherwise!
FATHER
  (mollified) Good child.

The chaplain beckons the altar boy to bring forward a black velvet,
gold-fringed cushion on which two wedding rings are placed in
readiness.

CHAPLAIN
  (to Fernando) Be pleased, my Lord, to take this wedding band
  and place it upon your bride's finger. (to Lucinda) And you,
  good lady, take that wedding band and place it upon your lord's
  finger. And each say together: With this -

But now Lucinda screams, rises, shouts *no, no, no*! Startled, the altar boy drops the cushion. The rings roll anywhere.

LUCINDA
   Cardenio! Save me! Protect me! Oh!

She sways then faints in front of the chaplain. Fernando's on his feet, so are Lucinda's parents, but the chaplain remains an unshaken pillar of rectitude. Lucinda's mother rushes to her unconscious daughter.

FERNANDO
   (outrage) What foolery is this?

Downstage Cardenio urges himself to action.

CARDENIO
   Strike now, my sword! Or never! Strike!

But, to his dismay, he discovers that words do not necessarily become deeds. He remains, despite every intention, exactly where he is. And what he is - a sensitive, frightened teenager quite incapable of righting wrongs by force. Meanwhile Lucinda's mother has withdrawn a paper folded and sealed around a tiny stiletto from her daughter's loosened bodice. Horrified she hands both to her husband.

MOTHER
   Look what's here!
CARDENIO
   Not move? Not strike? Cardenio coward?

Simultaneously Fernando snatches both the stiletto and letter from Lucinda's father.

FERNANDO
   No! These are mine!

He breaks the seal, unfolds the letter. Still Cardenio cannot move.

CARDENIO
   I'm as a willow rooted by a brook

16

That weeps for shame. Not stir, Cardenio?
FERNANDO
  Hear this, sir. Hear what your own daughter's writ.
CARDENIO
  No hand to do it? Myself by self betrayed?
  Oh, coward Cardenio, get you gone!

Cardenio goes, overwhelmed by shame, as Fernando, his anger mounting, reads out Lucinda's letter.

FERNANDO
  "I cannot be wife to Lord Fernando. I am vowed body and soul to Cardenio. And he to me. Our love is indivisible and I shall die rather than yield to any other man."

Fernando crumples the letter in his left fist while hefting the stiletto in his right.

FERNANDO
  She his? Forsworn? If this is so she dies!

He lunges forward but the chaplain intervenes.

CHAPLAIN
  This chapel's sacred, no blood must it defile.

Fernando draws back, takes breath, recovers his poise, but then, out of sheer immaturity - like Cardenio, he, too, is a teenager of his time - he patronises everyone present in a final, would-be heroic couplet.

FERNANDO
  So be it, father! But I shall have my due.
  I swear it here! Upon this whore, and you!

He goes without noticing that Lucinda is recovering consciousness. And speech. A heart-stricken murmur.

LUCINDA
  Pardon my frailty, good Cardenio.
  I could not do what I had sworn I would.

MOTHER
  (furious) Hush, child.
FATHER
  All's lost.
MOTHER
  And done.
FATHER
  Our name disgraced.

Blackout except for the two green exit signs behind us, as required by statutory fire regulations.

Act One - Scene Two

Had the preceding scene been played at Whitehall in 1613 the actors would have had to get off stage in full candlelit view rather than half-vanish into semi-electric darkness as visualised here. Doubtless, whoever directed the play at that time (and with the proliferation of scenic effects within indoor theatres the role and power of the director must have increased enormously), he would have distracted that gala audience's attention from this routine denouement occurring on one side of the acting area by at once bringing on the actors of the next scene on the other as energetically and as loudly as possible. If this were so then they could well have been Don Quixote himself and his squire, Sancho Panza, plus a hobby horse playing the part of Rocinante, the wandering knight's skeletal charger.

    But this isn't the case here. Here in my fringe theatre we have a puff of red smoke ballooning up from the floor. A childish pantomimic effect, I admit, but even so to my mind it's just the thing to announce an interruptive re-entrance of *Cardenio*'s co-author, John Fletcher. If the smoke still lingering above his head looks incandescent he is even more so. He's beside himself, virtually dancing with indignation.

FLETCHER
  God Almighty and all the Host of Heaven! Was that opener *really* supposed to be what I'd written? Never! My verses were far, far lighter on their feet. What do these post-modern pentameters think they've come as? With their heavy duty tread? Off-road John Webster, would you say? Four by four Tom Middleton, is

it? No! Why, even clapped out Frank Beaumont sported better radials than these -

Shakespeare is heard off.

SHAKESPEARE
(off) Jack! Some of us would like to hear this play rather than you bellyaching about it.

Shakespeare enters, still talking.

SHAKESPEARE
It may not be entirely to your taste but it's early days yet. Speaking for myself I'd say this make-over of what we did has begun efficiently enough. As a miniature melodrama it groaned and gurned a bit, I agree, but it was faithful to the original. And, more to the point, it did its job. It's put the plumbing of the plot in place in four minutes flat - I timed it - so why complain? Here's the bulk of your romance action set up, Jack. We've already got three out of your four young lovers at useful, star-crossed purposes and ripe for dramatic development. All we need now is for the fourth one to appear. What was her name? Dorinda? No, Dorotea. A very sensible character, as I recall. But we didn't bring her on just yet, did we? No, I think I said, let's get the funnies on first, did I? Didn't I? Remind me.
FLETCHER
You did. But I cut that scene.
SHAKESPEARE
Oh? So you did. Yes. Yes.
FLETCHER
You say let's hear this play, William. But how can you of all people bear to listen?
SHAKESPEARE
Because I've heard worse. And why discourage a fellow author? We can leave time and market forces to do that.
FLETCHER
But -

Suddenly a horse neighs through the sound system cutting Fletcher short as the light changes

SHAKESPEARE
That sounds familiar. Reminds me of George Bryan at his best. Did you know him or was he before your time with us? What an artist. Took over from me as the Ghost in *Hamlet*. A truly disconcerting mimic and totally outrageous with his animal noises, off stage, on stage. Horses, donkeys, cows, sheep, hounds in full cry - all conjured up as to the life. And birdsong! You should've heard his nightingales. Perfection. He could even do cicadas for outdoor continental scenes such as this one, from the look of it aspires to be -

Shakespeare and Fletcher go. We might now perhaps imagine them joining us in the audience. Why shouldn't the past sit in judgment on the present? Since we're only too ready to refashion the past to suit our present preconceptions?

Act One - Scene Three

A distant bagpipe evokes a hill path between trees with rocky peaks ahead and a dusty stubble plain below. We are - or at least could be - where Don Quixote's home province of La Mancha borders Andalucia. Noonday sunlight through overhanging branches speckles the knight and squire. The actors walk on the spot as if marching uphill. Sancho Panza, as I envisaged earlier, leads Rocinante in the shape of a toy hobby horse. This is a stick on wheels with a long equine skull for a head. But there's no sign of the squire's equally famous donkey. Surely the assistant stage manager hasn't forgotten to supply this vital property? No. His non-appearance here is a deliberate omission essential to the past, present and future action.

Don Quixote looks even worse than we might expect. He's as tall and thin as ever and the ancestral armour he wears (his great, great grandad's) is, as it should be, battered and dented. So is he. He could well have a black eye, or even two. After all, he's just been viciously beaten up and then stoned by a chain-gang of convicts he released in accordance with his belief in natural justice. His lance, too, is broken, thanks to a previous decision that a long line of windmills was, in fact, a squadron of giants requiring instant immolation. Unfortunately Don Quixote's lance got caught in the first windmill's sail and was broken into bits even as he and Rocinante were whirled up into the air only to fall headlong into folklore.

The only bright thing about him is his helmet. Except it isn't one. It's a highly polished brass basin that he's recently stolen from a travelling barber. To us it looks a bit like an eye-dazzling sun hat with a wide brim out of which someone, or something, has bitten a capacious mouthful. To Don Quixote, however, it looks like the upper half of a legendary helmet made of solid gold which he knows, thanks to his wide reading, once belonged to a Saracen warrior king called Mambrino, who thought the Middle East should belong to him, rather than to Christian crusaders.

Sancho is also badly bruised. The convicts stole his cloak but nothing else was worth taking. So he's been left with his old leather jerkin, filthy shirt, breeches worn under the belly but held up - just - by a wide belt, and his down-at-heel boots. Also, being less self-driven than his employer, Sancho is close to exhaustion. But even so he's the first to speak. In prose, naturally.

SANCHO
  About here's far enough, I reckon? Right?

To emphasise this he stops walking on the spot and proceeds to recover his breath emphatically even dramatically. Don Quixote does not stop. With his knees still pumping up and down (I presuppose a competent mime) he remains precisely where he is while addressing the air in high-flying terms which express his view of himself as a lovelorn lover out of a bygone age.

QUIXOTE
  Oh, peerless princess! Royal lodestar! Serenest Highness of my
  soul!
SANCHO
  (to us) Oh, no, not her again! Not Dulcinea!

Don Quixote's knees drop. He turns balefully towards Sancho.

SANCHO
  Heard enough about her! That Princess so-called. When she ent
  worth the half of my Dapple.
QUIXOTE
  Sancho! Have I not said I shall make good the theft of your
  donkey?

SANCHO

Aye, you have! But where's the comfort in that?

QUIXOTE

(tetched) You have my word. My word as a gentleman at arms.

SANCHO

Aye. (to us) And that's my worry, right?

If a laugh were to be heard here Don Quixote would be deaf to it because once again he's addressing his absent mistress. Sancho, not to be outdone, mourns for his lost donkey.

QUIXOTE

Oh, Dulcinea, your faithful knight -

SANCHO

Oh, Dapple, dearest donk as ever was -

QUIXOTE

Your humble servant -

SANCHO

Child of my bowels -

QUIXOTE

Your champion -

SANCHO

Comfort of my wife -

QUIXOTE

Defender of your virtue -

SANCHO

Sport of my kiddywinks -

QUIXOTE

I, Don Quixote of La Mancha, will never cease to serve you, oh peerless Dulcinea.

SANCHO

And never you doubt it, Dapple, I'll kill them bastards what stole you!

QUIXOTE

Patience, my squire, patience -

SANCHO

And my bag! And the money you said I was to keep safe for you. And all our eatables. Oh, my belly. You should hear it talk.

QUIXOTE

I can. It's volubility itself.

SANCHO

Do you wonder? It's had nought but nowt since the day before
yesterday.

QUIXOTE

Sancho, how many times must I tell you I shall set all things right?
I shall write a letter for you to take back to my housekeeper,
who, upon receipt of it, will deliver to your charge the two
young ass-colts I have, together with their dam, to more than
replace Dapple.

SANCHO

When?

QUIXOTE

When what?

SANCHO

When'll you write this letter?

QUIXOTE

As soon as may be. When else?

SANCHO

When's that?

QUIXOTE

After I've gone mad for love of the Princess Dulcinea. Up there.

He points upwards and outwards to somewhere above our heads.
He's indicating a bulky range of mountains to be seen through a
gap in the trees. Sancho is appalled at the sight of them.

SANCHO

Us? Climb up there? All the way up there?

QUIXOTE

Yes. Now you've got your breath back.

SANCHO

I haven't. I'm still gasping. Listen.

He gasps theatrically but somehow continues to speak.

SANCHO

Can't you go mad down here? It'll be mortal cold up there.
Look at them crags. When I said best get out of the road I didn't
mean go mountaineering. I meant make ourselves scarce lest
the law comes after you for all the damage you've done. Them
windmills, for a start -

QUIXOTE

(firmly) Giants.

SANCHO

Never! But enough said. We've been into that. As well as you harassing them flocks of sheep -

QUIXOTE

No, Sancho, that's you misreading the facts yet again. If you recall they happened to be two opposing armies requiring armed intervention in order to establish an honourable truce acceptable to both factions.

SANCHO

That ent what the shepherds said. And as for that chain-gang you set free -

QUIXOTE

Liberty is every man's birthright, Sancho.

SANCHO

Tell that to the law when they catch up with you. Reckon it was one of them rascals stole my Dapple.

Quixote turns aside, preferring to be platonically and despairingly in love with Dulcinea del Toboso who doesn't exist rather than listen to Sancho who does.

QUIXOTE

Oh, Dulcinea, discreet and silent beauty -

SANCHO

And now this mullarkey! You going mad for love. Up there of all places. Do you have to? With respect, sir, you're barmy enough already so why overdo it? Eh? You with me? Eh?

Quixote comes back to reality with a blink and a sigh.

QUIXOTE

My dear squire, use your thick head if you can. In order to be a knight-errant complete in every part - to become such not merely in theory but in practice - I am as much obliged to go mad for love as did Sir Roland of Brittany who was seriously unhinged by his love for Angelica the Fair, and just as Sir Amadis of Gaul was driven to distraction by Lady Oriana. Understood?

SANCHO

Not really, no. Why? Why did they go crackers?

QUIXOTE

Because - oh dear! - the ladies in question either played them false or else disdained them.

SANCHO

Leaving your lads a bit short like?

QUIXOTE

(pained) If that implies what I suspect, no, Sancho, no. Their love was - at that stage - platonic - as is mine.

SANCHO

Oh, aye, you've told me about that, haven't you? Platonic - aye. That means no nooky, right?

QUIXOTE

(even more pained) I would prefer to say they regarded their ladies, in ideal, even spiritual, terms.

SANCHO

And when them lasses didn't live up to all of that, your blokes went mental?

QUIXOTE

(sigh) Popularly put, yes.

SANCHO

Got you.

Pause for thought on both sides. Predictably Sancho's are more temporal than spiritual and Don Quixote's the other way round.

QUIXOTE

On reflection, I think it better if I imitate not Sir Roland the Furious but Sir Amadis the Agonised. You ask me why - ?

SANCHO

I don't.

QUIXOTE

(oblivious to this interjection) I will tell you. Because Sir Amadis retired to a very great height -

SANCHO

But I said -

QUIXOTE

(unstoppable now) There to express his misery amidst ice, snow, rocks and so forth. Yes, Sir Amadis is the one for me. What a man! His fits of fury outshone even Sir Roland's! Both tore up trees by the roots, of course, but only Sir Amadis turned somersaults in the nude.

Hearing this Sancho is not only shocked but alarmed.

SANCHO
  The man stripped off?
QUIXOTE
  Superman would be a better description given of whom we
  speak.
SANCHO
  And then went head over heels?
QUIXOTE
  Unquestionably.
SANCHO
  Oh, no! Promise me you won't do that, sir!
QUIXOTE
  That, my good squire, I can in no wise promise.
SANCHO
  Oh, my sakes! You? In the nuddy?
QUIXOTE
  As Venus commands Mars must obey.
SANCHO
  Oh, dear, oh dear, oh dear. (calculating outbreath) Yes, well, at
  least promise me you'll write that letter giving me them donkeys
  before you start cavorting about bollock naked, all right? Got
  me?
QUIXOTE
  All in good time, my squire. On we go. Ever upwards.

Don Quixote goes, leaving Sancho to share his concerns with us.

SANCHO
  Holy Mary! Had I known when I started what I know now I'd
  never have taken on this job - squire to Sir Daftee himself. I'm
  not saying -

And he isn't because a sudden realisation has interrupted his
train of thought which I see as a long line of pack animals toiling
across the high tablelands of New Castile. But putting that mildly
evocative historical image aside the thought Sancho's had, or
rather is having as we watch, cannot be shrugged off. For him its
implications are far too crucial for that.

SANCHO

Hey up! Hold on, lad. How the heck's he going to write this letter of his so I get my donks? Answer me that, eh? Where's the pen? Where's the ink? Where's the paper in this wilderness? I mean, I ask you, did you ever see a more unlettered, ignorant, dumb as they come stretch of mother Nature as we've got round here? Oh, my sakes! How's he going to do it? We're strapped before we start!

Sancho, leading Rocinante, goes after Don Quixote, calling to him urgently.

SANCHO

Wait for me, sir. Wait for me - !

The lights change and a wind machine (an old-fashioned theatrical device discovered by chance at a boot sale by the assistant stage manager) whirrs into action.

SANCHO

(offstage now) Master Quixote, wait for me, sir, I've had a thought! A right pig of a thought, sir. Wait for me -

Act One - Scene Three

The assistant stage manager who now appears is a girl just out of drama school. This fringe job is her first professional engagement which means she doesn't get paid anything - not even the Equity minimum wage - and survives on a heady mix of youth, enthusiasm, social security and ambition. She's a pretty girl of nineteen. Let's call her Lily. She's brought on an extruded polyurethane rock and placed is just to the right of centre stage. She goes off on the prompt side where Bill the stage manager is now winding the wind machine with increasing vigour. Perhaps I should point out here that left and right are contrary concepts for actors, for audiences. An audience observes an actor entering from the right and going off to the left. But for the actor it's the other way round. He or she has come on stage left and gone off stage right. Prompt side, by the way, is stage left and stage right is known as the O.P. side (opposite prompt). If this were a conventional chocolate box theatre Lily would now be out of view behind the gilded proscenium arch and 'on the book' as actors say. In other words she'd be the prompter following this text with an eagle eye until some playful performer gooses her. But as this is an open studio space there's no way of doing this so my actors need to know their lines thoroughly and be quick to improvise fluently if not. And Lily can go backstage and finish her mug of tea.

Another change of light, the presence of the rock, the sound of the wind augmented by music now suggest an open grassy upland dominated by outcrops of limestone. Kindly imagine dozens of them, like and unlike this one, that have been sculpted by weather and time into curiously threatening shapes redolent of myth and legend. Huge stone presences open to any interpretation you wish. Is that one a mastadon? This one an ogre? Are those over there a series of enormous organ pipes? The undulating grassy spaces between them offer harebells and sheep-droppings (the shepherds bring their flocks up here in high summer) as well as enough room for anyone to turn as many cartwheels or somersaults as they might wish. With or without clothes on. Enter Cardenio, stage right. If he was distressed before he is now utterly possessed by the sense of his own inadequacy - social and emotional. This will be expressed by anger. He will direct the anger he had for Fernando, but failed to act upon, first at himself, and then at anyone he happens to encounter who interrupts his interior monologue or exterior expression of it. From time to time he will become his trusting sixteen year old self again but such moments are yet to come.

The first thing he does is hurl aside a well-packed, expensive leather satchel, then he somersaults wildly, once, twice, three times, before tugging off his boots and stockings. During all these actions he talks to himself in furious iambic pentameters.

CARDENIO
  Love's either ignorant or merciless,
  Or else my mind's unequal to the cause
  That here condemns me to a living shame.

He throws off his jerkin.

CARDENIO
  Though Love's a god he's also blind,
  A silly, laughing, naked child.
  What malice can there be in such a one?

He now unlaces his fine cambric shirt.

CARDENIO
  Why then this hurt my brain divides?
  Why then this shame that in my soul resides?

He flings off his shirt.

CARDENIO
  It cannot be Lucinda is the cause,
  Such evil never dwelt in one so good.

Pause.

CARDENIO
  No! I myself am cause and fault alone,
  And only death can cowardice atone.

He buries his head in his hands and weeps. Then he looks up as he hears voices carried up from below on the wind. They are Sancho's and Don Quixote's.

SANCHO
  (off) Hold on, sir. Hang about.
QUIXOTE
  (off) Oh, peerless princess, disdain me not.

Cardenio rises and backs away leaving his belongings where they lie as he spits out his thoughts in chopped-up prose

CARDENIO
  Others haunt these crags? Begone! My wits are spent. Quick, Cardenio! Be seen by none. Be off with you. And you! And you!

He goes, fast. After a moment Don Quixote appears. He looks up and around, then comes to a halt,. Being so preoccupied with impersonating his chivalric self he doesn't notice Cardenio's bag and clothes scattered at his feet and beyond.

QUIXOTE
  Are these heights high enough, I wonder? These rocks cruel enough? This air bleak enough? This vicinity heroic enough?

29

Sancho arrives with the hobby horse.

SANCHO
  (out of puff again) Phoo! What a scramble! Stopping here, are
  we? Phoo. Hope so.
QUIXOTE
  The very question I'm asking myself, Sancho.
SANCHO
  I've got a question, too, sir.
QUIXOTE
  Hush, squire -
SANCHO
  About that letter, sir. Like how are you going to write it without
  ink nor -
QUIXOTE
  Silence, squire. I'm thinking.

Sancho makes a face then speaks to the hobby horse.

SANCHO
  Hear that, old son? Your lord and master's thinking. So why
  don't you chew the odd bit of this grass while you can, eh? Off
  you go. Get some flesh on you. But what we do about that letter
  I just don't know. Hey up.

He releases the hobby horse to graze with a well-timed slap on
its invisible rump and then sees Cardenio's bag. He stares at it
intently.

SANCHO
  Hey! What's that?

Quixote turns, regards it.

QUIXOTE
  A satchel?
SANCHO
  Aye! And stuffed full at that.

He comes to it. Views it warily yet rapaciously.

SANCHO

Calf skin? Silver buckle? Very grand, eh?

QUIXOTE

See what it contains, squire.

SANCHO

Won't I just! Don't need no second bidding for that, do I? Could be the gubbins, eh?

He kneels and unbuckles the bag. The first thing he pulls out is a green silk handkerchief with coins knotted into it. Full moon smile as he weighs it in his hand.

SANCHO

Hey, hey! Now this feels pleasing to the palm.

He unties the knot, laughing.

SANCHO

Oh, my sakes! Here's gold! And silver, sir. Oh, my beauties. Look at you! Pure gold, pure silver. See the King's shield on 'em? And how they shine! Strike a man blind they could and him not complain neither. (he turns to Don Quixote) Well, sir, here's a proper chance come like you said it would. Your worship's a real venturer, after all.

He feels in the bag again. And brings out a small, leather-bound notebook. He opens it.

SANCHO

Here! Somebody's written in this. Look. Have a read of that, sir.

He holds out the book. Don Quixote takes it.

QUIXOTE

You guard the money, Sancho, until we find its owner.

SANCHO

Right. But with any luck we won't, will we? And besides, finder's keeper's, ent it? And possession's nine tenth's of the law and -

QUIXOTE

Proverbs, Sancho. Remember? We agreed to eschew them, did we not?

SANCHO
  Aye. But with me they keep on coming back - like pickled
  gherkins.

He burps demonstratively before rummaging once more in the
bag while Don Quixote leafs through the notebook.

SANCHO
  What else we got, eh? Eh?
QUIXOTE
  We have a nice hand here. And verses. These denote a person of
  some breeding, I daresay. Yes. They do. They do.

Sancho, open-mouthed, pulls out cheese and bread in a napkin.

SANCHO
  (explosive joy) Mother of God, sir! Food, sir! Food! Would you
  believe?

He eats at once, tearing at the bread with his teeth. This isn't greed
this is genuine hunger.

QUIXOTE
  And here's a letter begun. Listen to this. (he reads aloud)
  'Madam, my miseries have brought me to such a place -'
SANCHO
  (mouth full) Up here does he mean?
QUIXOTE
  Patience, Sancho. He goes on, 'whence you shall receive news
  of my death.'
SANCHO
  (chewing the cheese now) Oh? He's dead then?
QUIXOTE
  Not necessarily.
SANCHO
  Sounds like it. Hope so. (belch) Pardon me.
QUIXOTE
  'I am repulsed, etcetera, etcetera, because - ' Ah, yes. All's
  clear now. The author of this letter, Sancho, considers his merit
  outweighs that of his rival who has supplanted him in his lady's
  affections.

Sancho has meanwhile found a silver flask in the bag. He holds it up.

SANCHO
  Glory be!
QUIXOTE
  Aqua vitae?
SANCHO
  Moonshine!

He takes a swig, then another.

SANCHO
  Pure brandy as ever was!

Don Quixote turns over another page in the notebook, scans it beadily.

QUIXOTE
  Ah, the truth unfolds. Yes. Mm. Yes.
SANCHO
  (after another gulp) Aye, it does. In all its glory. Phoo!
QUIXOTE
  The young gentleman writing here - for his youth is evident in
  every word he writes - this gentleman, I say, is plainly of two
  minds. On the one hand he's aflame with fury and on the other
  he's possessed of normal commonsense.
SANCHO
  Remind you of anybody?
QUIXOTE
  No. Who?

The childlike simplicity of this reply from Don Quixote throws
Sancho, as actors say. He gulps (and not from the brandy). Should
we happen to laugh at this reaction of his - we might - he won't
let his answer get lost, he'll time his next line with delicate, tactful
precision just as any noise from us subsides.

SANCHO
  Well, sir. Let's say, look who's talking, shall we?

QUIXOTE
  If you mean me, my friend, the answer is no, not so. I am always
  of one single mind, whole and indivisible.
SANCHO
  'Cept when it comes to your monsters, giants, wicked wizards
  and such, right?
QUIXOTE
  Exactly. You prove my point. Who else continue to oppress the
  earth? And who remains, save myself, to oppose them?

Pause because Sancho's realised it might be better not to continue
this discussion any further. He eats instead, but less voraciously
than before, while Don Quixote turns over yet more pages.

SANCHO
  (eventually) So you reckon there's two of him then?
QUIXOTE
  No. He is one person who is not always the same person. He's
  two in one, Sancho.
SANCHO
  Right. But which one of him's dead? Answer me that.

Don Quixote doesn't.

SANCHO
  Any road, let's hope we don't meet neither. They could ask for
  their bag back, couldn't they?

Don Quixote, disgusted by Sancho's pragmatism, sighs heavily,
snaps the notebook shut and changes the subject by reverting to
matters chivalric.

QUIXOTE
  'Tis meet now, squire, I attend upon mine own misfortune rather
  than reflect upon another's.
SANCHO
  Still of a mind to go mad for love, are you?
QUIXOTE
  Naturally. On we go.
SANCHO
  Won't here do? Looks horrible enough to me.

QUIXOTE

No. I require true desolation. Some crest or summit eternally chastized by sharper winds and icier blasts.

Don Quixote goes grandly. Sancho pulls a face before turning to address us, in confidence.

SANCHO

Fine words. But they don't butter this parsnip - no. Shall I tell you the real reason we've come up here? Shall we get to the guts of it, shall we? Well, then, forget his fancy love talk. And his so-called princess. That Dulcinea. And him thinking he's God's gift in shining armour to all and sundry. No, it's none of that, no. No, we're up here, out of the road, on account of his latest mad prank. Like he took the law into his own hands, so now the law aims to get its hands on him, right? You see there was this chain-gang. A load of convicts loaded with padlocks. He released 'em! Said nobody - not even the king on his throne - had the right to chain up any bugger else. So off you go, lads. But don't forget to go back to El Toboso with that chain of yours and lay it at the feet of my Princess Dulcinea and tell her what a good knight I've been giving you your freedom, all right? Which made them laugh, didn't it? So this one gets cross, doesn't he? So then it's a free for all, isn't it? We get beaten up and now he's a wanted man, just like them criminals. We're on the run. Only him on his way up there won't believe it, never mind how often I tell him.

Don Quixote is heard calling to Sancho from above.

QUIXOTE

(off) Mount on high, faithful squire, mount on high.

SANCHO

What did I say? Up the flue of his own chimney that one is, believe you me.

Even so Sancho shoulders Cardenio's bag, takes Rocinante's leading rein, and follows in Don Quixote's footsteps. As he goes he speaks to the hobby horse.

SANCHO

Hope you've got a better head for heights than me, old son. Hey up.

Was it a trick of my imagination or a clever property device that's made me think Rocinante nodded his head at Sancho? Either way it's too late to be sure. Both have gone.

Blackout.

End of Act One

1st Interlude

When *Cardenio* was first performed this interlude would have been marked by music and some replacement of scenic effects together with the trimming of candles and the bringing in of yet more as daylight faded from the high windows of the hall at Blackfriars or at the palace of Whitehall.

Such interludes weren't intervals as we know them. Audiences didn't push their way to the bar or lavatory, let alone outside for a furtive cigarette. No, this pause - the first of four - indicates what would have been the structure of *Cardenio* as a Jacobean play in five acts with its action punctuated but not brought to a stop by four such moments as this. Doubtless as the musicians played in the gallery above, the audience, still in their seats, discussed either what they had just seen or heard, or, perhaps - let's be realistic - their own affairs.

I'm going to assume the latter since this gives me licence to say what I want. Which is, that if, in fact, *Cardenio* was printed and sold after being registered for publication at the Stationers' Hall in 1653, then it would have appeared in the bookshops around old St Paul's in this classic five act form. But to be read rather than performed.

By this time Cromwellian decree had closed London's theatres; acting companies had been disbanded or reduced to makeshift touring and former managers, desperate for cash, sold off the publication rights of all the scripts they owned. Perhaps *Cardenio* was exploited in this way? The names Shakespeare and Fletcher were still remembered. If so then, who knows, a printed copy may yet be lurking, nibbled by dormice, on the cobwebbed library shelves of some neglected country house? But no, that I suspect, is a romantic thought as out of step with now as any of Don Quixote's then.

But if, during the Protectorate, *Cardenio* was enjoyed by readers rather than by theatregoers it could be that my re-invention of it here is at least in line with its registration as a text to be printed, whatever it had once been like on the stage?

Also, if such a five act play were available for production in the theatre today (as are *The Two Noble Kinsmen* or *Henry VIII*) then it's more than likely the management would chop it in two. An interval, of the sort we're familiar with, would occur almost certainly after the end of Act Three. Thus turning the five acts into two acts and creating a different theatrical beast. I do of course accept that a drink is often urgently needed after sitting through three fifths of a Jacobean drama re-interpreted for today and should you point out that re-interpretation is precisely what I'm up to at this very moment then, yes, I plead guilty. But I must add, in mitigation, that in my case, unlike that of a theatre director, I haven't got an existing play-script to work from. For me there's no well-sprung Shakespearean trampoline or Fletcherian bouncy castle upon which I can display my prowess as a dramaturgical gymnast. No, I've had to fashion this dramatisation for myself, while mindful that the formidable above-mentioned duo, along with that world-famous failed playwright Miguel de Cervantes Saavedra, have already dealt with this subject. But that said - oh, the music's changing and so are the lights. This supposed interlude is over. Gone as if it had never been.

Act Two - Scene One

Here's a shrine to the Virgin and Child at a country crossroads. The sun is high overhead. Unfortunately the stage management hasn't provided a clip-clop soundtrack of a donkey trotting by. If they had I might have thought we'd glimpsed Sancho's donkey, Dapple, ridden by whoever stole him, disappearing into the heat haze. But no. I daresay Lily and Bill were too busy bringing on the shrine in the blackout.

Instead a girl has appeared. She waits. We observe her. She is gravely beautiful but at past her middle twenties she's older than she would wish, given her present predicament. She is modestly dressed as befits her former status as a respectable farmer's daughter. Her name, as Shakespeare on second thought remembered, is Dorotea and she's waiting for someone.

She looks in the direction from which she has come, shading her eyes with her hand.

DOROTEA

No sight of you, dear nurse, despite the hour?
You know this holy place as well as I.
Here did you bring me when I was a child.
To place my daisies at the Virgin's feet.
Pray God you've met no mishap on the way.

Dorotea sinks to the ground choking back tears.

DOROTEA

And you, my lord, how could you break our troth?
Grave promises you made; then wrote with smiles
That by Midsummer we should married be.
Oh, how could you, so great, misuse my trust,
To make of me an object of your lust?

She weeps as her old nurse appears carrying a covered basket.
Her name is Costanza and she takes no part in Cervantes' original
work so I suggest we accept her as my homage to John Fletcher.
After all, he in his turn could well have introduced her here as
a compliment to his distinguished collaborator who, in his early
success *Romeo and Juliet*, had created just such an archetypal
peasant woman.

COSTANZA

My goodness me, girl, when you said meet me here I'd clean
forgot what a step it was. But these old legs soon told me. And
my heart. How it beats.
DOROTEA

Oh, nurse, good nurse, forgive me. I only had myself in mind.
Sit you down here. Rest now.

She helps Costanza seat herself before turning away, trying to
control her distress. But she can't.

COSTANZA

Hush, girl. Take heart. There's little or nought time don't mend.
DOROTEA

No, not so! No. You know my condition.
COSTANZA

That I do not! Nor do you neither! 'Tis too soon to say if you're
with child or no. And happen you are, well, so be it, there's

38

plenty of lads in our parish for you to choose to make an honest woman of you soon enough.

DOROTEA

But, nurse, you were witness to the betrothal Lord Fernando made with me. You saw him sign the paper - this paper!

She pulls it out from her cuff. It is a small sealed document.

DOROTEA

And heard him swear before God what it says here.

COSTANZA

Aye. But paper don't count with the likes of him. You're crying for the moon, girl. These days great men break their sworn word as fast as they break wind. But who dares say they mark the stink? No, my dear, you come home with me now. This instant.

Costanza hauls herself creakily to her feet.

COSTANZA

Confess all to your dad. He'll huff, he'll puff, then hold you to his heart. And with me at his back he'll get you another man before the month is out. By my reckoning a dowry of twice the tithe-rent your dad pays on those few acres up over Ladywell will get you a proper man - a man as will last you.

For a moment Dorotea considers Costanza's advice. She is not someone who dismisses other people's views too lightly or too quickly. But in this instance she's directly at odds with Costanza. She can't agree to such a compromise. It may be practical but it's also abject.

DOROTEA

(calmly) No. I want justice.

COSTANZA

(appalled) Oh, my Lord above! If that's what you're after, child, nought'll come right. Not now, not never. Oh, dear, oh, dear.

Dorotea picks up the basket her nurse has brought.

DOROTEA

Are these the clothes to keep me safe?

COSTANZA

Aye. And a weight they was. But, girl, hark, I beg you! Come home with me.

DOROTEA

With their help I'll find justice. You'll see. Wait, nurse, wait.

She goes behind the shrine with the basket, leaving Costanza to shake her old head to herself and to confide in us.

COSTANZA

Mainstay of our house she was. Now look what she's come to! And all for love of our duke's second boy - young Fernando. They're ever the worst, ent they? Pop eyes, bulgy britches. What girl's safe? But she loves him. Told me times. Her as was so capable, such a head on her shoulders, clever as she was fair, managing house and farm since her old dad lost his sight. And what've we got now? Thanks to love? A lass as daft as maybe. Looking for justice, she says! Some chance of that. Might as well look to pluck pears from an elm tree.

Dorotea reappears in breeches, boots (they added real weight to the basket) shirt and jerkin. She's tucked her hair up into a wide-brimmed hat. I can't say I'm entirely sure she looks convincingly male but we can discuss this Renaissance cross-dressing convention later. For the moment let's simply enjoy the look of her/him.

DOROTEA

When you get home, nurse, you must say you looked for me but couldn't find me.

COSTANZA

(shocked, indignant) Nor have I, child! Look at you! You in boots and trowsies! No, this is the Devil's doing, girl! For love of God, change your mind and them clothes. Come back with me.

DOROTEA

No, nurse. Lord Fernando must honour his promise to me. The law demands it quite as much as I do.

COSTANZA

Happen it won't. Not when the Duke his dad tells the judge what to say. You'll get short shrift. They'll mark you down for a whore. Folk'll laugh, say, fancy a doxy like her asking for justice. What's the world come to?

DOROTEA

I must chance that - for as it is I'm what you say already.
Farewell. Pray for me.

She kisses Costanza and goes.

COSTANZA

God go with you, child.

She crosses herself and then, with tears in her eyes, addresses the
Virgin.

COSTANZA

And you guard her, Our Lady, if it please you. Young folks reck
nought these days. Gone for good and all - our Dorotea. Who'd
have thought it? Not me, for one.

She curtseys to the statue and goes back the way she's come
looking older than ever.

Act Two - Scene Two

As a reader with a sharp eye I'm sure you noticed that in that
last scene it wasn't until the last speech that Dorotea's name was
spoken. Until then she'd only been addressed as 'girl' or 'child.'
And Costanza was never named aloud at all. She was just 'nurse'
or 'dear nurse.' This goes against much classic theatrical practice
in which the characters call each other by their names far more
frequently and indicatively than people do in reality. For the
sake of knowing who's who playgoers accept this convention.
Shakespeare, for example, peppers his dialogue with signpost
names and titles. But audiences, I've found, are also happy to
go along with much broader signifiers such as: the pretty one,
the ugly one, the happy one or that pain in the neck over there.
Furthermore, when the leading roles are played by star actors the
characters often become simply Sir Marvellous rather than King
Lear, or Dame Wonderful rather than Lady Bracknell.

Which means that here, in this hybrid fiction, I can allow
the people caught up in the action to name each other only as
much (or as little) as they would in life. And this brings me back
to Dorotea. She's one of Cervantes' best characters and, as you

41

will have guessed, she completes the standard quartet of lovers Shakespeare reluctantly allowed John Fletcher to flesh out. If, that is, we can believe Fletcher's account of how their collaboration on *Cardenio* was divided up. Assuming we can, then I suspect the chief reason Shakespeare might after all have wanted one last go at such a well-worn comedy convention would have been the character of Dorotea. This might just be because she reminded him of his wife. Anne Hathaway, after all, had also been a farmer's daughter who'd needed, at the comparatively advanced age of twenty six, to marry her teenage lover in some haste if their prospective baby was not to disgrace her.

Geography next. Because now we're at one of the higher points of the Sierra Morena - that range of mountains in the middle of Spain Sancho so dislikes. Cervantes doesn't in fact tell us exactly where in this wilderness his hero pretends to go mad for love of Dulcinea but I've chosen this location which is three thousand, five hundred and sixty seven feet above sea level. Plus the odd inch, of course. The map I've consulted calls it Mojina (which could perhaps be translated as Pudding Peak) but please don't accept this, nor my selection of this spot, as anything more than reasonably well-researched speculation. We're in Quixote country now. Here geography dances a different measure to what we usually expect. Luckily theatre is equally adept at such metaphysical footwork. It too can go anywhere, become anything.

In this instance a change of light and the revelation of a Don Quixote who isn't Don Quixote will do the trick. What we now see at the start of this next scene is, we realise after a blink of non-recognition, Don Quixote de La Mancha in effigy. That is to say a transmogrification of himself achieved by his hanging up his arms on his lance stuck in a convenient socket in the stage. On the splintered end of it he's placed his golden helmet - that barber's basin made of polished brass. Buckled below it we see his dented breast-plate and rust-pocked shield. And hanging below these chivalric bits and bobs is his ancestral sword in its decayed leather scabbard. Here we have the armoured shell of Don Quixote ablaze with whatever other-worldly radiance the lighting plan can supply and the budget afford.

Sancho stands stage right on this peak of unpleasantness, waiting, without enthusiasm, for his employer to demonstrate the sheer power of courtly love upon knights-errant past and present.

Enter Don Quixote in shirt and breeches but also head over heels. He's somersaulted on stage to land, puffed but upright, in front of Sancho.

QUIXOTE

There! How about that? Point taken?

SANCHO

(fearful of worse to come) Aye. That's it, sir. You've proved it. Aye. We can now say you're daft as they come and can still go arse over tit as well as any other gent else. Aye. So let's go down now, shall we? Bit chilly up here.

QUIXOTE

No, good squire, no. Now it is requisite you observe me do precisely the same - stark naked. As did -

SANCHO

Oh no! No, sir! Like I've said! No need of that! No! You keep your old cods to yourself, sir, if you please. Besides, you'd catch your death. No, sir, no. You'd do better, better by far, to write that letter you spoke of. To your housekeeper. About them donkeys. To hand over to me. You swore you would, sir. Swore blind, you did!

QUIXOTE

Indeed so. And I would, I would. More than gladly. But where, where are pens, ink, paper, at this altitude? And that, as I recall, was the very question you asked me earlier. On our way up here. Correct?

SANCHO

Aye! And I got my answer, didn't I?

QUIXOTE

Did you?

SANCHO

And I've still got it. Here! Here in this bag. Look!

Sancho swings Cardenio's bag from his shoulder and brings out a well-corked ink-horn, four stripped-down goose quills looking like giveaway white biros, and a silver pen-knife. He holds all this literary equipment up in triumph.

SANCHO

There, sir! How about this lot, eh? Didn't reckon on them, did you? But that's what we got. Enough for you to write all the letters in the world.

QUIXOTE

True, my squire, true. But where is paper in this void? Have you asked yourself that?

SANCHO

(promptly) Yes, sir. That fellow's notebook. In your pocket there. Snitch a page out of that.

QUIXOTE

Ingenious squire. Resource is in your blood. And furthermore-

He takes out Cardenio's notebook.

QUIXOTE

Furnished thus -

He tears out a spare page.

QUIXOTE

I can write to the absent mistress of my heart -

SANCHO

Aye, sir. And to Doña Knob-Polisher as well.

QUIXOTE

(out of chivalric reverie) Who?

SANCHO

Your housekeeper, sir. Her as has sorted you out since I was a lad.

QUIXOTE

Ah, yes. She has. Yes. An excellent woman on every count. Yes, I can also write to her. Yes. Bid her release unto your charge those patient creatures I've promised you, yes.

SANCHO

That's it, sir! Them two little 'uns and their dam. On you go, sir. Giddy up. Get writing - scritch scratch -

QUIXOTE

Hush now, Sancho. I must first distill each and every errant thought into Love's quintessence. To accomplish that behoves perfect silence.

SANCHO

Right. Not another word. Leave you to it, sir. But don't forget them donks.

He tiptoes dramatically away, hoping his action will make us laugh. It does. Don Quixote composes his thoughts and his

44

writing materials. Another property rock might provide a seat or table. Sancho, downstage, confides in us.

SANCHO
What a character, eh? Got the answer to everything, he reckons, ancient and modern. But has he? That's what I ask myself. Take his lady love. This Princess Dulcinea of Toboso he keeps on about. Well, look at it like this. El Toboso's the next village up the road from us. And it don't do princesses. No, what he's not telling you, me and everyone else, is like his princess, is, in fact, just a big, fat, miller's daughter. Name of Aldonza Lorenzo and - between you and me - a bit of a goer. Has a voice on her as loud as she's outspoken. And grows hair on her titties, they say. So, if you ask me, she don't really measure up to what you'd call a noble knight's guiding star whatever this one at the back of me may say. As I keep telling him. But does he listen? Never. All I get for answer is: "I speak of Dulcinea not as you say she is, my squire, but as I wish her to be - beautiful beyond compare, virtuous beyond doubt. A peerless princess just as every woman should be." He don't add so shut your gob but you can see him thinking it.

Don Quixote rises up from his rock, calling downstage to Sancho. He's agog with self-induced literary enthusiasm. The act of writing his letter to Dulcinea has reinforced his opinion of himself not just as the epitome of medieval chivalry but as the ideal Renaissance soldier-poet as well.

QUIXOTE
(bellow) Listen to this, good squire! Hear my letter.

He reads it aloud from the torn-out page shaking in his hands.

QUIXOTE
"Serene and Sovereign Madam, Beauteous Ingrate, Dearest Enemy, if Thou pleasest to cast thy orb-like eyes upon me I am Thine for all Eternity."
SANCHO
Sounds a bit old-fashioned to me, sir.
QUIXOTE
I am old-fashioned. Hark. "But if Thou disdainest me then I must herewith end my life."

SANCHO

(alarmed) Oh, no, sir! Think of me! I'd get the blame! And any road you can leave all that rubbish to that other fellow who's cut himself in two.

QUIXOTE

Have no fear, Sancho. I'm writing poetically.

SANCHO

Meaning you don't mean it?

QUIXOTE

Oh, no, I mean it. But as a perfect lover does - such as Sir Amadis of Gaul or Sir Roland of Brittany.

SANCHO

Meaning they didn't mean it either?

Don Quixote catches his breath, praying inwardly for patience.

QUIXOTE

All platonic lovers when disdained do, Sancho.

SANCHO

But how can yours disdain you, sir? When she ent who you say she is?

QUIXOTE

(sigh) Listen to my letter, Sancho. All great squires were good listeners who rarely, if ever, spoke unless spoken to.

SANCHO

I know. But with me it's different. With me speaking's like breathing. If I can't talk -

QUIXOTE

(roar) Silence!

SANCHO

Right.

QUIXOTE

Listen!

SANCHO

I'm all ears. Like my Dapple as was.

QUIXOTE

(reading again) "I must terminate my life, madam, thus satisfying Thy tyrannical cruelty bred of Beauty and my Despair bred of Fidelity. But even so I remain Thy Loyal and Obedient Servant, until Eternity itself doth end, Don Quixote of La Mancha also increasingly well-known as the Knight of the Sad Countenance."

Pause because Sancho's been thinking and is continuing to do so. Eventually he realises what to say next and says it.

SANCHO
  Right. That's you done, is it?
QUIXOTE
  (still exulted) It is indeed. Take this letter, squire. And my steed. Ride with all due diligence even unto my lady's palace. And may God go with you!

He offers the torn-out page to Sancho who shakes his head, refusing to take it.

SANCHO
  (resolutely) No, sir. Not yet. What about my letter? About my donks? We'll be wanting another page for that, I reckon.
QUIXOTE
  Ah, yes, your letter, yes. I take your point.

Don Quixote leafs through Cardenio's notebook.

QUIXOTE
  Alas, good squire, all these other pages are replete. On both sides.
SANCHO
  How about yours, sir?
QUIXOTE
  Mine?
SANCHO
  Give me.

Sancho now takes the letter and turns it over.

SANCHO
  Pure as driven snow! Look. You can write mine on the backside of yours, sir.
QUIXOTE
  (doubtful) I hardly think -
SANCHO
  I can show mine to your housekeeper first, then go on with your poeticals to Toboso after, right? Business first then pleasure, eh?

QUIXOTE

(not entirely convinced) One has heard it said.

SANCHO

No one'll notice. Least of all your ladylove. I doubt she ever looks at the backside of anything or anybody - from what you say of her. (to us) Though I know different, aye, aye.

QUIXOTE

True, squire, true. Very well. As you say there's ever an obverse to everything. Two sides to every question.

SANCHO

All the more reason to tell your housekeeper straight - hand over them donks or else - on the back of that.

Pause. Don Quixote nods resignedly.

SANCHO

Put it like this: Madam, I hereby command you, on receipt of this letter -

Don Quixote writes submissively to Sancho's dictation.

SANCHO

Deliver to the said bearer thereof, that is Sancho Panza herewith, my three donkeys left in your charge aforesaid, together with their harnesses, halters, bridles, appurtenances, garnitures and so on. All this same I order you to execute without hindrance, delay, niggle, complaint or shilly-shally. From my hand here, wherever I am, on this day, whatever it is, blah, blah, etcetera. And make sure you sign it with your real name, sir.

Pause. And my advice to the actors here would be to hold it for as long as seems feasible. Or even longer.

QUIXOTE

(eventually) Don Quixote of La Mancha, yes.

SANCHO

No! Don Alonso of our village, right?

QUIXOTE

No. I no longer answer to that. Either I am Don Quixote or I am nobody.

SANCHO

Not to your housekeeper you won't be. Stick to your real name, sir, or I won't never get my donks. She'll say your letter's from somebody else.

QUIXOTE

She knows perfectly well who I am.

SANCHO

(balefully) And I know what she's like, too. An awkward cow.

Don Quixote reflects then acquiesces.

QUIXOTE

Yes, you could be right, Sancho. Doña Veronica can be contrariwise upon occasion. A good soul but full of doubts and fears.

He finishes the letter with a flourish and hands it to Sancho.

QUIXOTE

There.

SANCHO

Hey. You wrote that quick.

He looks squintingly, suspiciously, at what's been written. It's a moment when a director might well have to restrain the company's clown from, as actors say, milking it.

QUIXOTE

(grandly) The hand appertaining to a cultivated mind, good squire, moves at speed.

SANCHO

Deceiving the eye, sir?

QUIXOTE

Putting everything in order. What was needful I have written. And signed as you would wish.

He moves away, leaving Sancho free to examine the letter even more closely.

SANCHO

Aye but did you write what I said? Don't look much. Three lines at most. Oh, I wish I could read. I can reckon up - but as for your ABC - (he sighs) still look at it this way, the old lad's a gentleman and so -

He turns to see Don Quixote unbuckling the belt of his breeches.

SANCHO
  Oh, no! That ent you stripping off, I hope?
QUIXOTE
  It is indeed, Sancho. 'Tis meet you witness -
SANCHO
  Oh, no, sir! No, my heck! Spare me that! Don't need your old
  ding-dong flopping all over, do we? I'm away now. Hey up,
  noble steed.

Sancho starts to lead the hobby-horse off but stops immediately
as Cardenio enters and Don Quixote steps out of his breeches.
Cardenio is naked down to the waist, Don Quixote naked up to
the waist.

SANCHO
  Lord help us, sir! Here's you know who!

Don Quixote sees Cardenio. And he Don Quixote. Pause as each
regards the other.

SANCHO
  (to us) Least this one's kept his trowsies on.
CARDENIO
  (to Don Quixote) Good sir, if you have any food, I beg you spare
  me some of it.

Don Quixote turns to Sancho.

QUIXOTE
  Squire Sancho. Food? Sustenance? Vittles? Have we any?
SANCHO
  No, sir. All gone. Whatever we had I ate to give me strength to
  serve you, sir, at this altitude.
QUIXOTE
  (to Cardenio) We have nothing, young man. Not a crumb. But if
  I can assist you in any other way, speak. I am yours to command.
  Since I have sworn to aid all those who are unfortunate.
CARDENIO
  I am.

QUIXOTE

Excellent. Then speak. My vocation as a knight-errant requires
me to redress all miseries, either by force of arms or power of
reason. That is to say reasonable force or forcible reason - as
appropriate. Speak.

Pause in which Cardenio wonders if he can trust himself to tell
this middle-aged scarecrow of a man, who stands beside ancestral
armour set up on a pole, about his predicament.

CARDENIO

I will speak, sir. But upon one condition.

QUIXOTE

(crisp patrician) What?

CARDENIO

That at no time you interrupt me - or my history.

SANCHO

(to us) Hear him out? Oh no! I'll never manage that! (to Don
Quixote) Right, I'm off, sir, right?

QUIXOTE

No, stay, squire, stay. 'Tis fitting you hear this gentleman's
account of his sufferings. Doubtless they are as dolorous as he -
from the sound of him - is well-born.

CARDENIO

Should you break the thread of my discourse I cannot answer
for my conduct.

QUIXOTE

Why not?

CARDENIO

Because at one moment I'm one person - at another - someone
else.

Sancho and Rocinante now come downstage to act as a subversive
chorus to the next unit of dialogue (to use a theatrical term)
between Cardenio and Don Quixote. Rocinante's contribution
will, I suspect, be the occasional soft whinny or more reverberative
expulsion of wind. What you, the audience, will add, I can't say.
But do feel free to express yourselves.

SANCHO

I knew it had to be him! I just knew it. Him of the bag! And
the notebook. Young Double-Trouble himself. Mister Who am

51

I? Him or him? That one! Or should I say them? Either way a
right pair, right?

Pause.

CARDENIO

(to Don Quixote) And that other is my enemy and yours, sir.

QUIXOTE

Could betrayal in love have brought you here, perchance?

CARDENIO

It has.

QUIXOTE

Then speak freely, sir, to a fellow sufferer.

CARDENIO

(trembling) You won't interrupt me?

QUIXOTE

You have my word, provided you do not touch upon matters
chivalric, that is.

CARDENIO

Why should I? That's all long past. My story's no older than I
am.

QUIXOTE

Then, by all means begin.

Cardenio takes breath, then speaks softly but quickly under
increasing tension, which he knows he will be unable to control,
should the slightest occurrence (or person) intervene in almost
any way whatsoever.

CARDENIO

(with further breath control - you don't get a part like this
unless you can deliver) My name is Cardenio. My place of birth
Córdoba. My parents wealthy. Close by, in that same city, lived
an angel in human form -

SANCHO

(to us) Girl next door? The old story? What d'you bet?

CARDENIO

Her name Lucinda. Of a degree commensurate with mine. She I
loved from my infancy and she, likewise loved me.

SANCHO

(to us) What did I tell you?

CARDENIO
Our parents knew of our love and we thought that in due course it could have no other fulfilment than holy matrimony -
SANCHO
(to us) But one day - what's the betting? - something happened much like it always does -

Cardenio has overheard Sancho.

CARDENIO
Did your man speak?
QUIXOTE
Possibly. He's prone to. (turning to Sancho) Did you say something, squire?
SANCHO
Only to myself, sir. (he winks at us) And a few old friends. Hope this fellow don't spot his bag or he'll want his money back.

Cardenio, meanwhile, has reacted quickly, angrily.

CARDENIO
(to Don Quixote) You swore not to interrupt!
QUIXOTE
(equally quick to react) I did indeed, sir. Nor have I. Your embargo was between me and you, no one else. We need not heed what squires speak. I pray you, woeful knight, continue with your unhappy history as befits a gentleman.

Cardenio recovers somewhat, curbed by Don Quixote's bark of authority.

CARDENIO
At your request, sir. Time increased our affections. Lucinda's father forbade me the house. This prohibition inflamed our desires further. We reached for our pens. Oh, what letters we wrote! What verses! At last we agreed I should demand Lucinda's hand in marriage. I went to her father. He said my father should make the proposal for me. Overjoyed I ran home, knowing he would agree -

Cardenio pauses. Sancho looks round then stage whispers at us. Fortunately Cardenio doesn't hear him.

SANCHO

And? But? Both, I reckon.

CARDENIO

My father was reading a letter while a booted and spurred messenger in ducal livery waited. My father said, we are immeasurably honoured, Cardenio. The Grand Duke of Montoro requires you -

SANCHO

(astonished outburst) Him! Why, even I've heard of him! Owns half the country!

QUIXOTE

(angry hiss) Be silent! (quickly to Cardenio) He didn't speak. A break of wind. Either from him or my noble steed. (Rocinante whinnies) There! My mount acknowledges the fault. Continue.

After a moment of doubt Cardenio does so.

CARDENIO

The Grand Duke required me to attend him as a companion to his second son, Lord Fernando, and in return my father said Duke Ricardo would advance me beyond all expectation -

QUIXOTE

(erupting both chivalricly and genealogically) Did you say Ricardo de Montoro? He - as all the world knows - is a direct descendent in the maternal line of Dardinel de Almonte, the former possessor of King Mambrino's helmet! And have I not, but yesterday, sir, recovered the same from shameful obscurity? There! Regard it!

He points at the barber's basin on top of his broken lance.

QUIXOTE

There! The helm, the casque - or to employ the correct armorial term - the 'skull' of Mambrino, king of the Saracens. There! The stuff of epic and romance itself. Of purest gold, of potent magic, since whosoever wins it becomes invincible. Invincible, sir!

If Cardenio reacted violently to Sancho's earlier interruption this one from Don Quixote disturbs him even more. We now see him change from a pink-cheeked youth of conventional nurture into a sweating, jugular and temple-vein bulging killer. If this weren't a comedy this transformation would be frightening.

CARDENIO

You cut me short for that? For a barber's basin on a stick? A
brass bowl to trim a beard into? You break your word for that?
I'll kill you! You see if I don't! You old idiot!

And he butts Don Quixote head first in the solar plexus knocking
him down before trying to strangle him. Sancho intervenes fast,
surprisingly so.

SANCHO

Hey! You let go! You let go of him!

And he drags Cardenio off Don Quixote with brutal peasant
efficiency hurling him aside onto his hands and knees.

SANCHO

(justly enraged) Get away, you mad bastard! Who do you think
you are? You keep off! Get away with you!

But Cardenio's on his feet again. He seizes Don Quixote's lance
sending the basin, armour, shield and sword anywhere with huge
clatterings. He brandishes it in a frenzy of murderous delusion.

CARDENIO

I know you! You work for Fernando, don't you? The pair of you?
Hand in glove! Spies! Sent you to follow me, hasn't he? Provoke
me! Oh, yes. He's up to every trick. Look how he stole Lucinda!
And now he's here. In you. You may look like an old fool and a
young one but I know what you are! Fernando's eyes! Fernando's
ears! And I'm going to kill you - kill you - just you see.

Cardenio stops, lost for breath and words. He sobs as Sancho
advances towards him. Don Quixote, recovering consciousness,
staggers upright.

SANCHO

(truly heroic) You're out of your mind, boy. Take your troubles
back where they belong. We've got enough of our own without
yours. And we ent no spies. Got me?

Cardenio drops the lance with another sob then falls to his knees
while Don Quixote, on his feet, wobbles.

SANCHO
  Spoilt baby, you are. Denouncing your elders and betters.
CARDENIO
  (tears in his eyes) Forgive me.
QUIXOTE
  I forgive you, sir.
SANCHO
  Well, I don't! Clear off!

Cardenio rises, tears running openly down his cheeks.

CARDENIO
  I will, I'm sorry. I was my other self.

He goes, sobbing.

SANCHO
  Well! I've seen some half-wits in my time -
QUIXOTE
  (chivalric self again) Such is the tyranny of love, Sancho.
SANCHO
  Aye but why take it out on us? Eh?
QUIXOTE
  Doubtless that Lord Fernando he referred to has supplanted
  this young man in that young lady's affections? She he called
  Lucinda.
SANCHO
  Maybe. But that don't excuse him half-killing you, sir.
QUIXOTE
  Possibly not. But then again one half of him regretted it.
SANCHO
  Aye. But the whole of me wishes I'd clobbered him once and
  for all. Still I'd best be off myself, hadn't I? About your business
  and mine. But do put your breeches back on, sir, and keep your
  sword about lest that loony comes back, all right?
QUIXOTE
  I shall, good squire. Your advice is sound. God speed you to
  Toboso.
SANCHO
  And God guard you, sir. He needs to.

Sancho leads the hobby horse away.

SANCHO
Down we go, lad. Be warmer down hill. And safer.

Rocinante whinnies - a romantic sound lost in an epic resurgence of the wind. Sudden after-image inducing blackout.

Act Two - Scene Three

The lights have come up again but how can I, even in a theatre of the mind, create a road across La Mancha four centuries ago? For this scene I can't even use a shrine to evoke the location. It's a seemingly endless high road, a dirt road, where every foot-fall pothers dust at this season of the year: the dog days of July. Stubble fields, lately harvested by scythe and sickle stretch away on either side to what ought to look like infinity. No shade. No wind. Only occasional thistles tall as a man.

And here, on cue, the stage management in the form of Lily is bringing on a cut-out replica of just such a thistle. She sets it down and goes. Good girl. It looks most convincing. I must ask her who made it. It's at least five feet high, fiercely, even tortuously prickly - the spines on it are sharp as daggers - and though only in two dimensions rather than three it's been ingeniously painted to be given apparent substance in the light of the shadows among its wicked grey-green leaves.

Cervantes does not describe such a road as this - for him, as arguably the Western World's first novelist, landscape is not a subject worthy of evocation. And we can be sure Shakespeare and Fletcher didn't bother either. I doubt their script of *Cardenio* even included a stage direction for such a scene as this beyond, at most: Enter Priest and Barber.

Once on stage however - and here they are - these new characters would have informed us through speech and mime what they were doing (walking); where they were (on the main road south of Valdepeñas); who they were (friends and neighbours of Don Quixote and Sancho Panza) and why they have appeared at this moment (in search of the errant pair.)

They mime walking on the spot quite as expertly as Don Quixote and Sancho Panza did earlier. This fringe group takes its craft seriously - in fact the actor playing Nicholas the Barber leads their warm-up movement classes before every rehearsal. But now they stop.

PRIEST

Ah. The road bifurcates, it would seem.

BARBER

Mm. (deft double-handed gesture.) Do we go left? Or right?

PRIEST

Quite so. Down or along?

BARBER

Choose wrong we could miss them.

PRIEST

Exactly. We need help, do we not?

Conjectural pause.

And now, while Father Perez tells his beads in quest of divine
guidance, and Nicholas mimes eeny-meeny-myney-mo childishly
to himself, I'd like to point out a small yet significant geophysical-
cum-literary feature of the high tableland of New Castile. And of La
Mancha in particular. This apparently monotonous plateau is riven
with underground rivers which often emerge into sheer-sided
valleys, opening surprisingly at your approach. When the sun's
high the green shade of these valleys, with their cooling streams
glimpsed sparkling between the trees below, and the sudden
singing of birds, offer a welcome you didn't know was there.

This unexpected world below land-level also includes
deeper, drier passages and caves, such as the one Don Quixote
delved into. But not here, not in this play tonight, no. Because
when Shakespeare and Fletcher put *Cardenio* on stage Cervantes
hadn't yet published the sequel to his knight's initial history. So
his adventures in that second book were not then available for
dramatisation.

Oh, look. Something's occurred to Nicholas. A second
thought it would seem. And not a nice one - if the face he's pulling
is anything to go by.

BARBER

Father?

PRIEST

What, my son?

BARBER

If our friends have done even half the mad tricks everybody
we've met so far says they've done - those millers, those
shepherds, and that chain-gang guard with the horrible gash on

his head - couldn't our trying to get them home before the law catches up with them, couldn't that make us accomplices to all their crimes?

PRIEST

No. Not if the law's capacity for absorbing emoluments in the name of justice remains what it has always been.

BARBER

Especially coming from the likes of you, father?

PRIEST

Exactly. Not from the Hand of God, of course, but as if from the Hand of God. (he looks from left to right) Now. Which is it to be? This way? Or that?

More conjecture before Sancho, astride the hobby-horse, enters from the left, downstage. He sees Father Perez and Nicholas but, thanks to theatrical convention they needn't see him if I'd rather they didn't. Nor do they. Not for the moment.

SANCHO

Hey up. Whoa, old lad, whoa. That's got to be our priest. And our barber with him. What are they doing out of our village? Could be more to this than meets the eye. Back off, do we?

But the hobby-horse whinnies loudly and piercingly. Father Perez and Nicholas turn at once and see Sancho on Don Quixote's old horse. All are surprised.

BARBER

Sancho!

PRIEST

Panza!

SANCHO

Mm. Me. Aye. Bit out of your road, ent you, father? Nicholas?

PRIEST

We could say the same of you.

SANCHO

Aye, you could. How's the wife and our kids?

BARBER

All well but worried sick about you, Sancho.

PRIEST

As we are about Don Alonso.

SANCHO

Hold on, father. He don't answer to that no more. Either you call
him Don Quixote or get your head bashed in.

PRIEST

Where is he?

SANCHO

Up there.

PRIEST

Alive or dead?

SANCHO

Oh? Alive all right but in the raw. Well, half of him. He just
won't keep his breeches on for being in love.

PRIEST

Oh, no! And his horse? How have you come by him?

SANCHO

Loaned him me he did. Seeing as my donkey got stole. So I can
take a letter to his lady-love.

BARBER

Who's she, Sancho?

SANCHO

His princess.

BARBER

Princess? What princess?

SANCHO

Where've you been, Nicholas? Her Royal Highness the Princess
Dulcinea of Toboso. Who else?

PRIEST

There are no princesses in Toboso, Sancho.

SANCHO

You try telling him that! The times I've said! But will he have it?
No, oh, no.

PRIEST

And the letter you say he's written to her? Where is it?

SANCHO

Here. Read that if you don't believe me. Proof positive, right?
All big ideas and bigger words. Right?

And he thrusts the letter at Father Perez in anger at having being
doubted. Pause as Father Perez begins to read aloud the torn-out
notebook page.

PRIEST
(with growing concern) "I hereby command you, Doña Veronica, to deliver to the bearer hereof, to wit Sancho Panza, three donkeys - " ?

SANCHO
No! Not that side, father! T'other side.

PRIEST
Yes, but - ?

SANCHO
You see! It's full of his speechifying! Like I told you. Look!

Father Perez scans the other side of the page.

BARBER
What does it say?

PRIEST
Quite a lot. And yes, Don Alonso does indeed address a certain - how shall I say? - putative princess. A Dulcinea of Toboso. In what I can only describe as high-flown terms. See for yourself.

He hands the letter to Nicholas to read before speaking to Sancho.

PRIEST
But now, Sancho, where exactly are you going?

SANCHO
Home.

PRIEST
Home?

SANCHO
My house first then Don Alonso's to get them donkeys he's giving me to replace my Dapple.

NICHOLAS
How did you come to lose Dapple?

SANCHO
I said - he got stole. By convicts.

PRIEST
And once you've received these replacements, do you intend to stay at home?

SANCHO
Oh, no! No, I'll come back. He needs me. Else he gets into pickles. And I'll tell him his princess loved his letter and says he can put his trowsies back on again.

PRIEST

Will he believe you?

SANCHO

Oh, aye. He'll believe anything if you put it to him talking his language.

Pause.

PRIEST

Are you aware the Holy Brotherhood is in search of Don Alonso?

SANCHO

Didn't I tell him the law was going to? That's why we took to the hills, Of course he says it's for love and all that bollocks, but we know better, don't we? Still, anyroad, I'd best be getting along now, hadn't I? Gee up, Paco.

Father Perez puts his hand to the hobby-horse's bridle.

PRIEST

Whoa. I'm not sure you should, my son.

SANCHO

Oh?

PRIEST

You'll do even better to help us find your master.

SANCHO

Oh, you can't miss him. Just go on and up till you see him all topsy-turvy.

BARBER

No, Sancho. You'd best come with us. That way we can all go back together.

SANCHO

You aim to bring him home?

BARBER

Of course.

SANCHO

He won't like that. He's after adventure.

PRIEST

It's for his own safety. If he's with us we can vouch for him.

SANCHO

Protect him from the law?

BARBER

Yes. And you, too, Sancho.

SANCHO

(shock) Me?

BARBER

Mm. We've heard the Holy Brotherhood also want to question you.

SANCHO

Why? What have I done? Oh, Holy Mary, Mother of God.

Panic-stricken, Sancho crosses himself at speed three times. Or more if the actor wishes.

PRIEST

So you see, one way and another, you'll be safest with us, all things considered.

Sancho grunts and nods miserably, acknowledging cogent but unwelcome reality.

SANCHO

Aye. Mm. I reckon so, father, but at this rate it'll be Michaelmas before I get my new donks.

PRIEST

Better late than never, my son. Lead the way.

SANCHO

(on the outbreath) Hey up. Back we go, old lad. Win one, lose one.

They go. Unsudden blackout.

End of Act Two

2nd Interlude

A green spotlight turning to warm amber discovers John Fletcher, as the musicians (well, the sound system) begin to play a set of variations by Robert Johnson (1583-1633) on what could be a Spanish folk-tune, if, that is, recent speculations about *Cardenio* are correct. They don't have to be, of course. Theatre is a far more elusive and an even shiftier art than many of its historians - and more pompous practitioners - care to admit. Shakespeare would, however, have been happy to agree. Indeed he often said so. What

Fletcher thought, I don't know, but the errant-playwright in me is prepared to guess it would be much the same, put less politely. If anything he now seems more arrogantly camp than before. But don't be deceived by his manner - Fletcher knows his craft.

FLETCHER

(to us) Look, I want this clear, crystal clear! No one, but no one, has done more than me to bring cutting edge Spanish literature to the English stage, all right? Especially the work of Michael Cervantes who, in my view, was way ahead of the field - his field, any field. Still is, come to that. I've used his stuff time and again for basic storylines, for flip-flops - otherwise known as unexpected reversals of fortune - for happy coincidences, double deceptions, comic cutaways, you name it, I've deployed it. Plus truly awesome psychological insight, correct? Talk obsession, talk compulsion, talk madness, you're talking Cervantes. And on top of that - would you believe? - he does tolerance of human folly like no one else, before or since. We're all indebted to him. Take the writer of this present piece - (self-interruption) - has anyone seen him, by the way? He must be somewhere around, surely? I mean, I've never known a playwright - except William when we tried out our version of this story at Blackfriars - not attend a first performance. Looking more like a ghost than a person, of course, and most probably pissed to the eyebrows. If you do spot him, let me know, I'd like a word with him if he's capable of coherent conversation, that is. Chiefly because what I've seen so far I've found fairly unsatisfactory as well as unsettling. Put it this way - on the one hand he seems to be using pretty much the same material as I did but on the other his characters speak a language - especially in prose - which certainly isn't mine or William's - let alone that of the translation we worked from - William having no Spanish. As it happened the English version was by a friend of mine. A hugely talented Irishman called Thomas Shelton who knocked it off in six weeks, for Christ's sake! All three hundred and twenty five thousand words of it! William's publisher Ed Blount published it and it was a sell-out. Walked out of the shop. Talk about word of mouth! As did the sequel when that came out. Four years after William's death - pity that, though I expect he's caught up with it since. That, too, would make a great play, but I based our effort on what was then available. But back to what we seem to be witnessing here. Don't get me wrong, I'm not saying it's not sort of valid, no. I'm just saying its wierdly different from what we worked up from exactly the same material. Funny that. How it goes. But then again, like it or not - and often I don't - now is now, right? And then is then, isn't it? And theatre's always now whenever it happens and whatever its subject, past or present, correct? It's like T-shirts used to say: Just Do It. By definition it's here 'n' now, at the edge, on the button. And who's the character benefitting most tonight from this immediacy? Yes. Absolutely! Sancho Panza, who else? And this to my mind is a question that needs to get addressed pretty soon if not sooner. Sancho is God's gift of a part, of course - comic servants sending up self-important masters never fail, do they? But given that, how's Don Quixote going to get his necessary dramatic due? It's a real problem theatre-wise. Inherent in the original material, of course. And it rears its ugly head the minute you try to put the old sod on stage. Once you start work it becomes as plain as a pikestaff up a Beefeater's bum that our Knight of the Sad Countenance is only dramatic if - or when - he relates to other people. When he charges off on his own into chivalric fantasy-land he's spectacular - sort of - but dramatic he ain't. Did I hear someone out there protest? Did you say but surely he does amazing, unforgettable things? Charges at windmills, attacks funeral processions and whatever? All that? Yes, he does. And, yes, they work a treat on the page, in the mind's eye. But they don't make for drama on stage. They can provide set pieces, trigger special effects, inspire designers, but that doesn't make for action, that's just decor, right? For drama, real drama, you've got to have people bouncing off - and on - each other, interactively. Which is why, speaking as the first truly committed dramatiser of Michael Cervantes's work, I would urge the present writer to make sure his Don Quixote (a) doesn't get upstaged by his Sancho Panza and (b) gets plenty of other characters to relate to - for better, for worse. And also to concentrate, as William and I did, on the knight and squire as sub-plot, not, repeat not main plot. Use them as comic relief, happy cutaways from the quadruple romance thrust, arc, whatever. That way this show could yet be in business. Oh, and here's one other thing while we're at it - this music we're hearing is by another mate of mine, Rob Johnson. A very upmarket songsmith. By Appointment to all the Royals. Rob did the music for William's *Cymbeline*, *Winter's Tale* and *The Tempest* as well as loads of my stuff including *Cardenio* so it's like pretty appropriate here. Beautiful. Enjoy.

Spotlight off - Fletcher's gone. And, as the last Robert Johnson variation on Juan Carnago's courtly love song *¿Que es mi vida preguntais? - What is my life you ask?* resolves, the lights change to alert us to the first scene of the next act.

Act Three - Scene One

We're once again at what I called Pudding Peak in the Sierra Morena. Don Quixote's arms and lance have been put back in place as an eerie effigy of himself. The wind is still whistling. Don Quixote enters and exits swiftly - cartwheeling from stage left (prompt side) to stage right (opposite prompt side) in his shirt-tails. Did I hear a giggle from Lily at this now you see it, now you don't piece of business? Don Quixote re-enters, breeches in hand. He speaks to himself informatively as he pulls them on, tucking in his shirt and buckling his belt.

QUIXOTE

Sixteen cartwheels, twenty four somersaults and nine handstands. Not a bad score. Not for someone of my age. Coming up to fifty next Lady Day. Indeed, though I say it myself, these figures add up to my being, as it were, head over heels in love. Younger fellows might do more, I daresay, and all honour to them, to prove their love, but, that accepted, I doubt even they could match Sir Amadis of Gaul for sheer physical fitness. He, upon his eightieth birthday - and this is vouched-for by a host of independent witnesses - pulled off one hundred and fifty nude cartwheels non-stop. And all for love of his Lady Oriana, who was as incomparable as my Princess Dulcinea, and equally ageless, as befits all gentlewomen.

Pause in which Don Quixote indulges in further romantic speculation. If he's just expressed himself comparatively sensibly, but rather pedantically, he now employs more archaic speech patterns as Don Alonso turns into Don Quixote again.

QUIXOTE

Perchance e'en now my egregious squire (he checks himself) - or do I mean exiguous squire? Well, never mind, both epithets apply. He's outstandingly bad at his job and small of stature. (starting again) Perchance e'en at this very momentous moment he hath accomplished his, that is to say my embassage? Surely I see him as he kneeleth before thee, oh princess mine? Whilst thou dost read those rude lines with thine ineffable orbs. Oh, look graciously upon your errant knight bereft of thee and should it hap my squire sayeth or doeth any untoward word or thing I beg thee to forgive him for he is not yet fully acquainted with all the practices of chivalry but e'en so is quite the best one can get these days. But now, glorious woman, whilst I await reply I shall again emulate Sir Amadis. But this time in verse. Herewith is my gloss on certain immortal lines he penned to his peerless one so they may apply equally to thee, my equally if not more so if that's possible, peerless one.

He pulls from his pocket another torn-out page from Cardenio's notebook and reads what he's written on it aloud and with feeling.

O'er craggy steeps I rove forlorn
To seek mischance from place to place;
Cursing the proud, relentless scorn,
That's banish'd me from human race.
To flagellate my wounded heart
Love brings his cruel whip in play;
I weep to feel the raging smart
Of absence from my Dulcinay.

Pause

QUIXOTE
As you will know, oh learned lady and effortless polyglot, it is permissible for a poet in the heat of literal and literate passion to transmute the name of his mistress to fit a rhyme. Thus here I address you in the elegant French fashion rendering homage firstly to you, oh my soul, and then to that mirror of chivalry, my hero, Sir Amadis of Gaul. Meanwhile pray advise my squire not to linger on his return. I burn to read whatsoever you choose to write. Farewell. All Toboso echoes with your fame and so does this inhospitable -

He stops short, taken short, clutching his stomach. Grimace.

QUIXOTE
What's this? A chill on the stomach? Whatever next? When did I

last have the gripes? Oh, forgive me, I must depart at once if not sooner! A call of nature. Most unusual for me. Oh, Ooh -

He goes fast and awkwardly.

Blackout.

Act Three - Scene Two

I've a couple of things to say before we discover a path through pinewoods thriftily indicated by Lily scattering large fir cones across the stage, and Bill's lighting plan nicely suggesting evocative shafts of sunlight as if between trees. The first is to explain Don Quixote's exit just now. The sudden attack of the squitters gag to get a character off is, I admit, always a playwright's last resort, but in this instance it has some relevance. In Don Quixote Cervantes has created a non-eating, non-excretory insomniac while, with one notable exception, leaving all the grosser natural functions to Sancho. But by deliberately exposing himself to the cold winds of the Sierra Morena it is, to my mind, physiologically feasible that Don Quixote gets a chill on the stomach. It doesn't just bring him back to reality it humanises him as well. So I make no apology for using this outworn and yes, crude, theatrical device. And like many an old joke judiciously performed by an experienced artist it got its laugh, didn't it? Well, it did from me. Did you ever see breeched buttocks more expressively clenched?

The second point is rather more academic. I'm wondering if I heard lute music on the wind as Don Quixote recited his poem to Dulcinea? If I did then it again sounded like Robert Johnson's work. If so the director of the play has shown that Johnson did set Thomas Shelton's translation of Don Quixote's verses to music. Just as Fletcher said. So here we may have heard an echo of an echo of the first but lost *Cardenio*. A romantic thought.

But back to my black box of a theatre as Father Perez, Nicholas, Sancho and the hobby-horse, on leading rein now, appear. They stop. Look about. Especially Father Perez.

PRIEST
 (to Sancho) Are you sure this is the right road?

Sancho glowers, grunts as the hobby-horse tosses his head and then whinnies emphatically.

SANCHO

There! What more do you want? If any of us knows the way, it's
this one.

BARBER

You definitely came down this path?

The hobby-horse snorts indignantly. So does Sancho.

SANCHO

'Course I did! Same as we went up it! Hey! Hark! Hear that?

All listen.

PRIEST

Water?

SANCHO

Just up and round above. A tidgy fall of water out of the rocks, a
bit of a pool, then it trickles away down to your left. (still miffed
at having his word and bump of direction doubted). Ask Paco
here if you still reckon I'm wrong - he wet his whistle both times
- going up and coming down.

PRIEST

(conciliatory) We simply wished to be quite sure, my son.

SANCHO

Aye. And some folk want to be believed, don't we, old lad?

The hobby-horse nods and exhales reverberatively.

PRIEST

Let us proceed. Up we go.

But before they start off again Cardenio appears from out of the
trees. He's half-naked as before and looking frenetically back over
his shoulder. Consequently he is, for the moment, unaware of
these others on the path. Sancho, of course, recognises him at once.

SANCHO

Oh, no, not this barmpot again!

BARBER

You know him?

SANCHO

Don't I just? Aye. And a real menace he is, too. Twice over.

Cardenio turns to face them. His eyes are fixed, focused on his inner world. When he speaks it is with febrile, whispered intensity. But not to them - to another, elsewhere.

CARDENIO
  Surely I heard your voice but even now?
  You cried upon the wind: I'm here above.
  Oh, stay, I seek you, though I know not how;
  Pray God you took this path, my purest love.
SANCHO
  (to us) Hear that? Verse. In my book that spells trouble. Only I
  can't read, can I?

Cardenio, oblivious to this aside, sinks down, crouching in upon himself hugging his knees.

PRIEST
  So you know this young man, Sancho?
SANCHO
  (nod) I wish I didn't. Calls himself Cardenio.
PRIEST
  Unusual name.
SANCHO
  Is it?
PRIEST
  I've never baptized anyone as Cardenio.
SANCHO
  Well, that's who he says he is, father. Anyroad one minute he's
  a real gent, next he's at your throat. Got anything for him to eat,
  Nicholas? If so give it him. For our sake, not his. He'll savage
  you as soon as look at you if he's starved.

Nicholas takes out bread from his knapsack and goes to Cardenio who accepts it calmly but without acknowledging him.

SANCHO
  He's from Córdoba. Lost his girl to some other fellow. So he's
  crossed in love, right? And very cross about it he is, too.

Cardenio rises.

SANCHO
  (lower, faster) Hey up. A word to the wise, father. If he starts
  telling you his tale of woe, don't interrupt him. Ever! Else he'll
  set on you, cloth or no cloth, got me?

Pause. Cardenio smiles. His eyes now register reality. He has
become youthful charm personified. He addresses Father Perez
deferentially.

CARDENIO
  Father, forgive me. Your calling requires more courtesy than I
  have offered. My mind, I am sad to say, is not always my own.
PRIEST
  (scrupulous diplomat) Is that so, sir?
CARDENIO
  It is. I can be other than myself. May I speak further?

Pause while Father Perez considers his reply. He may be an
obscure village priest but he's no pushover, nor is he afraid to
put others to the test. Indeed in the time it's taken me to tell you
this he's decided to do just that - to probe Cardenio's politeness
by way of a sententious answer appropriate to his vocation and
to the theatrical conventions of his era - whether played out in
England or in Spain.

PRIEST
  (adamantine) Age must endure what youth must speak, my son.

Flashpoint.

CARDENIO
  (outburst) To hell with that! If that's what you think I'll say
  nothing! Nothing at all!

Father Perez smiles benignly at this other Cardenio, then quotes
Lucretius.

PRIEST
  Nothing can come from nothing, sir. Am I to understand you've
  been disappointed in love?

Cardenio breathes in, blinks, breathes out. Speaks politely again.

71

CARDENIO
    Yes, father, yes. I was sent as companion, friend, squire if you like,
    to Lord Fernando at the request of his father, the Grand Duke.
PRIEST
    Of Montoro?
CARDENIO
    Yes.
PRIEST
    Such advancement speaks highly in your favour, sir.
CARDENIO
    So my parents thought. But it forced my absence from Lucinda.
SANCHO
    His sweetheart, father, since time was.

Cardenio reacts sharply; so does Father Perez.

PRIEST
    Sancho! Let this gentleman speak! Speak for himself!
SANCHO
    Sorry. Only trying to help. But mum's the word - (he turns to us
    with a wink) - as dad said to the new milkmaid with his hand up
    her skirt. Whoopsadaisy, Daisy.

Cardenio meanwhile is once again in conflict with his second self.

PRIEST
    (placatory) Never mind him, good sir.
BARBER
    He's known in our village as a mouth with feet on.
PRIEST
    Please continue.
CARDENIO
    (trembling, eyes blazing) You don't fool me! You think you can
    lie! Cheat! Pull the wool over my eyes! But you can't, no! Nor
    can that fat clown there. Oh, I know him! Nor that old idiot up
    there! Way up there! Telling me a brass basin's a gold helmet!"
BARBER
    Brass basin?
CARDENIO
    Yes!
BARBER
    The sort barbers use?

CARDENIO
  Yes!
BARBER
  I know exactly what you mean, sir. I have several in my shop.
PRIEST
  But he thinks it's a helmet?
CARDENIO
  Yes!
PRIEST
  Was he wearing it as such?
CARDENIO
  I've no idea. When I met him he'd stuck it on a pole.

Pause as his first self returns tentatively to him.

CARDENIO
  Where am I? Here, there, where? My head's bursting. So's my
  heart. So many places, people, so much shame! Shame, yes
  shame. Where was I?
PRIEST
  (very gently) You were in the service of the Grand Duke, sir.
CARDENIO
  So I was. Yes. (with fragile lucidity) Lord Fernando, hearing
  me talk of Lucinda, offered to carry my letters to her. Thinking
  him my friend I trusted him. But when he saw her - her beauty,
  her innocence - he resolved to have her for himself. Without
  my knowing it he demanded her hand in marriage. Lucinda's
  father, dazzled by the honour - and the wealth - that this union
  would bring to him and his wife, agreed.

Cardenio stops. He is lost for words. This time no one speaks, not
even Sancho, thanks to eloquent warning looks from Father Perez.

CARDENIO
  (eventually) Lucinda got word to me. I contrived to be present
  at the wedding in order to prevent it. Lucinda had written to tell
  me she would never say 'I will' to anyone but me. But then when
  asked at the altar by the chaplain, she did! Hearing this I drew
  my sword. Not to kill her! As if I would! No! To kill Fernando!
  But my mind could not command my arm, my hand. There and
  then I found myself a coward!

Cardenio sinks to his knees, burying his head in his hands.

PRIEST
  No. God guided you. Was the ceremony then concluded?
CARDENIO
  I don't know! He'd said 'I will' and so had she.
PRIEST
  Were rings exchanged?
CARDENIO
  I don't know!
PRIEST
  Did the chaplain say: I declare you man and wife?
CARDENIO
  I don't know! Don't ask! I ran away.

Silence before an unaccompanied voice is heard singing as if from higher up the path. All listen.

  Song

  Belief in Love begets deceit;
  Justice engenders unjust rule.
  Who can I trust who next I meet?
  How shall I know them false or true?

BARBER
  A boy's voice? A girl's voice? Wait. I'll go and see.

Nicholas goes, thus allowing time for Sancho to speak to us. In support of Cardenio for once.

SANCHO
  This Cardenio lad's right about one thing at least. There's more folk hereabouts than you'd think. Up hill, down dale. Best hope they don't bring us yet more trouble, eh? Seeing how much we've got already.

Nicholas returns on tip-toe.

BARBER
  A wonder. Come. But walk softly.

All follow him with varying degrees of stealthiness. Father Perez steps lightly, Cardenio neatly, Sancho clumpily, while the hobby-horse's wheels squeak like mating sparrows.

Act Three - Scene Three

Remember what Sancho remembered just now? Rocks, a fall of water, a pool so shallow it might be a plate of glass, a trickle of overspill? What he didn't mention was that here the pines have given place to a grove of sweet chestnuts and holm oaks providing chequered shade from the sun.

Of course none of this is present here. What we have instead is an actor seated on a plastic rock we've seen before with her feet planted on a piece of mirror. Fringe theatre at its most demanding. Again Bill's done pretty well with the lighting, but even so it's up to us to imagine together, out of such bits and bobs of natural history as our various memories possess, light and shade through foliage, liquid reflections, sunbeams bright with butterflies. Music can help us here and I think Lily has just put on a rather delicate guitar treatment of the song we've just heard.

The actor is Dorotea, still dressed as a boy, as I'm sure you've guessed. She's taken off her boots and is cooling her feet, in mime, on the mirror. Enter Father Perez, Nicholas, Cardenio, Sancho and the hobby-horse. All adopt furtive positions as if peering through conveniently low-slung foliage.

As Dorotea continues her song we lose the guitar so she sings unaccompanied. Also she takes off her hat, allowing her long, lustrous hair to fall.

Song

My sighs, my tears, in stone make print;
But not in you, harder than any flint.
Who can I trust who next I meet?
Since lust in love begets deceit?

BARBER
(whisper) There! What did I tell you? A woman! And a handsome one at that.

CARDENIO
  (equally unvoiced) Since she is not Lucinda she can be no human
  creature.
PRIEST
  (naturally discreet) Diana at the least, one might say.
SANCHO
  (too loud) With hot feet from look of it!

Nicholas shushes Sancho but it's too late, Dorotea has heard his
voice. She jumps up, justifiably alarmed.

DOROTEA
  Who's that?

She grabs her boots and hat.

DOROTEA
  Robbers? Bandits?

Father Perez breaks cover, confident his cassock will proclaim his
good faith.

PRIEST
  Honest travellers, madam, at your service.

Cardenio now steps forward and bows graciously. His ragged
appearance however is not quite so convincing as his manner.

CARDENIO
  Yours to command, lady.
DOROTEA
  (still afraid) Who? Who are you? Who?

Sancho and the hobby-horse appear, with Nicholas. Seeing them I
think Dorotea might be somewhat reassured. They look relatively
harmless. Hardly the outlaws she feared at first.

SANCHO
  Well, miss, since you ask, that one's Father Perez, our priest,
  and this one's Nicholas, our barber. He shaves us Saturdays,
  delivers babbies any time, sets our bones if we break 'em. And
  this gentleman, lower half in rags, calls himself Cardenio.

DOROTEA
  And you, sir?
SANCHO
  Me? I'm Panza. Sancho. But I'm no sir. Just squire to the world
  famous knight Don Quixote of La Mancha 'cept nobody's heard
  of him as yet. (patting the hobby-horse's head). And this is his
  horse, or, as he would say, his mighty steed. Name of Rocinante.
DOROTEA
  (puzzled) Squire? Knight? Mighty steed?: I'm not sure I
  understand?
PRIEST
  Nor need you, madam. But rest assured you're safe with us.
  And if we can help you we will But first we must know what's
  brought you here?
SANCHO
  Got up as a lad.
DOROTEA
  To protect my honour. Such as is left of it.
PRIEST
  Ah.

Pause broken tactfully by Nicholas.

BARBER
  Where do you come from, madam?
DOROTEA
  Montoro.
CARDENIO
  (sharply) Montoro?
DOROTEA
  You know the town, sir?
CARDENIO
  I do! Too well! It's the seat of the Grand Duke Ricardo.
DOROTEA
  It is. Yes. His son - the younger one - Lord Fernando -
CARDENIO
  Him!
SANCHO
  (to us) Didn't I say? Small world, big trouble?
PRIEST
  Shush, man, shush!

Dorotea holds out her left hand to show Father Perez and Cardenio a gold ring on her wedding finger.

DOROTEA

This ring came from him. He placed it here himself as pledge of his honourable intent.

CARDENIO

You're betrothed?

DOROTEA

I am. And so is he. He promised me we should be married. He signed and sealed this paper.

She produces the document she showed her nurse at the beginning of Act Two. She hands it to Father Perez.

PRIEST

May I ask your name, madam?

DOROTEA

Dorotea. The only daughter of my widowed father who has no son to take his name. Our farm's close by Montoro.

PRIEST

Are you tenants of the Grand Duke?

DOROTEA

Yes. His family claims half our harvests. On occasion, more.

PRIEST

Ah.

DOROTEA

But read that paper, if you please, father.

Father Perez opens the document. As he reads it we become aware that Cardenio is now consumed with further justifiable hatred of his rival.

CARDENIO

When did Lord Fernando sign that promise?

DOROTEA

Three weeks ago.

CARDENIO

And do you know he's since married another?

Dorotea is horrified.

DOROTEA
  Oh no!
CARDENIO
  I was witness to it!
DOROTEA
  Then I am beyond help. Beyond justice!
CARDENIO
  As I am! As are we all - except Fernando!

He goes, getting himself off stage with a blood-curdling yowl of teenage despair. Pause. Then Dorotea looks up at Father Perez who has just finished reading the marriage pledge.

DOROTEA
  (hardly able to speak) Can I believe him, father?
PRIEST
  I don't know. But he has told us he did serve as a companion to this young lord.
DOROTEA
  Oh, no!
BARBER
  And that he's lost the love of his life to him. A lady called Lucinda.
DOROTEA
  Worse still.
SANCHO
  Sent him cuckoo it has.
DOROTEA
  I'm sure. Oh, Holy Mary, help us.
PRIEST
  With our prayers she will, madam, she will.

Cardenio returns. He's calmer than he was and he's smoothed down his hair and straightened his torn breeches. He's still bare-chested and bare-foot, of course, but his late Renaissance manners are now more impeccable than ever, and his sentiments - expressed in verse as he kneels in front of Dorotea - would win even Don Quixote's approval.

CARDENIO
  Madam, your plight's concurrence with my own,
  Half-broke my brain but now I'm whole again,
  And here, upon my knee, I swear to right

These unjust harms we both do suffer.
Let me your champion be, and with one stroke,
I shall at once avenge both you and me.
SANCHO
(to us) More verse but I've heard worse. Not too bad for a lad of
his age up his own jaxie, right?

Father Perez clears his throat warningly at Sancho.

SANCHO
(to himself) Hey up. Shut gob, mister you, meaning me.

Father Perez, having now fully considered Fernando's paper
promise of marriage, addresses Dorotea and Cardenio formally.

PRIEST
Doña Dorotea, Don Cardenio, allow me to advise you both. For
your best sakes, proceed with caution in this matter. And let me,
if you will, assist you in your mutual quest for justice. All may
yet be resolved - nothing it seems is quite so certain here as first
appears. (to Cardenio in particular) Have you not said, sir, that
the wedding ceremony of Lady Lucinda to Lord Fernando may
not have been concluded?
DOROTEA
Could this be so?
CARDENIO
Don't ask! I quit the place too soon!

He bows his head in anguish, but even so this latest outburst
has been less emphatic than others we've heard from him.
Furthermore, his shame-faced silence after it gives Nicholas and
Sancho a chance to tell Dorotea what they know about Cardenio.
Both seize it - sotto voce.

BARBER
You see - he meant to stop the wedding -
SANCHO
But at the last moment he got the jim-jams! Since when - well,
look at him, lady. I wouldn't count on him as a champ, would
you? All balls one minute, all boo-hoo the next.

To her credit Dorotea takes Sancho's assessment of Cardenio seriously. I have the feeling she could turn out to be as shrewd a judge of character as he is. But then again I'm partial; I like the girl. She's a rare one, as Sancho would say. And doubtless will.

DOROTEA
Well, at least he's as unfortunate as I am. (to Father Perez) We can go together to Montoro, father, and with your help - and may God reward you for it - we can, I hope, discover -
PRIEST
Wait, my child. We have - Master Nicholas and I - an immediate task of our own to conclude hereabouts.
DOROTEA
And what is that?
BARBER
To fetch a neighbour home.
SANCHO
(ever helpful) Him as I said I was squire to. Our local loony 'cept he isn't. He comes and goes, off and on, like your lad there. But in a sort of different, more big-headed manner, somehow, if you know what I mean?

Dorotea doesn't. But before she can query Sancho's report of his employer's eccentricities Cardenio looks up.

CARDENIO
I'm myself again.

He rises, lucidly.

CARDENIO
Father, if you're to complete your mission, let me help you if I can. I've seen the unhappy gentleman you speak of and he too needs good counsel -

Sancho is indignant.

SANCHO
Hold on! He gets that all the time from me! I'm always telling him what's best.
BARBER
(sharply) Sancho! Enough said, all right?

SANCHO
  No - !
PRIEST
  (firmly) Yes, Sancho, yes. Time flies. The world wags. God waits.
  Let us all go on - in peace - together. And do His will.

They all go.

Act Three - Scene Four

I very nearly wrote *exeunt omnes* just now but I didn't because
to use Latin for stage directions (and indeed for act and scene
announcements) struck me as too old-fashioned for this present
version of *Cardenio*, which, although it owes its being to the past
is nevertheless happening now. And besides, if it's been said (and
it has) that all novels are historical, then it's equally true, as John
Fletcher pointed out, that all plays, whenever they are set, are
contemporary.

Doubtless the lost printed text of Shakespeare and Fletcher's
collaboration would have used this classical convention but until
a genuine, carbon-dated copy turns up we must make do with
supposition. Mind you, actors still say they make exits and entrances
so I could have written *they exit* which though ungrammatical is
exactly what would be said in a theatre. I can just hear a director
at rehearsal shouting: "Go on, exit all revolting citizens, drunken
soldiery, harlots and catamites now!" Shakespeare himself said it,
through Jaques in *As You Like It*, apropos the seven ages of man.
And, by the way, though theatre folklore suggests Shakespeare
may have played Adam, the faithful old servant, in that comedy,
I wouldn't be surprised if he sometimes took on Jaques. On tour
perhaps? It's such a mature actor/playwright's part - that of
the wryly ironic commentator to one side of the story. Another
role he's thought to have played, the ghost of Hamlet's father, is
more crucial to the action - physical and metaphysical. The ghost
may be a small part but it's so densely packed with consequence
it demands the most careful casting. You don't hand the part to
just anyone. After all it sets the whole tragedy in motion and is
in a sense the infernal machine itself - the past literally haunting
the present. This suggests to me that Shakespeare was a far more
considerable actor than many literary people have given him
credit for. There's a tendency to suppose that because he wasn't

a star actor like Edward Alleyn playing Tamburlaine at the age of twenty one or Richard Burbage playing Hamlet at the age of thirty four, that he wasn't that good. But I've seen dozens of what are called character actors get better and better, subtler and more charismatic as they grow in age, experience and authority. Surely Shakespeare could have been like that? Most scholars tend to identify with the writer in Shakespeare and seem sometimes to deplore and then ignore the actor in him. In essence it's that age-old snobbery about *luvvies* (journalists are particularly prone to it), but a moment's thought should remind us that if Shakespeare hadn't been a natural actor he wouldn't have got a job in the theatre in the first place, and so might not have discovered his genius as a playwright.

But I've digressed - a fault that may be forgiven in a novelist but never in a playwright. So music, please. A change of light. And enter Don Quixote. He's re-armed. I can't say he looks magnificently Arthurian, Wagnerian, or Tolkienian, but then again he doesn't look entirely ridiculous. Is this a trick of the light or something to do with the present performer's physique? Possibly both, plus something about the original concept of this tall, thin middle-aged idiot which commands our respect even as we laugh at him. Could he be what we will become?

If Richard Burbage did play the part, as John Fletcher claimed in Act One, then he must surely have supplied true star quality: a something instantly recognisable but not easy to define. It's there in how an actor looks, sounds, moves. It's in the voice, the body language, the eyes - especially the eyes that make their contact so directly with us as rows of shadows - to him or her - beyond the electric dazzle of the lights out front.

But here Don Quixote (whoever may be playing him) has no audience but you, me, William Shakespeare, John Fletcher and Miguel de Cervantes Saavedra. Unless, that is, the last three of them have popped out to the pub opposite. I can't say I'd blame them if they have. After all, they do know the story, don't they?

Anyway, Don Quixote is now alone on stage and free to address himself, us, and a stuffed griffon vulture, borrowed by Lily from the Horniman Museum in Sydenham, South London, perched on that other plastic rock we've seen before when our hero was less completely dressed. Or, to put it in military jargon, when he was in shirt-sleeve order. But now, armed more or less *cap-à-pie*, as the French chroniclers said, he presents his lance and sword aloft as if on parade at a tournament.

QUIXOTE

(quoting Virgil) Arma virumque cano! I sing of arms and the man. Or should I say: arms and the hero? Translators differ on this point, I find. But be that as it may, it's time once more for action. Both manly and heroic. Yes! Time to put the chronicler of my deeds to the test. Can his words match my prowess? Give me my place in history? Make my name resound forever? Putting it bluntly I wish to be immortal. I certainly need to be. Look at it this way, even Achilles, a born demi-god, needed his Homer. And Aeneas, prince of Troy, founder of Rome, had to have a Virgil to make his mark. And my latter-day heroes - Sir Amadis, for prime example - all had their distinguished and devoted biographers, many with a magical, nay transformational turn of phrase. So where is mine? He must be somewhere?

The stuffed griffon vulture croaks as if clearing its primordial throat. Ideally it would also clap its vast, plank-like wings - I quote the Shell Easy Bird Guide to Britain and Europe here - but this arresting stage effect is beyond even Bill and Lily's ingenuity so please take it as read. As it is the vulture's croak serves as a perfectly acceptable cue for Don Quixote who turns to address it.

QUIXOTE

You? Are you he? Why not? You could be. I've read of any number of spell-binding, word-spinning historiographers assuming all sorts of different forms, whether of birds or beasts. Therefore let it be so, sir. Mark me, follow me, as I now set forth. First in quest of my squire whom I fear may have fallen by the wayside, such is his propensity for mishap. He could be - even now - in need of rescue. And then, once I've brought him back into my service - for with me the word spoken is the deed done - then I shall engage in some mighty exploit worthy of record. For know you this, sir, my war is against the unacceptable wheresoever it is to be found and my purpose is to restore - single-handed if need be - Peace and Justice worldwide. No more, no less.

Don Quixote marches off to a sudden burst of military music. The stuffed vulture remains. When the music stops, as suddenly as it began, the bird caws. Aptly enough it sounds tersely derisive: cor!

Act Three - Scene Five

Somewhere else lower down the mountain. Lily's removed the vulture and turned the fake rock round to give it a different aspect. We could well be close to the spot where Sancho found Cardenio's bag in Act One. Some mournful music here would help the illusion. But no. The sound system's playing up, it seems. Doubtless Bill is coping even as the show goes on.

Father Perez and Cardenio are walking round Nicholas, appraising him from all angles. He wears a neatly trimmed false beard made from a cow's tail, huge pebble glass spectacles and a chain mail jerkin several sizes too large for him. There is no sign of Dorotea or Sancho but the hobby-horse is grazing contentedly close by. Nicholas, however, is becoming increasingly irritated by the scrutiny he's undergoing. Finally he speaks.

BARBER
  Well? What do you think? Do I convince or don't I?
CARDENIO
  (non-committal) Mm.
PRIEST
  Well -
BARBER
  For heaven's sake! Do I look like a Lord High Steward to a Princess from the Back of Beyond? Yes or no?

Tact gathering pause.

PRIEST
  It could be the spectacles rather diminish the effect, Nicholas.
BARBER
  But they hide my eyes.
PRIEST
  True.
BARBER
  He might recognise my eyes.
PRIEST
  Yes. Also true.
BARBER
  He may be nuts but he isn't daft.
PRIEST
  Indeed so. Keep them on. (turning to Cardenio) Nor ideally

85

should he recognise us.

CARDENIO

I'm sure he'll recognise me.

PRIEST

I daresay. So you and I, sir, must keep well back. And allow our Lord High Steward here to conduct the usurped princess into the presence of that mirror of chivalry, Don Quixote of La Mancha. (to Nicholas) You look fine. After all, let us remember, he'll want you to be who you say you are quite as much as you do. In fact - more so.

BARBER

(not entirely convinced) Mm. (eternal actor) Let's see how it plays.

PRIEST

(to Cardenio) Only by entering into his fantasies can we lure our good neighbour home without his knowing it so he can become who he really is again - Don Alonso the Good.

Dorotea appears. She's wearing the dress she wore before she changed into boy's clothes. Cardenio is impressed, as well he might be. Dorotea is not.

DOROTEA

I'm not sure this dress turns me into a princess really -

CARDENIO

Oh, it does, madam, it does!

DOROTEA

And I've forgotten her name. Who am I going to be, did you say?

PRIEST

The Princess Micomicona.

BARBER

Of the kingdom of Micomicon.

CARDENIO

In Ethiopia.

DOROTEA

I knew it began with M. Micomicona, yes. Princess of Micomicon, right. Got it.

BARBER

And you've come with me as your Lord High Steward to beg a boon from Don Quixote who -

Dorotea interrupts him, laughing.

DOROTEA

Oh, I can manage all of that side of it! It was only the name
escaped me. I know all about knights, giants and monsters. And
dwarves, and elves, and wizards, and magic rings and steaming
mirrors in which you see things at your great peril. Don't worry,
I've read all the books.

PRIEST

But they haven't driven you mad, have they?

DOROTEA

I don't think so. Not so far. But I do love them! Your friend won't
catch me out when it comes to any of that silliness.

Sancho enters at a belly-shaking run.

SANCHO

He's coming down! He's on his way! In all his gear. Heard him
a mile off - clink, clonk, clank. And bawling at the sky as usual.

PRIEST

Then we must meet him. Confront him with a boldness equal to
his own. But first, Sancho, be sure to remember that the lady here
is now the great Princess Micomicona and that she commands
your squire-like respect and loyalty, is that clear?

Sancho looks at Dorotea. If Cardenio was impressed, Sancho is
bowled over.

SANCHO

Oh, my sakes, girl! You look lovely. A real beauty you are. Far
more so than my one's lady. His princess Dulcinea's a pig's ear
compared to you, Doña Dorotea.

BARBER

No, Sancho! Princess Micomicona. And you must address me as
her Lord High Steward, understood?

SANCHO

Hope so. But it'll take some doing, Nick. You in that beard - cow's
tail, is it? And them dirty great spectacles. And Meecomeemona's
a bit of a mouthful, you know.

BARBER

No! Micomicona. It ends with *cona*, Sancho.

SANCHO

Right. Mona-Coma. Right.

BARBER

No -

PRIEST

(intervening) Why don't you just stick to Your Royal Highness, Sancho?

SANCHO

Oh, I can say that! No trouble at all. Why didn't you say so before?

PRIEST

(with a sigh) Let us go.

And they do. In the following order: Dorotea and Nicholas first, then Sancho leading the hobby-horse, with Father Perez and Cardenio behind. Father Perez may pull his biretta well down in an attempt to mask his face in readiness for their encounter with their quarry. As soon as they've gone off stage right Don Quixote enters stage left.

Act Three - Scene Six

Don Quixote takes centre stage and marches on the spot. Clink, clonk, clank. If the thought of a suit of ancestral armour on the move occurs to us so much the better. After a moment he stops and speaks directly, confidentially, to us. As his rational, country gentleman Don Alonso self.

QUIXOTE

Speaking frankly, a knight errant without a horse is not at his best. One might even say he becomes a rather pedestrian contradiction in terms. Of course I had no choice but to lend Sancho dear old Paco, also celebrated, as you know, as Rocinante. How else was he to get to El Toboso and back? But now it seems they've been held up for some reason. Rocinante could've thrown a shoe, perhaps? Pray heaven he hasn't gone lame. So here I am without a mount. Irksome really. After all, horse-power is also man-power, is it not? It puts the fellow on top - oneself - at a level with others of an elevated kind, and above those of a not so elevated kind. Not that I would ever dream - God forbid - of riding roughshod over ordinary people, oh no, quite the reverse! But the truth is one can do lower, less fortunate souls so much more good from the saddle, can't one? And also, fittingly enough, help those even higher up in the scale of things than oneself. I'm thinking here of troubled princes - male or female - and also of lords and ladies at the mercy of untoward events - dishonour, death, drought, dearth, disability, delusions, etcetera. In other words a knight-errant is, by definition, charity on a horse. But should he be without one he's - well, let's face it - he's - how shall I put it? - less effective. And as for surgically eradicating rogues and monsters on a global basis, well, without a warhorse, where are you? (he looks round) Good question. Where indeed?

Horse whinny as the sound system functions again. Don Quixote spins round, reactivated as his heroic self.

QUIXOTE
Rocinante! His voice! He's back! My mighty steed! My squire as well, I trust? Oh, praise be! (another whinny) There! He smelleth battle not so far off!

He adopts an exultant chivalric pose. Enter Dorotea as Princess Micomicona. But that's putting it mildly. What she in fact performs is an amazingly athletic knee-slide of an entrance so that she falls, whoosh, at Don Quixote's feet in a desperate but intensely elegant, even regal, sort of kneel.

DOROTEA
(her bosom heaving impressively) Great knight, we, Princess Micomicona, shall not arise from this spot, here at your feet, unless Your Magnanimousness grants us one boon.

Don Quixote registers some surprise. This is, after all, the first time anyone has deliberately entered into the spirit of his delusion. Meanwhile Nicholas enters in his disguise (such as it is), followed by Sancho, very much as himself, and the hobby-horse as Rocinante or Paco - take your pick. Beyond them Father Perez and Cardenio appear as invisibly as is humanly possible.

QUIXOTE
(no longer surprised) Your Royal Highness - I shall not answer you one word, until you rise.

DOROTEA
Your word is our command, illustrious knight.

She rises. Don Quixote kneels.

QUIXOTE
As yours is mine, majestic madam.
DOROTEA
Nay! Arise, exalted sir, that we may speak as equals - you, by reason of your valour and renown, and we, by reason of our blood and rank.

Don Quixote rises, firmly convinced that his dream of an age of gothic derring-do has now come true.

QUIXOTE
May it please your Highness to know that the boon you crave is already granted and therefore in effect achieved however out of the question it may prove to be. Speak, I pray you, I am all ears, forsooth.
DOROTEA
Then know again great Don Quixote of La Mancha we are the Princess Micomicona of the kingdom of Micomicon.
QUIXOTE
An African state, if I am not mistaken, conjunct with the realm of Prester John, is it not?
DOROTEA
Polymathic sir, your knowledge is boundless, but, woe are we, our kingdom is usurped, despoiled, ravaged by a giant whose name must not, shall not, cannot, just won't befoul our tongue. But our Lord High Steward here, may voice it to you.

And she turns, with a questioning smile, to Nicholas, thus neatly covering this moment of forgetfulness. It's only the odd name that escapes Dorotea, nothing else. Nicholas, however, is reluctant to speak directly to Don Quixote in case he recognises his voice. So he grunts before mumbling the giant's name.

BARBER
Hmmm. Panda - hmm - filando.

90

Don Quixote now looks more closely at Nicholas. Until this moment Dorotea's beauty, presence, and delightful distress have distracted him. But Nicholas's disguise is another matter. Even Don Quixote may now be permitted to query it.

QUIXOTE
This gentleman is your steward, madam?
DOROTEA
He is, sir. The Lord High Steward of our royal house. We should be as nothing without him.
QUIXOTE
(still doubtful) High Steward, kindly repeat the name of that giant aforesaid. Panda - something, was it?

Nicholas coughs as if to clear his throat but in fact in an attempt to alter yet again the timbre of his voice. This time he speaks with catarrhal hoarseness. Plus further coughing.

BARBER
Filando. Pandafilando.
QUIXOTE
Thank you, sir. Pandafilando. Yet your voice, sir, seems strangely familiar to me. Do I not know it? You sound very like a neighbour of mine suffering from a heavy cold. Is not that peculiar?

Awkward pause cut short by Sancho barging forward with the hobby-horse to interpose himself between Don Quixote, Nicholas and Dorotea. Oddly enough this rough and ready intervention saves the situation. Chivalry comes in many forms.

SANCHO
Right, sir, let's get this straight, shall we? With less fancy talk! Look, sir, like you see, I'm back. And so's your old nag, sir. Went like shit off a shovel, he did, bless him! And your lady love was knocked out by your letter, sir. But I never had time to get my donks 'cos who should I meet but these grand folks looking for you, sir. Yes, you! No bugger else. They know all about you, sir, and they reckon you're just the man for the job, sir. And I agree with 'em. A dirty great adventure setting everything right so we can all live happily ever after? And rich! So come on, here it is, handed you on a plate. The big one. Yours for the asking. A princess to rescue, a giant to kill. What more d'you want? And

while you're at it, sir, you can forget your Toboso lady because here's a better one. I mean, just look at her! Pure gold in person. And what's the betting if you do what she wants you can marry her? You'll be her hero forever. Her one and only. Her consort. Her king! And -
QUIXOTE
Enough, Sancho, enough! Let Her Highness speak. It does not fit you to intervene so rudely between great ones.

But, as said, Sancho has already saved the day. The dragon of doubt has, for the moment, been dealt with. Nicholas is no longer under scrutiny and Dorotea has recovered her poise.

DOROTEA
And yet, great knight, your good squire's words contain much truth. Wilt thou kill us this giant?

Formal pause while Don Quixote concocts the correct wordage in which to accept the quest. Unfortunately this delay causes Sancho to explode yet again. Unfortunately is both the right and the wrong word, of course. At one level - let's say reality - it's true. But at another level - let's call it drama - it couldn't be better. And Sancho, a consummate performer at both levels, times this next interruption to perfection.

SANCHO
What you waiting for? Here's a real princess!
QUIXOTE
(supremely tetched) Hold your tongue, vile squire!
SANCHO
Look at her! It's now or never!
QUIXOTE
Silence, bottlehead!
SANCHO
Never! She's all yours for the taking. You'll be king of wherever it is! Get on with it! You'll never get another like this one whoever you are! She's gorgeous!
QUIXOTE
(exploding) Be quiet!

Sancho subsides into a sulk.

DOROTEA

Pardon him, indomitable hero, he is but young.

QUIXOTE

(still supremely vexed) Not so young! Well over thirty and well overweight. A tub of loquacious lard!

Although Sancho's first intervention just about deflected Don Quixote's doubts concerning Nicholas as a steward to royalty he has nevertheless decided to seek diplomatic refuge in shadow alongside Father Perez and Cardenio. This leaves Dorotea alone to cope with an indignant mirror of chivalry and his infatuated squire. Who would have thought Sancho would have fallen for her - apart from me, of course?

DOROTEA

(managing majestically) Great sir, you do your squire wrong. Is he not, as yet, perchance, unskilled in the service of so punctilious a knight-errant as your unparalleled self?

Buttered up like this I regret to note that Don Quixote responds rather too smarmily.

QUIXOTE

Your Highness, you do me too much honour. I am a nobody, a non-entity, a nothing, save in the service of the Great and the Good.

Hearing this, Sancho turns to us.

SANCHO

Hear that? The old bastard can lay it on thick when he chooses, can't he? Mind you, I don't blame him. (indicating Dorotea) I mean - well - just look at her. Ent she lovely? Pure perfection. And know what? I tell you no lie. Oh, dear. Oh, wibbly-wobbly! I haven't felt like this since I was a lad too big for my breeches. What will the wife say? Won't tell her, ooh!

He sighs, besotted, as Dorotea returns to the other subject in hand.

DOROTEA

We, the Princess of Micomicona, await your answer, great sir. Will you undertake this perilous quest?

QUIXOTE

I shall, great lady, I shall. Command me as your champion.

DOROTEA

We do. Forthwith. And forsooth.

QUIXOTE

But upon proviso.

DOROTEA

Oh? What's that?

QUIXOTE

When I bring you this giant's head, upheld by my invincible arm despite its weight, do not, in gratitude, I pray you, offer me your royal hand in marriage since I am bespoke already to that lodestar of luminosity, Princess Dulcinea of El Toboso.

DOROTEA

That is understood, sir. Your constancy to her is as world-famous as your prowess in the field.

SANCHO

(outburst) Oh, no! How about that? The old so and so's done for us now.

QUIXOTE

Did you speak, squire?

SANCHO

What if I did? You never listen, do you?

QUIXOTE

Then hold your tongue.

Sancho makes a give-up face at us as Don Quixote kneels in front of Dorotea.

QUIXOTE

Here I kneel, Your Highness. Here I swear my fealty as your chosen champion.

Another shout of denial - louder even than Sancho's - from upstage. Cardenio rushes forward before either Father Perez or Nicholas can stop him.

CARDENIO

(raging) No! No! No! I'm her champion! Me! Not you! Me! Me! Me!

QUIXOTE

(surprised) You? You again? What are you doing here this time?

CARDENIO

What I say! Defending this lady's honour. Her real honour! In the real world!

QUIXOTE

The real world? What world's that?

CARDENIO

This one!

Now it's up to Father Perez to reveal himself in order to save the situation. Clearly, with so many fantasies and emotions in conflict, it isn't going to be easy. For once he's flummoxed. And Don Quixote is, of course, genuinely surprised to see him.

PRIEST

Before we go further -

QUIXOTE

Father Perez?

PRIEST

Don Alonso -

QUIXOTE

Don Quixote, if you please.

PRIEST

My mistake. Of course. Don Quixote.

QUIXOTE

Exactly. But what are you doing here, father?

PRIEST

Toiling as ever in the Lord's vineyard. I'm on leave of absence from our parish as counsellor and confessor to Her Royal Highness the Princess Micomicona and her retinue.

CARDENIO

Look, I want this clear -!

PRIEST

Patience, sir. And a word of advice - !

He draws Cardenio aside.

PRIEST

(fierce whisper) The aim is to humour him, remember?

CARDENIO

(loudly) Maybe! But I'm not having that old fart as her champion.

Dorotea joins them urgently. She's as concerned as Father Perez.

DOROTEA
  But we agreed, Don Cardenio -
CARDENIO
  (overlap) Oh, no, we didn't! Not to you having two champions!
DOROTEA
  But this is only make-believe -
CARDENIO
  (on the edge of relapse) Look! I swore to avenge you, didn't I?
  On an exclusive basis? Agreed? And never mind who it was. Or
  is. Lord Fernando or this giant Pandafilando - who cares? I'm
  the one to do it! No one else. And that's that! There's nothing
  more to say!

Don Quixote's overheard all of this so he's in a position to refute
Cardenio's final statement.

QUIXOTE
  But there is, sir. I've sworn the same.

Sharp, double-edged pause. Don Quixote and Cardenio confront
each other. This time the knight is in control, secure in all his
delusions, while Cardenio, his fragile hold on reality stretched to
the limit by the charade Father Perez, Nicholas and Dorotea have
set in motion, snaps in two.

CARDENIO
  (at all three) It's a plot! You've planned it! All of you! Not just
  this crackpot here but you, father whoever you are, and you, sir,
  in that stupid beard! And you, too, madam, with all your airs
  and graces!

All three protest. *No! No! Be reasonable* etc. But Cardenio's now
dangerous frenzy shouts them down.

CARDENIO
  Don't think I don't know! You can't fool me. You've done it to
  provoke me, haven't you? To get rid of me! Destroy me! You've
  chosen that one there - him! - to be your champion! Not against
  any damn fool, non-existent giant but against me! Me! Me! Me!
  I'm the one you're really after, aren't I? I'm the one you want

96

to drive mad! Prove a coward. All of it thought out, worked out behind my back. But you mistake your man! I'll show you! You'll see!

And with a lightning lunge he seizes Don Quixote's lance out of his hand before he can react and wields it around himself as it if were an enormous baseball bat. Then he freezes, deliberate aggressive stance, and challenges Don Quixote.

CARDENIO
Right! So now, you old idiot, let's see who's the champion. You or me? Right!

He charges, lance level, straight at Don Quixote who side-steps neatly. General consternation including Sancho now. Don Quixote draws his sword. More consternation as Cardenio recovers his physical balance and turns to face him. Acute pause.

QUIXOTE
(calmly) I'm for you sir. Stand your ground, sir, if you dare.

All protest again.

ALL
No! Hold on! Wait! Listen! Look! Use your head!

Cardenio heaves up the lance again. Dorotea rushes in bravely to try and stop him.

DOROTEA
No! We're all friends - all of us! Please -

Cardenio thrusts her aside.

CARDENIO
Never! You all lie. All except me. You all pretend to be what you aren't. (at Dorotea) And you're the worst! False! False as Fernando! Oh - aaaah!

And with a prolonged howl he rushes away, taking the lance with him.

SANCHO

Looks like you've lost your old poker, sir.

QUIXOTE

Possibly. But he's quit the field, has he not, and I still have my sword? My ancestral blade known to one and all as the Flame of the West.

SANCHO

First I've heard of it.

QUIXOTE

Well, now you have.

Don Quixote turns to Dorotea and as he speaks we become aware, even if we haven't before, that only he among the present company is truly expert at tailoring reality to suit himself. He's the professional, the others amateurs compared with him. This, of course, makes them more like us and Don Alonso/Don Quixote all the more exceptional. A living star on earth, you might say - however out of this world he almost always happens to be.

QUIXOTE

Should I require a lance in combat with your giant, madam, I shall tear off the living branch of an Ethiopian oak and brain him with it. But now let us go, as Father Perez and your noble steward who looks and sounds so like our village barber - a mischievous device doubtless of some ill-intentioned wizard - have advised.

DOROTEA

(relieved) We are agreed, great sir. We shall go e'en as far as Fortune necessitates. And yet we are loath - in all royal conscience - to lose that other champion. So young, so troubled.

SANCHO

Oh, don't you worry about him, ma'am. He'll be back when it suits, I'll warrant. He was before and will again. Lads of his age are always trouble, if you ask me.

QUIXOTE

We don't, Sancho.

SANCHO

Maybe but -

PRIEST

(getting a grip) Let us proceed. And may the Blessed Virgin smile upon our quest.

All start to go by walking on the spot. Dorotea, beside Don Quixote, makes polite conversation as if they were strolling through a royal park.

DOROTEA

We are informed, sir, that among many other scarcely credible exploits you have, single-handed, already conquered forty giants?

QUIXOTE

That was indeed my intention, madam, but as it happened they cunningly avoided combat. Tell me, Your Highness, are there windmills in your country?

DOROTEA

Not to our knowledge, sir. The kingdom of Micomicon is blessed only with the gentlest of breezes. We enjoy a climate and fertility not seen in this world since the Age of Gold.

QUIXOTE

I'm glad to hear it, madam. Many evil but lily-livered giants like nothing better than parading about as windmills.

Slow blackout so the cast can walk off stage in reality. Bring up houselights if any. If not, open the exit doors so the audience can get a breath of air by street light outside, or a drink in the pub opposite.

End of Act Three

3rd Interlude

No music this time because this is the big break in the action I mentioned earlier. The interval favoured by most modern productions of plays written in the classic five act format. So I see no reason why we, too, shouldn't enjoy a similar sort of relief for twenty minutes or so. But also, since this is page not stage - and reading usually a less strait-jacketed pastime than theatre-going - I'm in a position to offer you another diversion out of the Renaissance repertoire of fun: an interlude that isn't musical but instead is mildly histrionic. Think of it as a fledgling play hoping to take flight from a twig of plot.

The antecedents of these inconsequential playlets were the medieval mysteries and moralities but as late as the early 1600s interludes (by then of a more secular nature) were still enjoyed in England, not in the middle of the play as here but at after-dinner banquets where cream cakes, baked custards and sweet wines were served. Today we would regard these sketches, if comic, as slices of life and, if serious, as conversation pieces. What now occurs is a mixture of the two.

Fluctuating stage lights irradiate Miguel de Cervantes with all the colours of the spectrum. He's on stage, sitting in what will appear to be an arch in a cloister, once the action starts up again. He's making a glass of white wine he holds in his good right hand last as long as possible.

CERVANTES
(to us) I've just met John Fletcher. He's gone in search of William Shakespeare. Wants to introduce us. I told him I'd be honoured to make his acquaintance. Mind you, I must say no word of your Shakespeare reached me during my lifetime - let alone anything about John Fletcher. I've heard of both since, of course - the afterlife tends to live in the past - but this is the first time I've come across either of them in the flesh, as it were. Fletcher struck me at once as rather too full of himself for his - or anyone else's - comfort but at least he's bought me a drink. And if he can locate William Shakespeare, well, so much the better. As I say, in my time, Shakespeare's fame was pretty insular, even parochial, but since then he's gone global, hasn't he?

Enter John Fletcher bringing a bottle of wine, a corkscrew, and two glasses.

FLETCHER
Guess where William's got to?
CERVANTES
Where?

Fletcher puts down the wine and glasses and points out front and upwards with the corkscrew.

FLETCHER
Up there. Playing with the lighting console.
CERVANTES
I thought the lights kept changing.

FLETCHER
You can just see him - through that little window. There! His bald head. He's driving the lighting designer potty. Typical. Hard to please is William. But he'll be down any minute he says. We'll see. Shakespearean production minutes can take forever.

He's now inserted the corkscrew so he can pull out the cork with a nicely timed plurp. He refills Cervantes's glass generously. Then his own.

FLETCHER
(toast) So, cheers, Don Miguel.
CERVANTES
God's light upon you, Mr Fletcher.
FLETCHER
Jack, please. Call me Jack. Everyone does.
CERVANTES
To you, Jack.
FLETCHER
But not Jack of All Trades, thank you. Oh, no! No, not me. I'm no Johannes Factotum. Never was, never will be.
CERVANTES
I'm sure not.
FLETCHER
William, yes. In his younger days. He was anybody's. And how! Towards the end, too. Wow!
CERVANTES
(diplomatically) Well, that's the theatre for you. It consumes even as it gives life - like the fire and the phoenix.
FLETCHER
Could be.

They drink.

CERVANTES
(savouring the wine) Mmm.
FLETCHER
Chilean Chardonnay. Relatively unboiled. Said to be organic. Flown here in bottle by jumbo-jet.
CERVANTES
Mm. Reminds me a little of what I used to enjoy from my wife's vineyard. The grape there was Albillo not Chardonnay, of course.

FLETCHER
  You're a wine buff, Don Miguel?
CERVANTES
  For my sins, yes.

They laugh convivially.

FLETCHER
  So, Don Miguel, your verdict on the show to date? What d'you
  reckon? Five stars, four stars, three stars, two stars, one star, eff
  all?

Pause.

CERVANTES
  Well, I never like to judge too soon. But - and I'm not at all sure
  this is much of a compliment to the present writer - this version
  of my story is rather as if I'd adapted it for the stage. And as you
  may be aware, Jack, I had a very limited success as a playwright.
  I never reached your heights, let alone William Shakespeare's.
FLETCHER
  And the verse? What d'you think of the verse?
CERVANTES
  Workaday.
FLETCHER
  I'd call it flat-footed.
CERVANTES
  Mm. As you said at the start, yes. And as mine so often was. But
  verse isn't really expected from playwrights these days, is it?
  Prose is what matters now. Highly charged, of course, and often
  ornately punctuated. And some of this chap's prose does seem
  to have a certain something about it, now and then.
FLETCHER
  You're far too generous, Don Miguel. If you ask me the actors
  are mounting a superb rescue operation on a script that isn't -
  for me - delivering.
CERVANTES
  It's a very good cast, I agree.
FLETCHER
  Some of them getting on for A-list, I'd say.
CERVANTES
  But I do think you should give the script a little more credit. It's

got quite a lot of laughs so far and may yet improve. I love the Dorotea, by the way.

FLETCHER

Me too. Isn't she great? The fringe is where it's all at these days, of course. Amazing actors are only too happy to work for peanuts in little black boxes.

CERVANTES

I could wish the Sancho Panza was rather less robust occasionally.

FLETCHER

(laughs) A bit OTT?

CERVANTES

OTT? I'm afraid my English isn't up to that?

FLETCHER

Acronym. Meaning over the top.

CERVANTES

Ah, yes, of course. OTT.

FLETCHER

But then that's clowns for you. You should've seen our Sancho. Bob Armin at his best! Or should I say worst? Naughty!

CERVANTES

But ultimately forgivable, would you say?

FLETCHER

Not by William. He was forever coming down hard on the clowns.

CERVANTES

Really? With his marvellous sense of humour?

FLETCHER

Precisely because of it. He adored getting laughs. But they had to be his - not other people's.

CERVANTES

Oh, I see. Not too keen on too much ad-libbing, was he?

FLETCHER

No. One tough cookie, our William. Under all that celebrated charm.

Pause. Fletcher refills their glasses. A dog's bark is heard off.

FLETCHER

Hullo, here he comes plus horrible dog. He could at least have left it in his Land Rover. But no, inseparable they are.

William Shakespeare appears with Jessop straining at his lead, wagging his tail, and barking enthusiastically.

SHAKESPEARE
  Just stop that, Jessop! You silly, silly boy. We're about to meet the world's greatest novelist, so just behave yourself.

Jessop gulps. And is silent.

FLETCHER
  (wary eye on Jessop) Don Miguel, allow me to introduce Mr William Shakespeare. William, I present Don Miguel de Cervantes Saavedra.

Shakespeare comes forward with Jessop - now obedience itself - to meet Cervantes who has risen.

SHAKESPEARE
  How do you do?
CERVANTES
  How do you do?

They shake hands.

SHAKESPEARE
  Forgive me, Don Miguel, I intended to be here sooner but I felt I just had to do something about the lighting of this show. To my eye it's been a tad basic so far. Not that I blame the stage management or the lighting designer - they've done wonders with antiquated equipment and a nothing budget. But even so I thought some fine-tuning was still possible.

Fletcher offers Shakespeare a glass of wine. Jessop growls.

SHAKESPEARE
  (warningly) Jessop. (To Fletcher) No, thank you, Jack. You drink it for me. The grape and I are still rather off hooks with each other. Even now. After all this while.

Fletcher smiles and refills Cervantes's empty glass with what's left of the bottle.

FLETCHER
  I daresay you and I could manage another of these, don't you,
  Don Miguel?
CERVANTES
  Might there be a red, Jack? A Shiraz or Tempranillo? I don't like
  to stick with white for too long.
FLETCHER
  (smile) Of course. Yours to command.
CERVANTES
  Thank you.

Fletcher swigs the wine he offered Shakespeare at a gulp and
goes, taking the empty bottle with him. Jessop barks again.

SHAKESPEARE
  That's enough, Jessop. Jack's gone now so relax.

Cervantes and Shakespeare sit together in the arch of the cloister
with Jessop at their feet.

CERVANTES
  Well - apart from the lighting of the show so far - what do you
  think? Mr Fletcher doesn't seem too impressed.
SHAKESPEARE
  (laugh) Jack's never impressed. Point of honour with him. As
  for me -

Shakespeare pauses.

CERVANTES
  Yes?
SHAKESPEARE
  No. No, I'd far prefer to hear what you think, Don Miguel. After
  all it's your story revived here on stage.
CERVANTES
  True. But you had first go at it, didn't you? At least in English.
  So your view is perhaps more to the point than mine. So do
  say.

Shakespeare pauses again before speaking.

SHAKESPEARE

Let me put it this way - I've heard and seen worse. The text, for the most part, allows the actors to act which, of course, is no small thing in itself. Did Jack, by the bye, tell you he thought they were performing wonders with a poor script?

CERVANTES

He did, yes.

SHAKESPEARE

He always does.. That's his line on any show not his own. His version - frankly he took over the whole thing - made far, far more of the romance plot than this one has to date. But then that was very much Jack in his heyday. His lovers' verses ran as sweetly and profusely as summer morning milk into a dairymaid's bucket. Here we get far more burlesque - a tricky genre in my view, asking for a very light touch.

CERVANTES

Which - on the whole - it's getting, I'd say. And of course my book started as burlesque.

SHAKESPEARE

Only to grow beyond it, Don Miguel.

CERVANTES

Perhaps. But this version's particular emphasis on the knight and squire's experiences - well, I put that down to a change in theatrical taste. What seems to have been subplot material for you would seem here to have become main plot. In prose. This present chap's keeping verse to a minimum, I'd say.

SHAKESPEARE

Understandably - from what I've heard. But you're quite right. Jack and Dick Burbage insisted I stay with the subplot. And I did. With huge pleasure, I might add. What a delightful double act your knight and squire make. I loved them both. Mind you, had our script survived, I suspect my contribution - despite Jack's rewrites - would be somewhat incomprehensible nowadays. Nothing dates faster than up to the minute backchat, does it? But even so, what a pair they are. And they get even better in your sequel.

CERVANTES

Oh? You've read that too?

SHAKESPEARE

Oh, yes. It came out in English not long after I died. But that didn't stop me reading it. Purgatory runs a very good mobile library service, as I'm sure you've found, Don Miguel?

Pause.

CERVANTES
You died in the old faith?

SHAKESPEARE
(circumspect out of ancient habit) Ah. Put it this way - in my experience the afterlife tends to coincide with those beliefs you learn at your mother's knee. Anyway, your second part of *Don Quixote* bowled me over. Reading it I thought: here's the future. Off the stage, on to the page. That's the thing to do.

CERVANTES
(surprised) You'd write novels? If you were alive?

SHAKESPEARE
Yes. Why not? What doors you opened with that book.

CERVANTES
How odd. Novels are an awful grind. They can take you years. *Don Quixote* did. All I ever truly longed to do was write successful plays. Plays are so much quicker to write than novels.

SHAKESPEARE
Not in my experience. I was always revising mine.

CERVANTES
Really? Unlike Lope de Vega.

SHAKESPEARE
Who?

CERVANTES
(with rare animosity) My arch-rival. A prolific poet-playwright. Knocked off a play a week for thirty odd years on end *and* every actress in them. Grew monstrously rich and then arranged for himself a state of the art state funeral, would you believe?

SHAKESPEARE
Really? It sounds as if I should've heard of him. But I *did* know you had actresses in Spain. Jack told me.

CERVANTES
Mm. While you were obliged to make do with boys, I understand?

SHAKESPEARE
We were. But I'm not sure *make do* is the right phrase. Some of the lads were very, very good. Clever little devils. Utterly beguiling.

CERVANTES
Doubtless they were. But I still think a real girl dressed as a boy can be even more beguiling. Look at Dorotea here tonight.

SHAKESPEARE
(ambiguous smile) If you insist, Don Miguel. But how about a

boy playing a girl playing a boy? And then, why not have another boy playing a girl fall in love with this particular him or her who meanwhile has fallen in love with your uncompromisingly male juvenile lead playing the local duke? That, I would suggest, turned the theatrical reality of my day into romance at its delightful, unruly, gender-bending best.

CERVANTES

(laughing) It wouldn't have done for us! Not then, not in non-reformist Spain. We left all such transsexual shenanigans to you horrible English heretics. It just wouldn't have been countenanced. Not even at Epiphany.

SHAKESPEARE

You know my *Twelfth Night*?

CERVANTES

Only in translation. I seem to remember a rather sad clown singing rather sad songs - oh, and a pompous steward tricked into falling in love.

SHAKESPEARE

That's the one.

CERVANTES

But what about the mature female roles? Who played those?

SHAKESPEARE

(grin) The old queens, of course. Why do you think I wrote so many history plays?

Small pause then both laugh uproariously. This excites Jessop who jumps up, tail wagging, to lick Cervantes's maimed left hand.

SHAKESPEARE

What happened to your hand? Were you born with it like that?

CERVANTES

No. Most of it got shot off in battle.

SHAKESPEARE

You were a soldier?

CERVANTES

For five years. I loved the military life.

SHAKESPEARE

Really? You surprise me.

CERVANTES

I don't see why. I was very much of my time. Being of no family to speak of I aimed at becoming a well-known warrior poet.

SHAKESPEARE

A complete Renaissance gentleman, as it were?

CERVANTES

Just that. But poetry eluded me. Though I did get to be a decent shot. What's now known as a sniper. As a versifier I was, you could say, competent - but then who wasn't in those days? - but my verses never exploded in other people's minds. Unlike yours, William. May I call you William?

SHAKESPEARE

(charm itself) I was hoping you would, Don Miguel.

CERVANTES

Then I shall. But no - my verses jogged along like Sancho Panza on his donkey.

SHAKESPEARE

Your Don Quixote has something of the poet about him.

CERVANTES

Perhaps. But not when composing verses.

SHAKESPEARE

Well, prose can do just as well - sometimes better.

CERVANTES

True. But oh, so slowly.

They laugh again. Not so heartily as before but as like-minded craftsmen sharing a trade commonplace.

SHAKESPEARE

What was it like, fighting in battle? To kill or be killed?

CERVANTES

(equably) Wonderful.

SHAKESPEARE

Good heaven's above! Am I really to believe that?

CERVANTES

I hope so. That was certainly my experience.

SHAKESPEARE

I put dozens of battles on stage - some were quite spectacular, despite my telling the audience they wouldn't be - but I never, ever thought of the reality as wonderful. Quite the reverse! Wonderful?

CERVANTES

Perhaps I should've said full of wonders? From the worst to the best?

SHAKESPEARE

Mm. That I can imagine. Yes. Where was this battle - in which you lost the use of that hand?

CERVANTES

Bang opposite Arcadia.

SHAKESPEARE

Classical Arcadia?

CERVANTES

(nod) In the Gulf of Corinth.

Shakespeare's eternal passion for history and geography asserts itself.

SHAKESPEARE

A sea battle?

CERVANTES

Fought as if on land - every galley, boat, ship, grappled to its opposite - the infidel. Or as we now say - Islam.

SHAKESPEARE

Lepanto! You were at Lepanto?

CERVANTES

You've heard of it?

SHAKESPEARE

Heard of it! Lepanto! Oh, my God! I read all about it. Everything I could. Background reading for one of my tragedies. Which I set in the aftermath of that appalling battle. With all its consequences, political, commercial, private. And you were there! How old were you just then?

CERVANTES

Twenty four.

SHAKESPEARE

The same age as your Commander in Chief, Don John of Austria?

CERVANTES

Yes. But less well-connected.

They smile.

SHAKESPEARE

Your Holy League was heavily outnumbered - or so I read. Was that true?

CERVANTES
No, we were more or less evenly matched. The Muslims had a few more galleys but we had superior fire-power. Papal cannons from the Vatican. Mounted on Venetian merchant ships. Loaded with Spanish gun-powder. Firing Neapolitan balls.
SHAKESPEARE
And was it really all over in just four hours?
CERVANTES
Yes.
SHAKESPEARE
With their leader's head on a spike?
CERVANTES
(nod) Held up for all to see as a sign of Christ's victory.
SHAKESPEARE
And did you really kill thirty thousand Muslims that afternoon - between lunch and tea, as it were?
CERVANTES
Is that what your books say?
SHAKESPEARE
Yes. And that nine thousand Christians were killed. With even more wounded. Leaving the sea literally blood-red.
CERVANTES
I can vouch for that. But I didn't have time to count casualties - dead or alive. Many of us, on both sides, must've been wounded only to die later.
SHAKESPEARE
But you didn't? Clearly?
CERVANTES
No. I was lucky enough to live.
SHAKESPEARE
To fight elsewhere another day?
CERVANTES
Yes, but only after many months in hospital.
SHAKESPEARE
That hand took time to heal?
CERVANTES
It wasn't just my hand. I'd also been shot in the chest and shoulder. So all in all it was a long convalescence.
SHAKESPEARE
Was the hospital in Messina? In Sicily?
CERVANTES
Yes.

SHAKESPEARE

I thought it had to be. The Holy League set out from Messina, didn't it? So you were bound to go back there after your famous victory.

CERVANTES

The city greeted us with bells, flags, gun salutes and fireworks apparently. But I was too feverish to notice.

SHAKESPEARE

What a shame. I set one of my comedies in Messina. It had victorious Spanish and Italian soldiers coming back from the wars. Not from Lepanto. From Milan or somewhere. I left that side of it deliberately vague so as to concentrate on that peacetime speciality - the war of the sexes.

CERVANTES

Was it successful?

SHAKESPEARE

Hugely. But the play was never one of my favourites.

Pause. Could it be we've now, at last, heard Shakespeare's view of *Much Ado About Nothing*?

CERVANTES

And that other play you mentioned - the tragedy?

SHAKESPEARE

I set that first in Venice, then in Cyprus. After the break-up of the Holy League. When the Venetians were left to fight off the next challenge from Islam without your help or the Pope's. Its hero was an honest mercenary soldier who'd risen to the rank of general in the pay of Venice.

CERVANTES

Othello - the Moor of Venice? I've read it.

SHAKESPEARE

Not heard it? Sorry, I should say seen it, shouldn't I?

CERVANTES

Neither, thank God. That would be like being invited to watch a good man tortured to death. And his wife, too. For no discernible reason at all.

SHAKESPEARE

Just what I intended.

CERVANTES

You sound like your villain - Iago.

SHAKESPEARE
  Named after Spain's patron saint - the Moorkiller.
CERVANTES
  So I noticed. But at least *his* motives were clear.

Pause. Jessop looks quickly from one to the other, marking a blip
of difference - cultural and emotional - between our two authors.

SHAKESPEARE
  (to bridge the gap) I'm often told *Othello* is about jealousy -
CERVANTES
  (meeting him half-way) Only up to a point, surely?
SHAKESPEARE
  Exactly. Trust you to observe that, Don Miguel.
CERVANTES
  Beyond that it's a show of evil for evil's sake, I'd have thought?
  Plus the power of suggestion in a closed community? With a
  plot-mechanism that's like a procession of practical jokes - each
  one more sadistic than the last? Until Othello's world, and his
  wife's, implodes?

Shakespeare smiles.

SHAKESPEARE
  You should be a theatre critic.

Cervantes laughs.

CERVANTES
  (crossing himself) Holy Mary preserve me! I've committed my
  fair share of sins but I don't deserve *that* for a penance.

Shakespeare laughs. Jessop wags.

SHAKESPEARE
  My aim was Iago's. To destroy innocence.
CERVANTES
  Whose? Your hero and heroine's innocence?
SHAKESPEARE
  No. The audience's innocence. By obliging them to witness Iago
  at work.

CERVANTES
Thus making them - us - accomplices to his crime?
SHAKESPEARE
Just that. Theatre's event not explanation.

Reflective pause as Cervantes sighs before speaking.

CERVANTES
No wonder.
SHAKESPEARE
No wonder what?
CERVANTES
No wonder I could never write plays. Plays that worked, I mean.
That took audiences by storm. I was all for explanation. I never
stopped hoping to explain. To myself and everyone else.
SHAKESPEARE
That's why you wrote novels so successfully.
CERVANTES
Perhaps. But I do wish we'd met before, William. You - your
advice - could've saved me years of bother. I was still trying -
and failing - to get plays on while finishing *Don Quixote*. If only
I'd known why. What a thing! What a revelation! And like all
revelations only too obvious once revealed. Oh, dear, oh dear.

He laughs ruefully. Pause.

SHAKESPEARE
What did you do after you recovered from your wounds?
CERVANTES
I stayed on as a soldier though I had to give up the hookgun.
SHAKESPEARE
Hookgun?
CERVANTES
What the French called an *arquebus*.
SHAKESPEARE
Oh, yes.
CERVANTES
Essentially a musket on a stick.
SHAKESPEARE
The stick supported it?
CERVANTES
(nod) Brass hook under the barrel - ring on the end of the stick.

Needed two hands to load, prime and fire it. Then three years later I got taken hostage while sailing home on leave.

SHAKESPEARE

Where were you held - Algiers?

CERVANTES

(another nod) What a place.

SHAKESPEARE

I've read somewhere that in those days as many as twenty thousand Christian slaves were up for sale in Algiers?

CERVANTES

Perfectly true. People used to say it's raining Christians in Algiers. It was a boom city. Booming with living ghosts building it. Us. Beautiful, too, as it spread up the hill from the harbour - except for the sight of so many Christian men and women impaled on hooks set in the town walls. The penalty for minor offences such as stealing food or cheeking the guards. All the streets were scrupulously clean. Kept so by us, martialled in chain gangs to sweep and scrub by day, and cart off filth by night. The city's hanging gardens rivalled Paradise our guards said, but we didn't see them like that because we were weeding and clipping in the sun, while they sat in the shade sipping mint tea. That was our life in Algiers - unless we were chained-up in prison, of course.

He laughs. Shakespeare's surprised.

SHAKESPEARE

You laugh?

CERVANTES

Well, it's a long time ago now.

SHAKESPEARE

It still sounds dreadful to me.

CERVANTES

It was. But to quote you if I may: "the worst is not - so long as we can say this is the worst."

SHAKESPEARE

(more surprise) You've read *King Lear* too?

CERVANTES

Yes. It left me speechless.

Silence.

SHAKESPEARE
(eventually) I feel ashamed.
CERVANTES
Why?
SHAKESPEARE
At having written so much having lived so comparatively little.
CERVANTES
What does that matter when your work lives on?
SHAKESPEARE
A lot. It becomes a never-ending reproach. All that pretend violence instead of facing the reality of it. Which reminds me. I met a big fat fellow the other day. He told me every man thinks meanly of himself for not having been a soldier.
CERVANTES
Did he indeed? I'm never happy with generalities. I wanted to be a soldier certainly, but I see no reason why anyone should blame himself for not being one. I think observations of that kind come a little too pat.

Shakespeare is not convinced. Pause.

CERVANTES
(to cheer Shakespeare up) We had a game in prison. Betting who could jump highest in his chains.
SHAKESPEARE
You had money?
CERVANTES
Melon seeds. And of course we ran a handicap system based on the weight of our chains. Some of us being more heavily loaded with iron than others. The higher your ransom the heavier your shackles.
SHAKESPEARE
How long were you a hostage?
CERVANTES
Five years. I was thirty three when my family finally scraped together the money to redeem me.
SHAKESPEARE
Did people ever manage to escape?
CERVANTES
Every now and then, yes. I tried four times. But fate was against me. Always my hope was to save my family the ransom demanded. They weren't rich - far from it. Poor as dirt really -

116

except my mother and sisters were incessantly house-proud. Our house shone with nothing. The problem was my price had been set too high. I was thought to be worth more than I was - thanks to two letters I'd had with me when I was captured. We put up a good fight, by the way, but were outnumbered ten to one.

SHAKESPEARE

What was in those letters?

CERVANTES

Useful eulogy. They were testimonials. Recommending me for promotion from the ranks.

SHAKESPEARE

Despite your crippled hand?

CERVANTES

Certainly. After all, I could still wield a sword with this one, couldn't I?

He makes several fencing flourishes with his right hand. Shakespeare laughs. Jessop barks delightedly.

SHAKESPEARE

Ever the man of action. Down, Jessop!

CERVANTES

I was then. The prospect of promotion - to the rank of captain no less - had made me absurdly proud and insufferably happy.

SHAKESPEARE

That was a big step up?

CERVANTES

Oh, yes. For a nobody like me. I could see myself set on the path to glory. I couldn't have had better, grander referees. Those letters - to the King himself - came from Don John of Austria no less, and the Duke of Sessa, Viceroy of Sicily.

SHAKESPEARE

(impressed) You *had* distinguished yourself.

CERVANTES

Yes, I had. Do you like irony?

SHAKESPEARE

Dramatically speaking, yes.

CERVANTES

But not in life?

SHAKESPEARE

No. (changing the subject) Any road your captors thought you were a valuable commodity?

CERVANTES

Did you say *any road*?

SHAKESPEARE

(nod) It's a Midland usage.

CERVANTES

I like it. I think I heard Sancho use it, too, in the play just now? Did you?

SHAKESPEARE

I did. The part's written that way. And the actor's accent's almost up to it. A bit more Northamptonshire than Warwickshire, I'd say. But Midland - no question of that. A nice touch. So - what sort of price did they put on your release?

CERVANTES

Five hundred gold ducats hiked up to six hundred at the very last moment.

SHAKESPEARE

(grin) Allowing for inflation, were they? Over five years?

Cervantes laughs.

CERVANTES

I can laugh now but I didn't then. I was already chained to an oar in a galley about to leave - within the hour - for Constantinople. If the friars handling my release hadn't rejuggled their finances there and then I'd never have seen Spain again.

SHAKESPEARE

It was as touch and go as that?

CERVANTES

What's now called a cliff-hanger.

SHAKESPEARE

Six hundred ducats? I suppose that today would be - broadly speaking - twenty odd thousand pounds.

CERVANTES

Would it?

SHAKESPEARE

I'd say so. If not more.

CERVANTES

Money was always a mystery to me. I wanted it. Who doesn't? But at the same time I hated it. So it eluded me. But however you price yesterday against today six hundred gold ducats then was far too much for my family to find. Even with government grants available. Especially as my brother, Rodrigo, had been captured with me.

SHAKESPEARE

He was a soldier, too?

CERVANTES

Yes. So they also had to raise a ransom for him.

SHAKESPEARE

How much was that?

CERVANTES

Half me. Three hundred ducats.

SHAKESPEARE

Nine hundred ducats in all? For the pair of you?

CERVANTES

Mm. Rodrigo cost less because he hadn't had any grand testimonials with him. Also his slave-master was not so money-grubbing as mine. Our family, poor souls, did everything and more to get both of us out. Since I was older than Rodrigo I was supposed to be ransomed first but they couldn't scrape enough together to meet my price so I said use what's there to redeem Rodrigo.

SHAKESPEARE

How noble of you

CERVANTES

Not quite. It was rather more pragmatic than that. The plan being that once back in Spain Rodrigo could organise an escape operation - not just for me but for a lot of other hostages. Overall that would cost less than paying all the ransoms involved.

SHAKESPEARE

A mass escape?

CERVANTES

We thought the bigger the better would attract the best backing. Enough to hire a boat in Mallorca to pick us up at an already agreed point - a headland - three miles east of Algiers.

SHAKESPEARE

It sounds like a fairy tale.

CERVANTES

It felt like one to start with.

SHAKESPEARE

What happened?

CERVANTES

Rodrigo got the backing we needed in an incredibly short time - in just a month. And fourteen of us managed to escape from the city and hide out in a cave on an estate near our agreed pick up point. One of the gardeners there was from Pamplona - it was he who helped us, hid us, fed us. The boat arrived on time but then sheered off. We never knew what scared it away. It came back two nights later but in the meantime another slave on the estate betrayed us.

SHAKESPEARE

A Christian slave?

CERVANTES

Yes. But not that Christian. The Pasha's troops turned out in force and we were all marched back to Algiers, chained neck to neck, men and women alike. The gardener who'd helped us was hung up by one foot till he died.

SHAKESPEARE

And you?

CERVANTES

As organiser of the whole thing I thought I was as good as dead if not worse. But no, my inflated price saved me.

SHAKESPEARE

You were too valuable to kill or mutilate?

CERVANTES

(laughs) Yes. So I tried to escape again.

SHAKESPEARE

Now *that* was surely tempting Providence?

CERVANTES

I agree. But she likes a tease, doesn't she? Quite a frisky lady, Providence, in her way. Half-sister to Fortune.

SHAKESPEARE

(smile) She let you down?

CERVANTES

No, I did. With my own hand.

SHAKESPEARE

How?

CERVANTES

I wrote some letters and paid an Arab -

SHAKESPEARE

With melon seeds?

CERVANTES

No, with real money. Borrowed, of course. We hostages were forever lending or borrowing small amounts from each other. This Arab was to take these letters to Oran - to our governor there - just up the coast. In them I asked for a rescue party for me and three others. All to be paid for later out of the ransom money saved.

SHAKESPEARE

But your messenger was caught?

CERVANTES

And impaled alive.

SHAKESPEARE

After informing on you?

CERVANTES

No. He kept our trust. But those letters were in my handwriting and, of course, I'd signed them. My slave master, Hassan Pasha, read them and pronounced sentence - two thousand lashes.

SHAKESPEARE

But it can't have been carried out? You'd have died there and then. No one could survive so many.

CERVANTES

True.

Reflective pause.

CERVANTES

Many people have since speculated about this. Some have suggested it was because I was Hassan Pasha's favourite but I put that down to Freudian prurience. Others, more imaginatively but equally erroneously, have thought I told him bedtime stories - like Scheherazade - to save my life, and in this way prepared myself to become the first modern novelist - so called. Nonsense, of course. Who can imagine what they haven't yet dreamt of? Scholars, I'm sure, will disagree, but they only theorise after the event, or so I find, don't you?

SHAKESPEARE

Tirelessly, it would seem. My life and work have funded a myriad lifestyles.

CERVANTES

So have mine. Lord what fools these mortals be.

SHAKESPEARE

(more delight) You know my *Midsummer Night's Dream* as well?

CERVANTES

I've seen it twice. Once performed by a girls' school in a garden, and then, much later, in a powerful professional production with all the actors on trapezes in a white box. On both occasions your play survived triumphantly. I think it might be my favourite.

They laugh.

SHAKESPEARE
  Shall I tell you my favourite?
CERVANTES
  By all means.
SHAKESPEARE
  Love's Labour's Lost.
CERVANTES
  Don't know it.
SHAKESPEARE
  Please don't read it. Wait for any production of it anywhere.
  I wrote it in Hampshire. The plague had shut the theatres in
  London that summer. So we all went where we could. I was in
  love at the time with my patron. A very pretty boy much younger
  than me. Lord Southampton. All of nineteen. He and his friends
  concocted a rough first draft of the piece, then handed it to me,
  as the pet poet in residence, to sort out.
CERVANTES
  You rewrote it?
SHAKESPEARE
  Completely. I tore it apart and put it together again. My way.
  Then when we did it - with enormous, bucolic success - they
  took all the credit.
CERVANTES
  You still sound rather miffed?
SHAKESPEARE
  Do I? I ought not to. Perhaps it's only once we're dead we come
  to realise just how good we really were?
CERVANTES
  I always had a fair opinion of myself.
SHAKESPEARE
  Me, too. But, perhaps, even so, we underestimated our
  achievements?
CERVANTES
  Perhaps. Mind you, plays and novels weren't so respected then
  as now, were they?
SHAKESPEARE
  True. However, when it comes to *Love's Labour's Lost* I tend to
  get reminiscent, sentimental. It even had a sort of Don Quixote
  in it. Before the event. Your event.

CERVANTES
Really?
SHAKESPEARE
Don Armado I called him. So you could say I had a trial run at your gentleman.

Pause.

SHAKESPEARE
What happened next in Algiers?
CERVANTES
Reprieve from execution. Remission of Hassan Pasha's sentence. But with me incarcerated in the heaviest chains yet. In the most secure prison he'd got.
SHAKESPEARE
Date?
CERVANTES
I'd almost given up counting by then. But it must have been - let's think - 1578, yes.
SHAKESPEARE
The year I left the grammar school. Well-versed in Ovid and onanism, aged fourteen.
CERVANTES
While I listened to my fellow prisoners' life stories. I suspect I must've heard at least a thousand maybe more - all with the same ending.
SHAKESPEARE
Did you write anything? Apart from letters home?
CERVANTES
Two or three devotional lyrics of heartfelt solemnity.
SHAKESPEARE
No sonnets? Love songs?
CERVANTES
Some, yes. Half a dozen or so to a girl I'd left behind in Naples where I'd been stationed for a while. But I tore them up as unworthy of her. I did write a letter in verse to the King's private secretary trying to keep my hopes of promotion alive. Rodrigo took it back with him and delivered it. I never got a reply. It was too late. After that my dream of becoming a successful soldier-poet faded.

SHAKESPEARE
  But meanwhile you played jumping games and planned escapes
  for yourself and others?
CERVANTES
  Mm. And attended mass.
SHAKESPEARE
  That was allowed?
CERVANTES
  Tolerated. And became a card sharp.
SHAKESPEARE
  You cheated at cards?
CERVANTES
  Whenever I could.
SHAKESPEARE
  Only for melon seeds, I hope?
CERVANTES
  And for fun.

They laugh.

SHAKESPEARE
  Still sounds disgraceful to me.
CERVANTES
  It was. But it's a skill can keep you from starving.

He takes a pack of well-thumbed playing cards from his pocket
with his right hand.

CERVANTES
  Do you play, William?
SHAKESPEARE
  I've never gambled, Don Miguel.
CERVANTES
  How sensible of you.

He flicks and cuts the pack one handed with a conjuror's dexterity.
Shakespeare gawps.

SHAKESPEARE
  How *did* you do that?
CERVANTES
  Practice. And I can use my bad hand too. Look.

He flicks an ace of hearts at it. What's left of his fingers grips it and displays it.

CERVANTES

There! Now, while you're watching that card I can slip this one, the ace of spades, into this pocket, for use as appropriate. My horrible left hand, especially without a glove, waved about like this, always distracted my opponent or opponents. They were left wondering how it could possibly hold even one card - let alone two. There!

And he flicks another into it. Miraculously that's also held and displayed. Shakespeare is impressed, amused, but unable to approve.

SHAKESPEARE

Please assure me, Don Miguel, as a gentleman, that you never cheated for real money.

CERVANTES

Not in Algiers, no. But I did later in Seville. When I was an income tax collector. The treasury hadn't paid me for months on end. So I had to win at cards simply to survive. It was that or cook the books and embezzle the money I'd collected. Many did.

SHAKESPEARE

Your life gets worse and worse. You of all people - a tax collector!

CERVANTES

It was the only job I could get as an ex-hostage, ex-soldier, ex-playwright.

SHAKESPEARE

Explain.

CERVANTES

I'd rather not.

SHAKESPEARE

But it's what you're best at. You told me so yourself. Just now.

CERVANTES

Yes. But with regret.

SHAKESPEARE

Even so. Please.

Pause.

SHAKESPEARE

(cajoling) I'm all ears - like Sancho's donkey. I'm sorry he isn't in the play, by the way. The hobby-horse of Rocinante is very persuasive, I find, and I'm sure one of Rucio would be equally amusing. Rucio means Dapple, I believe?

CERVANTES

It does.

SHAKESPEARE

A proper country name.

CERVANTES

Mm. And the way this show's shaping up I've got a hunch he may yet appear. After all, he does in the book, and whatever else you or I might say about this version, it's sticking reasonably closely to what I wrote.

SHAKESPEARE

As I advised Jack we should. I was all for putting in both horse and donkey but he cut the pair of them. So I hope you're right, Don Miguel. And that this treatment of the story *does* produce Dapple. I love donkey masks - especially if their huge ears wiggle, their speaking eyes roll, and their elastic lips curl to reveal beastly yellow teeth. Think of Bottom in *The Dream*.

They laugh.

CERVANTES

I heard recently the Americans now floss their animals' teeth.

SHAKESPEARE

I can believe it. They love everything to be hygienic, whether it's sex or war.

CERVANTES

While we are past both.

They laugh again.

SHAKESPEARE

You were saying?

CERVANTES

I wasn't.

SHAKESPEARE

True. But I was hoping you'd explain how you came to be a tax-collector?

CERVANTES

It's not a pretty story. And it's in all my biographies.

SHAKESPEARE

I never read biographies.

CERVANTES

I'm sure you've suffered from them too?

SHAKESPEARE

(heartfelt) I have. That's why I no longer bother with them. Mine or anybody else's. To my mind they're simply novels by non-novelists. Or, in my case, pen-portraits - not of me - but of their authors. Did tax-collecting give you time to write?

CERVANTES

Now and then. When I wasn't on the move. I tried my hand at short stories mostly. Stuff people could read or listen to for an hour or so. Did you know it takes fifteen minutes to read two thousand words out loud? Intelligibly, that is?

SHAKESPEARE

And for readers reading silently to themselves?

CERVANTES

Much faster. But it also depends on the reader, of course. Some are speedier than others. Naturally that sort claim to comprehend far more than the slow ones - but then they would, wouldn't they? Being competitive souls bent on all sorts of supremacy over less quicksilver mortals.

Shakespeare smiles. He appreciates the point but -

SHAKESPEARE

You're still not answering my question, Don Miguel, are you?

CERVANTES

No, I suppose not. I did what I could when I could. As a hostage I met the world in a cage. As a travelling taxman I met it all over everywhere. And very evasive it was, too. And time-consuming.

SHAKESPEARE

To go back to your theatre ambitions - ?

CERVANTES

What can I say? Except they were never truly realised - for reasons I now appreciate. Also I loved a girl who wanted to be an actress. I couldn't get her a job, but I got her pregnant. We passed the child off as hers and her husband's because I was getting married to someone else.

SHAKESPEARE

How complicated.

CERVANTES

Life can be. How about yours?

SHAKESPEARE

(avoiding the question) Was the child a boy or a girl?

CERVANTES

A girl. Called Isabel. She took my name later hoping I might be able to support her. As an adult she proved to be a pain in the neck. But that often happens, doesn't it? Babies are one thing, grown people another.

SHAKESPEARE

I had a daughter like that.

CERVANTES

Illegitimate?

SHAKESPEARE

No, legitimate, but still a pain. Unlike her older sister Susanna, who was lovely. In every way. No, Judith was trouble. She ruined my last years. Mind you, she was a twin who lost her brother at an early age. When I wasn't there. Then, later, she married the wrong man - at least from my point of view. I can leave you to imagine the rest. So you gave up on the theatre?

CERVANTES

No. It gave up on me. But beside that Madrid was overrun with would-be poets all competing for success in the theatre. The companies couldn't get enough scripts and there were plenty of poets with money who didn't need a commission to get them started. Naturally the managers favoured them, saying they'd pay them later out of receipts. And then to cap it all along came young Lope de Vega to outdo us all in quantity - and let's admit it - quality.

SHAKESPEARE

We had standard rates for scripts in London. Twenty marks - that's just under four thousand pounds in today's terms - paid in instalments either to a single poet or shared between several. Most plays were collaborations - my works and Ben Jonson's were the exception rather than the rule, although we, too, worked with others - *Cardenio*, for example. And of course we tarted up old scripts all the time. Standard practice.

CERVANTES

You make it sound like a factory.

SHAKESPEARE

It was. But the only way to make real money out of it was to become a sharer in an acting company.

CERVANTES

How did that work?

SHAKESPEARE

Well, for a start, you needed to be a decent actor and then find a patron to buy you in. Unless of course you already had money, or a theatre manager for a father, like Dick Burbage, or craftily married a manager's step-daughter like Ned Alleyn. Our theatre was, after all, an actors' theatre. Who needed directors when the staging was always pretty much the same and the lighting either daylight or candles?

CERVANTES

Surely you supervised some rehearsals?

SHAKESPEARE

When I had time, yes.

CERVANTES

But you still haven't said how the sharing side of it worked?

SHAKESPEARE

Matter of capital. Investment in the company. If you were in a position to put in a lump sum - say fifty pounds - as was so in my case - then you had a share in all future profits. Usually this privilege was enjoyed by four or five leading members of the company.

CERVANTES

The rest were on wages?

SHAKESPEARE

Mm. Hired men we called them. Plus their apprentices - our boy actors learning their trade.

CERVANTES

I daresay fifty pounds was a pretty substantial sum at that time?

SHAKESPEARE

Oh, yes. I bought the second best house in Stratford-on-Avon for sixty.

CERVANTES

You had that sort of money at the start of your career?

SHAKESPEARE

Oh, no. My family wasn't wealthy - better off than yours from the sound of it but my dad was in big financial trouble at the time and I had a wife and children to support back in Stratford.

CERVANTES
You found yourself a patron?
SHAKESPEARE
Yes.
CERVANTES
Lucky you. I never did. Well, not to speak of. The Archbishop of Toledo helped me out towards the end of my life but that was about it. Who was your patron?
SHAKESPEARE
That young lad I mentioned. Southampton. A very pretty boy. Beautiful hair. When he came of age he put up the fifty pounds I needed for a share. Gossip at one time insisted he gave me more - even as much as a thousand pounds - but that's typical theatrical exaggeration. Still, spread over my twenty odd years with the company that share certainly earned me as much as that and more.
CERVANTES
A fortune!
SHAKESPEARE
Well, after all, by the time Jack Fletcher and I worked together on *Cardenio*, we were the equivalent of today's National Theatre. How long did your tax-collecting last?
CERVANTES
(smile) Always the quick question. And you never give up, do you, William?
SHAKESPEARE
No. Never have. How long, Don Miguel?
CERVANTES
Eleven or twelve years in all. Together with two or three spells in prison.
SHAKESPEARE
Prison? Oh, no.
CERVANTES
A routine experience for revenue collectors. Any discrepancies in your accounts and the Treasury put you in prison while they sorted them out.
SHAKESPEARE
That must have taken time?
CERVANTES
It did. Some people believe I wrote *Don Quixote* in prison. But I didn't. You can't. Such places are just too noisy, too crowded. Worse than Algiers. In many respects they're close to being

madhouses. Which reminds me I've been meaning to ask you about madness - quite a number of your characters are mad, aren't they? Or else go mad.

SHAKESPEARE

(laugh) Really? I'd have said lunacy was more your speciality?

CERVANTES

Oh, I won't argue with that but even so - look at your Hamlet and Ophelia, your King Lear, Othello driven to frenzy, Timon raving at the world from his cave, and that King of Sicily whose name escapes me -

SHAKESPEARE

Leontes.

CERVANTES

Imagining his heavily pregnant wife is having an affair with the King of Bohemia, for heaven's sake. And as for that deluded steward Malvolio, not to mention that young Gloucester boy pretending to be Tom of Bedlam -

SHAKESPEARE

(laughing) All right! Perhaps you've proved your point! So the answer must be: it's a mad world, my masters. And it makes for entertainment in depth - providing pity, fear and laughter.

CERVANTES

True. Who said *it's a mad world, my masters*? You? It sounds like you.

SHAKESPEARE

No, it was someone else. I can't remember who. But I must say, Don Miguel, I've never met anyone - such as your Don Quixote - sent mad by reading novels?

CERVANTES

Nor have I. I invented him. And for some reason the idea struck a chord. (he grins) But I've met several people driven pretty close to the edge through reading your sonnets, William.

Shakespeare roars with laughter.

CERVANTES

The theories I've heard. And read.

SHAKESPEARE

Me, too! And as for that misprint in the dedication -

Re-enter John Fletcher with a bottle of red wine.

FLETCHER

Jeez - the time I've had! What's funny?

SHAKESPEARE

(still laughing) The old, old story, Jack. The riddle of the sonnets.

FLETCHER

(grin) One day you'll have to come clean, William, once and for all. Give us your Who's Who. Plain and straight.

SHAKESPEARE

Never.

FLETCHER

Like did that Italian Jewess give you the pox or didn't she?

SHAKESPEARE

(no longer amused) Are you drunk, Jack?

FLETCHER

(unfazed) Not half so much as some. I met a guy - name of Theobald - in the pub. Tanked to the hairline except he was bald. What a motor-mouth. Kept on about our *Cardenio*.

SHAKESPEARE

You've met the author of this version?

FLETCHER

No, that eighteenth century character who stitched us up. The one who put it on at Drury Lane.

SHAKESPEARE

Oh, that one. I see. Yes. It's coming back to me now. Didn't you say he claimed he adapted it from an old prompt copy?

FLETCHER

I did. And so does he. Kept on at me about it. What a success it was blah blah.

SHAKESPEARE

When was this exactly?

FLETCHER

He did say. 1727, was it? Or '28? Anyway when he went to the gents I made my escape - like fast.

Thumps and bangs off before Lewis Theobald lurches on stage. Like the others present he appears at the age he died - fifty-six. I see him as tall but stooped; bald on top but with wispy grey hair, tied with a greasy black bow at the back of his neck, that almost gives the impression of an old, unkempt wig. He wears an unbuttoned double-breasted grey suit with an uptight maroon tie. He and his clothes have all seen better days. His manner is, to say the least, mannered.

THEOBALD

(still drunk, light tenor voice) There you are, Fletcher! Thought you could give me the slip, didn't you? But oh, no. No. No one escapes me, sir. And as I was saying - I've something more, yes, to - (self-interruption) but who are these gentlemen? Friends of yours, sir?

FLETCHER

I hope so. Surely you recognise Mr Shakespeare?

Theobald registers Shakespeare.

THEOBALD

Good Lord, so it is.

To Shakespeare's embarrassment he sinks to his knees.

THEOBALD

(breathless) Whoever would've thought it? I edited you, adapted you, championed you all my life, sir.

SHAKESPEARE

Please get up.

THEOBALD

Before the Swan of Avon, never!

SHAKESPEARE

Please. Let me help you.

He does. Theobald stands shakily.

FLETCHER

(enjoying the moment) And this is Don Miguel de Cervantes Saavedra.

Theobald registers Cervantes.

THEOBALD

Oh, my God. Too much. Another immortal.

He sinks to his knees again.

THEOBALD

I've adapted you, too, señor. Your *Captive's Story* made a - dare I say? - captivating opera but, alas and alack, it was never performed.

CERVANTES
  Up you get.

He and Shakespeare help him to his feet again.

THEOBALD
  (wobbling even more) Whoopsadaisy. Silly me.
SHAKESPEARE
  Perhaps you should sit down, Mr Theobald?
THEOBALD
  You know my name?
SHAKESPEARE
  Mr Fletcher has explained all about you.
THEOBALD
  (suddenly modest, perhaps maudlin) Not that there's that much
  to say really. One did one's best from 1688 to 1744 and then that
  was it. One was nowhere.
CERVANTES
  You'll feel better sitting down.

Cervantes and Shakespeare help him to sit where they were
sitting until his appearance.

THEOBALD
  Thank you. So kind. I do feel - what's the word? - disorientated.
  Yes. I had the devil's own job finding this place. Wrong stop on
  the tube then three buses so I've missed everything so far. But
  I did manage to get hold of a programme - (he produces it) - I
  read it in the pub together with the odd whisky - and I must say
  it doesn't seem to be anything like our play, William, I mean -
  correction - *your* play, William. May I, dare I, call you, William,
  sir?
SHAKESPEARE
  (so polite it hurts) If you wish, Mr Theobald. But if anything it
  was always Mr Fletcher's play more than mine.
FLETCHER
  Quite so. Dead right. Well said, William.

Cervantes requests Theobald's programme.

CERVANTES
  May I?

THEOBALD
Do. But I warn you it's full of inaccuracies. Not to say bloomers.

Fletcher uncorks the red wine.

FLETCHER
Australian Shiraz this time, Don Miguel.

He fills Cervantes' glass then his own.

SHAKESPEARE
Do offer Mr Theobald a glass, Jack.
THEOBALD
(coy) Oh, no, no, not for me. I shouldn't. I really shouldn't. Oh, well, if you insist, sir. So very, very understanding of you.

He takes the proffered glass.

THEOBALD
(toast) To all three of you. To the immortals. Whoops!

He slurps some of the wine onto his trousers. Brushes at it with his hand while spilling more onto the floor.

THEOBALD
Doesn't matter. It's an old suit. Charity shop. Oxfam.
SHAKESPEARE
Mr Fletcher tells me you retitled the play?
THEOBALD
(anxiously) I was obliged to. I do hope you don't object? The manager at Drury Lane insisted yours was not - well - a selling title. I fought my corner as we say nowadays - or rather yours and Mr Fletcher's corner, William, and also yours, so to speak, Señor Cervantes - but eventually it boiled down to either a new title or no production. And so, after much thought, I proposed *Double Falsehood* and the play went on. To great success I might add. It ran for ten nights to packed houses.
CERVANTES
Were you well paid?
THEOBALD
Alas, no. I'd already needed an advance. And that somewhat prejudiced my powers of negotiation contract-wise, as it were.

He laughs deprecatingly thus inciting a series of hiccups.

THEOBALD
  Pardon me.
SHAKESPEARE
  And what's this about an old prompt copy?
THEOBALD
  (trying to disguise his hiccups as genteel hesitations) Ah, yes!
  Yes, indeed. Mr Downes's - er - copy. The famous old prompter.
  He - er - passed it on to Mr Betterton, the great - er - actor who
  was even more - er famous. Er. I saw him play Falstaff when
  I was a - er - boy. What a performance! Er - some, no, I mean
  awesome - as current usage tends to have it, does it not?

He coughs and to his relief his hiccups stop.

SHAKESPEARE
  (still studiedly polite) I'm afraid I've never heard of Mr Downes
  or Mr Betterton, Mr Theobald.
THEOBALD
  Really? But apart from the Downes stroke Betterton copy there
  was another. In immaculate running-secretary hand. The one
  you gave to your natural daughter, William.

Pause in which the lukewarm social temperature plummets
alarmingly.

SHAKESPEARE
  (stainless steel) I never had a natural daughter, Mr Theobald.
THEOBALD
  (sobering up) Nor a natural son?
SHAKESPEARE
  No, sir. All my children were legitimate.
THEOBALD
  (eternal scholar) Not according to my researches, alas.
SHAKESPEARE
  (deadly now) Whose word do you prefer, Mr Theobald? Mine
  or yours?
THEOBALD
  (hurriedly) Oh, yours, of course, naturally, William sir or Sir
  William -

SHAKESPEARE
  (explosion) Explain, damn you! It's one thing to revise a play -
  another to revise a life!

Pause. Theobald gathers his wits together under Shakespeare's
basilisk glare. Tactfully Cervantes keeps out of it by studying the
programme.

THEOBALD
  Well -
SHAKESPEARE
  Yes?
THEOBALD
  History can bear me out -
SHAKESPEARE
  Really? How?
THEOBALD
  Well, as a young man I became acquainted with Mr Betterton in
  his later years. He frequently reminisced about the great actor-
  manager Sir William Davenant, poet laureate, friend of Mr
  Milton, etcetera. Mr Betterton had been the star of the company,
  you understand, but by the time I knew him -
SHAKESPEARE
  (interruptive) Yes?
THEOBALD
  Davenant was dead, sir.
SHAKESPEARE
  And - ?
THEOBALD
  Well, Mr Betterton always said Sir William Davenant claimed he
  was - forgive me for putting it so plainly - the fruit of your loins.

Fletcher can't help laughing - snort - while Shakespeare is further
displeased.

SHAKESPEARE
  (curt) Thank you, Jack! (to Theobald) How did he substantiate that?
THEOBALD
  Well, as it so happened, the dates could have fitted. Sir William
  was born during your lifetime. In 1606 Mr Betterton always
  said, and well - apparently - oh forgive me if I was misinformed
  but - oh,

137

He stops, bereft of words, reduced to silence by Shakespeare's unremitting gaze. To our surprise Fletcher intervenes.

FLETCHER

Perhaps I can help you here, Mr Theobald?

THEOBALD

(gratefully) You can? How kind. Please do.

FLETCHER

I've been urging William since forever to read Aubrey's *Brief Lives* which I'm sure you know? But he flatly refuses. I no longer read biography is his posh line. Despite the fact that Aubrey's stuff is wickedly full of fun. I feature in the *Lives* and so does he, but, even more to the point, so does this Sir William Davenant of yours. Luckily, among all my many talents, I can boast a photographic memory so I can quote you what Aubrey says. Take heart, Mr Theobald, you aren't alone in what you think.

SHAKESPEARE

(unamused) Jack -

FLETCHER

No, William, play fair. You really should've read Aubrey before getting on your high horse. He writes - I paraphrase without omitting the nitty-gritty - thus: "Sir William Davenant, Knight, was borne in the City of Oxford at the Crown Taverne. His father was a Vintner there. His mother a very beautiful woman. Mr William Shakespeare - "

SHAKESPEARE

Now, look, Jack - !

FLETCHER

I am. I'm looking at the entire printed page in my mind's eye, William -

SHAKESPEARE

That doesn't mean it's true!

FLETCHER

(grin) Of course not. But it does mean others may have *thought* it to be true. And what's more, William, the entry continues like this. "Mr Shakespeare was wont to go into Warwickshire once a yeare and did commonly lye at this house in Oxon." (to Cervantes) Oxford's on the way to Stratford - good stop-over point, right? (quoting again) "Now Sir William Davenant would sometimes, when he was pleasant over a glass of wine with his most intimate friends, say that it seemed to him that he writt with the very spirit that did Shakespeare and - "

138

SHAKESPEARE
Wrote like me?! How dared he claim that?
FLETCHER
Stay with us, William, it gets worse. "And seemed contented to be thought his son."

Prickliest pause yet.

SHAKESPEARE
Clearly the man was speaking metaphorically. To prop up his opinion of himself as a poet.
FLETCHER
No. Sorry. That won't do either, William. Because Aubrey keeps going. Like this: "He would tell them the story in which way his mother had a very light report, whereby she was called a Whore."

Shakespeare explodes again.

SHAKESPEARE
Stuff and nonsense!
FLETCHER
I'm sure it was. But which came first - the stuff or the nonsense? Or was it the other way round? Lots of jolly nonsense then the serious stuff?
SHAKESPEARE
A cheap joke, Jack, entirely typical of you.
FLETCHER
Maybe. But it could clarify how Mr Theobald came to believe what he did. However erroneously.
SHAKESPEARE
Yes. But let's not forget, Jack, that he's also supplied me with a natural daughter. Equally fictitious.
THEOBALD
No less a noble person than Lady de la Warr assured me that was so, sir.
SHAKESPEARE
No need to justify yourself or history any further, Mr Theobald, just accept my word instead. I had neither one nor the other.

He turns to Cervantes.

SHAKESPEARE

Forgive us, Don Miguel. What with Jack's flair for mischief and the theatre's delight in salacious rumour I'm afraid we must have tried your patience?

CERVANTES

Not at all. The conflicting claims of fact and fiction have always charmed me. As does this programme. Not that it tells me much about the author of this piece tonight. He keeps rather a low profile. But it does talk about your version, Mr Theobald, and suggests that within it there might well be a few echoes of Mr Shakespeare and Mr Fletcher's work. But what puzzles me is that it doesn't seem to have featured my knight and squire at all? And yet from what I've learnt so far today, Mr Shakespeare provided the comic subplot - deploying them to great effect - while Mr Fletcher concentrated on the romantic side of things, to earn equal applause?

SHAKESPEARE

Quite so.

FLETCHER

Exactly.

THEOBALD

Well, all I can say is they weren't in the prompt copy I worked from.

SHAKESPEARE

Then it must've been a fake. No question.

FLETCHER

Or some botched-up later job, William? After all, there was a civil war between our effort and whatever Mr Theobald's turned out to be. Call it theatrical fake blood under the bridge.

SHAKESPEARE

(easing up at last) Yes, Jack. You're right. Things change. So who cares anymore?

THEOBALD

(sober now) I do! And I did! I edited your collected works, sir. All of them. And took great pains to compare texts and correct compositors' errors. (bitterly) And small thanks I got.

CERVANTES

He's right, William (handing him the programme). According to this. Look.

SHAKESPEARE

(reading aloud from the programme) "Lewis Theobald is now recognised as a pioneer of Shakespearean studies. Modern editors continue to accept more than three hundred of his textual emendations"

CERVANTES

I wish I'd had a scholar like you, Mr Theobald, to correct *Don Quixote*. The first edition was riddled with misprints.

SHAKESPEARE

(still intent on the programme) It says here you offended the poet, Alexander Pope?

THEOBALD

That man! Or rather, manikin!

SHAKESPEARE

He appears to have edited me too. Did he?

THEOBALD

And how! Dreadfully! I pointed out his errors and in return he pillored me in print. Made me out to be a total dunce. The glitterati fell about laughing.

SHAKESPEARE

(laughing) Hey, what about this quotation, Jack? According to Pope you're "half-eaten Fletcher" and I'm "hapless Shakespeare, late of Theobald - spelt Tibbald - sore."

FLETCHER

Half-eaten by whom?

SHAKESPEARE

"Tibbald" presumably. That's to say Mr Theobald here.

FLETCHER

Let me look.

He takes the programme, scans it, laughs too.

FLETCHER

Jeez! What crap.

THEOBALD

It wasn't funny at the time. I did my very best for both of you (to Cervantes) And for you, sir.

SHAKESPEARE

(magnanimous now) I'm sure you did, Mr Theobald.

THEOBALD

And if I was otherwise misinformed about you then I can only say I was misinformed upon authority.

CERVANTES

Cheer up, Mr Theobald. All of us - with the shining exception of William Shakespeare here - we've all been targets for

141

abuse. When I published *Don Quixote*, Spain's most successful playwright sent me a sonnet in which he suggested its pages would best be used as lavatory paper. Many others have since echoed him, most recently the Amises, father and son, both formidable talents, I'm led to believe.

THEOBALD

The literary world is full of dangers.

CERVANTES

I can think of others more dangerous.

SHAKESPEARE

Forgive me, Mr Theobald, I overreacted. I only wish I had Don Miguel's generosity of spirit. You'd think eternity would mellow rather than intensify our feelings but in my case, no. If anything I feel more strongly than ever.

THEOBALD

Really? Not so with me. But then I never really knew what to think or feel from the start. Silly me. But there we are and now, now I'd like to ask all three of you what you think of this particular play - so boldly entitled *Shakespeare's Don Quixote*? Do you recommend it?

SHAKESPEARE

Well -

FLETCHER

Good question -

CERVANTES

The first thing I'd say is -

Sudden blackout.

ALL

(cut short) Oh!

A bell signalling the end of the interval pings off. Then the Assistant Stage Manager's voice is heard over the sound system.

LILY

(voice over) Please take your seats.

Various thumps are now heard as Bill, the stage manager, finishes setting up the next scene in the blackout. He does not hear or see Shakespeare, Cervantes, Fletcher or Theobald.

142

CERVANTES

It seems we must vanish once again.

FLETCHER

I'd say we already had.

THEOBALD

We are such stuff as dreams are made on, are we not, William?

SHAKESPEARE

(firmly) I wouldn't say so. No, not for myself. For others - perhaps.

Even though we can't see them all four have gone. The blackout continues.

End of 3rd Interlude

Act Four - Scene One

A cloister bell resounds steadily as light returns to the stage. A girl, whom we may not recognise at once, stands before the arch where Shakespeare and Cervantes sat. She, however, is much better lit according to the adjustments Shakespeare made to the lighting plan. In fact he's made both girl and cloister look lusciously Pre-Raphaelite. Ideally her fragile prettiness should beguile us even as we ask ourselves, who's this? And then answer, oh, yes, of course, that girl who fainted at the start of the action proper. That unwilling bride. In front of that fancy altar. At that forced wedding ceremony which her childhood sweetheart - that lad we've since seen torn in two by love and shame - failed to interrupt so that she was obliged to faint dead away in front of that cadaverous chaplain, that rapacious bridegroom and those social-climbing parents. An action to get the plot moving certainly, but no less true to life at the time for all that. And to pose a dramatic question: was this coerced but interrupted occasion valid or not? Is Lucinda - of course that was her name - is Lucinda now married in the eyes of God to Lord Fernando or isn't she? And if she is, does this make him, aged seventeen, and with what little brain he's got boiling in his balls, a bigamist? As we know from Dorotea, he and she were betrothed just before this supposed wedding and she wants justice. Breach of promise was a serious matter in 1605. With all this brewing I suspect Father Perez is going to have his work cut out reconciling the conflicting claims of flesh, faith and social propriety between the three of them. And that's reckoning without that wild card, Cardenio.

Anyway, by now, we've recognised Lucinda, thanks to her dress and also, perhaps, by the tip-tilt of her nose. Her dress is the same one she wore at the opening of the play. And this is a nice example of how a frugal theatre budget can be put to informative dramatic purpose. After all, we only saw her very briefly a good ninety minutes ago - and that's assuming playing time not reading time. Meanwhile most of the other characters have been able to establish themselves not just as who they are but to act out some of their hopes and fears, their certainties, their doubts.

So now it's Lucinda's turn to be herself, state her case, and share her predicament with us, while the convent bell counterpoints her thoughts, expressed - appropriately enough - as an echo of Fletcherian verse.

LUCINDA
Here must I dwell in doleful shade obscure;
Of hope, of love, of happiness denied.
But ever thus within my bosom pure,
This painted semblance of your face doth lie.

She takes out a gold-framed miniature of Cardenio and addresses it with tears in her eyes.

LUCINDA
Here is the relic I must yet reserve,
With all the fears my harsh misfortunes owe.
This, midst Fate's cruelty, may still preserve
My love for you, oh, lost Cardenio.

Lucinda falls to her knees weeping openly now. Enter a middle-aged Abbess, plump as a partridge, accompanied by a Nun carrying a novitiate's habit for Lucinda. These characters, and Lucinda are, for the moment, seventeenth century stereotypes but if, by professional inventiveness and natural ability, the actors can give them life and individuality, then Stanislavski's famous dictum: "there are no small parts only small actors" will have been vindicated. I should also add that I see the Abbess as being played by the actor who played Dorotea's nurse, Costanza; and that Lily, the ASM, is now the Nun. Her first part on the professional stage.

ABBESS
  (to Lucinda) My child, are you still resolved to accept our Rule?
  To become a novice in our sisterhood, renouncing all earthly
  things? Reflect once more, I beg you, before you answer. Your
  words, remember, will be weighed at the last day before the
  throne of God.

Pause in which the convent bell stops ringing thus creating a
deeper silence. Into it Lucinda sobs once. Then again. These two
sounds are sharply separated one from the other - the objective
being to make her anguish real to us.

LUCINDA
  Yes, good mother, I have resolved -

But she leaves this almost voiceless response unfinished and so
implies the opposite: that, at heart, she does not wish to enter this
sisterhood. How lucky playwrights are - compared with novelists
- to have actors and directors ready, willing, and eager to create
subtexts for them. As a playwright you can ask an actor to say
yes meaning no and then hear (and see it) happen. I'm reminded
of an anecdote concerning the always earnest Arnold Wesker,
who kept offering his thoughts during a rehearsal of one of his
early plays which was being directed by the waspishly mercurial
John Dexter. You don't need to know who either was to get
the joke. Dexter, exasperated by Wesker's well-meant but over
deterministic advice, finally turned on him to say: "Oh, do shut
up, Arnold, or I'll direct this scene just as you wrote it!" I have
no doubt that after that explosion the scene came subtextually to
life. Let's hope this one can do the same. The Abbess, meanwhile,
has accepted Lucinda's unfinished statement with a smile which
could suggest she knows something we don't.

ABBESS
  Then come with us, my child, and we shall dress you as a novice
  of our order.

Lucinda rises but as she does so two cloaked, masked men appear.
The first one brandishes a pistol rather than a sword or dagger.
Lucinda screams but the Abbess and the Nun are less alarmed.
In fact the Abbess simply crosses herself composedly as the Nun
says: 'Oh'. The first man speaks.

1st MAN
Stay back, Most Reverend Mother. We mean no harm to you or
any of your order. I claim my bride. She's mine, no other's, be
he Christ Himself.
ABBESS
(unconvincingly) Who are you, sir?
1st MAN
Lord Fernando of Montoro.

Lucinda screams again but now the second man clamps his left
hand over her mouth and pinions her arms behind her back with
his right. Forgive this banal stage direction but certain physical
actions in a play need to be spelt out for practicality's sake.

FERNANDO
No noise! Away with her!

The second man hustles Lucinda off while Fernando backs away
as if covering his accomplice's exit. Then, at the last moment he
produces a well-filled velvet purse with a flourish. The Abbess's
eyes gleam.

FERNANDO
Here, Most Reverend Mother.

He hands the purse to her.

FERNANDO
There. As agreed between us.
ABBESS
(curtsey) My gracious Lord.
FERNANDO
Never say this fugitive gentlewoman was here at any cost but
mine.

He goes.

ABBESS
(to the Nun) If only every distressed lady who comes to us for
protection were sought out so earnestly.
NUN
Indeed, good mother. But as you reminded me only yesterday,

Lord Fernando's father, the Duke, is your second cousin once removed.
ABBESS
He is. So now we may repair the dormitory roof, thanks be to God.
NUN
(to us, as they go) And to rich relations.

They have gone. Blackout.

Act Four - Scene Two

The last line of this last scene was an ad-lib from Lily. An unwelcome example of theatrical camp only slightly less flagrant than kicking up your heel to get an extra laugh on making an exit in some left-over West End comedy getting done to death in weekly repertory back in the '50s. And all the more surprising coming from our ASM. I thought actors just out of drama school these days were more conscientious than this? But perhaps not? Camp will out. And if theatre's anything, it's shameless. Quintessentially so. Lily will, on this showing, I'm sure, go far - provided she doesn't go too far, of course. Also, to be fair, her ad-lib has placed this charade-like abduction of Lucinda in a pertinent, historical perspective. Nunneries often served social interests quite as much as God's. But what this latest miniature melodrama has failed to do is to confirm whether Fernando and Lucinda are married or not. He has appropriated her as his runaway bride but is she really his wife? As a plot hinge it creaks, I agree, but there we are, it's central to the original story, and we can all blame Cervantes for making a meal of it. According to some, Shakespeare, in the lost script, went even further. He, it's said, smuggled Fernando into the convent in a coffin. This ruse to abduct Lucinda is planned and then reported as done in Lewis Theobald's version. Why it should be thought to be Shakespeare's idea rather than Fletcher's, I'm not sure. In *Cymbeline* the villainous Iachimo certainly gets into Imogen's bedroom by way of a large piece of furniture - a chest - but Fletcher could've borrowed this idea quite as cheerfully from Shakespeare as Shakespeare might have repeated it for himself. Writers, after all, are as indebted to themselves and each other as they are to life. Or Theobald - steeped as he was in Jacobethan drama - could easily have thought it up on his own account. Such exuberant deployment of containers (like wardrobes in later French farces) were comic or semi-serious staples of the entertainment industry of the day. Think of Falstaff in that laundry basket, or the box full of tennis balls brought by the French as a diplomatic insult to young Henry the Fifth. No wonder George Bernard Shaw, in his quixotic quest to surpass Shakespeare, produced his teenybopper Cleopatra as a dinky doll in a rolled-up carpet.

But apropos of Theobald's version of *Cardenio* two things are beyond dispute. First, however it happened in reality not report, he had to change the title to *Double Falsehood* because he - or that prompt copy - listed all of Cervantes' characters under different names. Cardenio becomes Julio, Dorotea - Violante, Fernando - Henriquez, and Lucinda - Leonora. Now Fletcher or Shakespeare could equally well have changed them - it was a common practice - but that then leaves us with a play which logically should've been called *Julio* not *Cardenio*. And all the earliest references to their work are to *Cardenio*. So perhaps these changes were made by Theobald? Only the discovery of that missing prompt copy can resolve this miniscule mystery. Perhaps some literary archaeologist will dig it out from somewhere eventually. And we'll all feel - well, some of us anyway - mildly relieved, historically speaking.

Meanwhile the cloister arch has been removed and as the lights come up again we realise we're back at that mirror pool where Dorotea bathed her feet so convincingly. But now the hobby-horse has been placed so he appears to be drinking from it, with Sancho beside him, lying on his stomach, Cardenio's satchel on his back, also drinking thirstily. Don Quixote stands close by, iron clad, still as stone. There's no sign of Father Perez, Nicholas the Barber, nor of Dorotea pretending to be Princess Micomicona. Don Quixote is waiting patiently for Sancho to finish quenching his thirst so he can question him - in confidence.

But before this can happen I suspect I ought to remind you of what all these characters were doing when we last saw them at the end of Act Three. At that moment you may recall Don Quixote had been chosen as a royal champion - mission to destroy the gigantic usurper, Pandafilando, and restore Princess Micomicona to her throne.

Meanwhile Cardenio had relapsed and charged off into the wilds again, as love-lorn and lacking in self-esteem as before. But now, as they descend from the Sierra Morena, Father Perez, Nicholas and Dorotea have gone in search of him like the three conscientious social workers they sincerely hope they are:

the priest with concern for Cardenio's soul; the barber as the seventeenth century equivalent of a village GP wondering if the boy might come to physical harm and need his help; and the competent daughter of a widowed tenant farmer, determined to see that he gets as much justice as she herself requires, from the man who has abused them both.

Having said this to you, the reader, I can now allow Don Quixote to say it again to you, the playgoer. But before he does so, the hobby-horse finishes drinking and lifts his head while Sancho continues to lap, head down, slurp slurp. Don Quixote registers this.

QUIXOTE
Rocinante's drunk his fill, Sancho. Surely you have, too?
SANCHO
(head up) He hasn't talked as much as me.

He continues to drink, head down.

QUIXOTE
(not especially surprised) I note you continue to keep that deluded boy's bag about your person?

Sancho now finishes drinking and manoeuvres himself upright, his mouth dripping rather more than Rocinante's did.

SANCHO
(back of hand wipe) Yes, sir, I do keep it. Right here (slaps the bag). Best place for it.
QUIXOTE
It is indeed. And I suggest you restore it to him at your earliest opportunity.
SANCHO
(truly , even honestly, astonished) You do?
QUIXOTE
Most assuredly. Always assuming, of course, our friends Father Perez, Barber Nicholas and that eminently sensible but unfortunate princess we've just met, can find the poor lad, that is.
SANCHO
(pragmatic peasant) Well, I hope they don't! Didn't I tell them not to bother? Didn't I say: if he comes back, he comes back, and if he don't, leave that sort of loony well alone? I mean, like how

many times has he tried to kill us? And even if they do find him
I still say, like my dad did, and his before him: what comes your
way, hold fast and what doesn't, go and get, before some other
son of Satan grabs it.

He slaps the bag possessively.

QUIXOTE
  Hardly a noble sentiment, Sancho.
SANCHO
  Well, I'm not noble, am I?
QUIXOTE
  You could be. Given time. But, be that as it may, I wish to speak
  of something else.
SANCHO
  (warily) Oh, aye? You do?
QUIXOTE
  Of Princess Dulcinea of Toboso.

Sancho turns to us. Every muscle of his face and body works
wordlessly to say: "Oh, no! Not her!" Here is physical theatre
personified - body language perfected. If anyone in the audience
laughs I do hope it's Shakespeare, delighting in such expressive
professionalism. Clowns may often say and do too much but if
they simply shrug and their trousers fall down, or, dancing a jig,
kick their own bottoms and then do a double-take wondering
who did it, we forgive them everything. I'm sure Shakespeare
did really. Whatever Hamlet may say to the Players he certainly
remembers Yorick the clown with affection.

QUIXOTE
  (not having seen Sancho's performance) And of my letter to that
  lady. That letter you delivered to her at her palace. Correct?
SANCHO
  (playing for time) Oh, that one, sir. Right. Yes. *That* letter. Got
  you now. The one I took, aye.
QUIXOTE
  There was no other, Sancho.
SANCHO
  There was! The one on the back of it! About them donks you're
  giving me!

QUIXOTE
Oh, that. That's beside the point at present.
SANCHO
Not to me, it ent! Them donks -
QUIXOTE
(firmly) Sancho, we are speaking of the peerless Princess Dulcinea not livestock.
SANCHO
(outbreath) Right. If you say so, sir. On you go.
QUIXOTE
No, Sancho. It is now your duty, as my faithful squire, to give me your report of your audience with her at the accomplishment of your mission on my behalf.
SANCHO
(to us) What *do* I say? Dunno. I told him I went there. To Toboso. But I didn't, did I? I mean you saw what happened as well as me, right? I met our priest, didn't I? And our barber not that far from where we are now. And - (self-interruption) - come on, Sancho, use your head if you've got one. Think! What does the old boy want to hear? Answer - what he likes to hear. And even if it doesn't please him he'll twist it so it does. So tell him anything you like. He'll believe it. Right. So here we go. Right.

He turns to face Don Quixote.

SANCHO
Well, sir -
QUIXOTE
I'm waiting.
SANCHO
Well - funny you should ask about that princess of yours, sir -
QUIXOTE
(tenterhooks) Yes?
SANCHO
Well, let's put it like this, shall we?
QUIXOTE
Yes?
SANCHO
Let's say she got your letter - all right?
QUIXOTE
(some doubt now) *Did* she?

SANCHO

In a manner of speaking, sir. After all, you sent it, didn't you?

QUIXOTE

By way of *you*, Sancho.

SANCHO

That's correct, sir.

Pause. Don Quixote would like to query what he's just heard but such is his need of a positive report from his squire he speaks meekly rather than demandingly.

QUIXOTE

I wonder if you could enlarge upon what then occurred, good squire? When you delivered my letter?

SANCHO

(fully in charge now) If you like, sir. But first why don't you tell me what you want to know? I mean you're better at this sort of mullarky than me, ent you?

Another pause.

QUIXOTE

(meeker yet) Possibly. At any rate you must have been ushered into her gracious presence? Were you not?

SANCHO

Could be. Aye.

QUIXOTE

And doubtless she was enthroned, dare I suggest?

SANCHO

If you like. Why not? Worth a go.

Clowns can be as cruel as they are funny and the actor here is no exception to this rule.

QUIXOTE

And virtuously employed upon some high born maidenly task? Such as embroidering an emblem or love-knot upon cloth of gold?

SANCHO

Sounds good, sir. Keep going.

QUIXOTE

A costly neckerchief, perchance, for this her knight - meaning oneself, me, that is - to wear upon his golden helm - this one - (he taps the brass basin on his head - it tings) - when I come to joust before her at the next royal tournament? That surely was how it must have been?

SANCHO

More or less like that, sir. Aye.

QUIXOTE

I've hit the mark?

SANCHO

Spot on. Well, sort of. Looked at your way, aye, it was. She was enthroned all right. On a hen-coop.

QUIXOTE

A hen-coop?

SANCHO

In a backyard.

QUIXOTE

Backyard?

SANCHO

Where else? But she wasn't at her needlework, no. She'd rolled up her sleeves and was riddling barley through a dirty great sieve. Weigh a ton they do. You should've seen her biceps! Bigger'n her titties.

QUIXOTE

Ah! A rustic idyll! Royalty often embraces the simple life. And without any shadow of doubt, excellent squire, those grains of barley in that sieve turned to seed pearls, did they not?

SANCHO

Did they?

QUIXOTE

What else? At the slightest shake of her delicate hands and lissom wrists - never mind her upper arms, which would, in point of chivalric fact, have been hidden from impertinent view in purest silk, would they not?

SANCHO

So they was! Got that wrong, didn't I?

QUIXOTE

I fear you did, my squire.

SANCHO

And I know why.

QUIXOTE

Why?

SANCHO

Because, sir, I was thinking of pearl barley - like you said, wasn't I?

QUIXOTE

Pearl barley? No. I was stipulating seed pearls.

SANCHO

Well, they look much the same, don't they? Sparkly bits of nothing you can almost see through. The wife makes a drink of pearl barley. To get our kiddies' bowels moving.

QUIXOTE

Spare me your family life, Sancho. Did my princess kiss my letter?

SANCHO

(retrenching) She could have, sir. I'm not saying she didn't.

QUIXOTE

I'm sure she did. What other ceremony did she use upon receipt of it? Did she bestow it in her bosom for later perusal? Or hand it to her most trusted lady-in-waiting for safe-keeping?

SANCHO

(thinking hard) No. She didn't do any of that. Just gawped at it. I mean looked at it. So I asked for it back.

QUIXOTE

(horrified) You asked for it back!

SANCHO

'Course I did! For what you wrote on the other side! Telling your housekeeper to hand over your donks!

Pause as Don Quixote is forced to recognise the reality behind his chivalric aspirations. But before he can construct another morale-boosting fantasy Dorotea appears, followed by Father Perez and Nicholas, with Don Quixote's broken lance.

DOROTEA

We found Don Cardenio again only to lose him again.

SANCHO

But you've got your old poker back, sir, from the look of it.

PRIEST

He threw it at us. Fortunately without harm.

Sancho takes the lance from Nicholas and hands it to Don Quixote.

SANCHO

Here, sir. Get a grip on that. You'll feel better with that in hand.

QUIXOTE

Thank you, Sancho - most squire-like of you.

PRIEST

The difficulty is Don Cardenio still insists he alone must be the champion of our princess.

He glances at Dorotea who takes the cue. Clearly they have agreed this account of their meeting with Cardenio beforehand. Dorotea turns to Don Quixote.

DOROTEA

(regally) But when we assured him he was our champion in peace and that you, sir, were our champion in war he -

SANCHO

He went loopy again, I bet.

PRIEST

Let us say he regressed, Sancho, shall we?

QUIXOTE

Can he not distinguish betwixt peace and war?

DOROTEA

Not at this time, sir. Nor between love and hate. For the moment he lacks your judgement in such matters.

QUIXOTE

Then he's beside himself indeed.

PRIEST

Not quite, sir, no. This latest relapse struck me as less profound than others we have witnessed. In my view he could be whole again once he is two in one.

QUIXOTE

Two in one? But he's that already?

PRIEST

He is. But if the cause of this division were to be removed by a reunion with his lady, Lucinda, then I'm sure he would be entirely himself again.

SANCHO

Like get his end in, he'll be all right?

Pause. All turn to regard Sancho with disgust at his crudely pragmatic approach to life, love and marriage. Sancho tries to face out their heavily silent disapproval, fails, blushes, hangs his head.

SANCHO

(murmur) Sorry I spoke. (to us) That'll cost me six Hail Marys come Friday, I shouldn't wonder.

PRIEST

(to Don Quixote) I fear your squire, great sir, is as yet unfamiliar with the niceties of chivalric speech.

QUIXOTE

Or any speech, father, except his own. But he means well and in time, I'm sure, will learn.

PRIEST

Let us pray so. I've frequently observed maturity emerge from simplicity (with a touch of snobbishness). And particularly in young gentlemen such as Cardenio -

Sancho snorts indignantly and turns away to pat the hobby-horse.

SANCHO

(whisper) Hear that, old lad? Like we're nobody compared with some. Ooh, I'm hungry, how about you?

The hobby-horse nods its head and vibrates its lips in agreement. Meanwhile Father Perez continues to address Don Quixote. If there's one thing theatre's good for, it's for doing two things at once (if not more).

PRIEST

Don Cardenio - once he is married to Lady Lucinda, will, I'm sure, prove to be his former self again. Such is the remedial power of holy matrimony.

SANCHO

(determined to bring this scene to a close and I tend to sympathise with him) What's that?

QUIXOTE

What's what?

SANCHO

I heard something. Listen. Nasty noise it was. And how.

Pause. All listen. Nothing is heard.

SANCHO

There it goes again!

QUIXOTE

It doesn't.

SANCHO

It does! Gurgle, gloop. Listen.

All listen again.

QUIXOTE

Nothing. You're making it up, Sancho.

SANCHO

Never! There it is! Tummy rumble. Telling me it's time to fill it. Yours too, sir. When did you last eat? Like an empty belly tells the time just as loud as any church bell, eh, father?

PRIEST

(won-over smile) Very well, good squire. In this instance your word is good. A mile from here there is a crossroads with an inn known as the Four Ways - a humble refuge for such as Princess Micomicona here -

SANCHO

Reckon she won't complain - I mean, just look at her. She's lovely. A true princess wherever she is. She'd make anywhere a palace.

DOROTEA

(to Don Quixote and Father Perez) Who says Squire Sancho is not, after all, the soul of chivalry?

Don Quixote sways, Sancho reacts at once.

SANCHO

Hey, hold up, sir! We can't have you with the staggers. (to the others) Like I said, Lord knows when he last ate.

PRIEST

Help him along, good squire.

DOROTEA

We shall take his other arm. After a good dinner our champion will reshape the world. And so will his faithful squire.

Dorotea and Sancho help Don Quixote off, followed by Father Perez and Nicholas, leading the hobby-horse. If the hobby-horse were to jib at Nicholas's beard and spectacles he could remove them and be heard to say as they go -

BARBER
  Steady up. It's only me, old fellow.

They've all gone.

Act Four - Scene Three

This scene follows immediately and takes place in a spotlight illuminating Cardenio's face only. He could be anywhere. We might, for instance, suppose he's following Don Quixote's party, or lurking in a thicket beside the road. Wherever he is, he's reverted to verse - heroic couplets this time.

CARDENIO
  All thoughts I have their opposites provide,
  My head and heart are lost in this divide;
  At ev'ry step another pulls me back,
  And ev'ry purpose all conviction lacks;
  My head condemns me for my cowardice,
  In shame my soul does ever count the price;
  My heart is rent for my Lucinda's sake,
  What dare I do to reparation make?

Lucid moment.

CARDENIO
  My enemy's without and not within!
  Forgive myself? Have my revenge on him?
  I fled too soon, at forfeit of my name?
  Take heart, Cardenio, reclaim your fame!
  That's easy said, but can I do it sure?
  Put to the proof will I prove fool once more?

The tightly focused spotlight allows the actor of Cardenio six seconds of self-doubt ameliorated by a growing sense of self-worth before flicking off. Blackout. If this vital moment of self-recuperation hasn't registered with us, please don't blame the actor, or me, or the lighting designer, blame William Shakespeare. After all, it was he revamped the lighting, wasn't it?

Act Four - Scene Four

Beautiful sunset effect warmly illuminating who else but Shakespeare? Here he is, with Jessop at his side, sitting opposite Cervantes at a table outside the roadhouse known as the Four Ways. Where before they appeared at one remove from the play now they seem to be actually on stage during the action. Or rather just before it resumes. How should we regard their presence? Perhaps as the equivalent of those wealthier patrons of the Blackfriars Theatre who sat on stage conversing with each other or any scene-filling spear-holder they fancied standing close-by? By the way, the Globe Theatre - just across the river from Blackfriars - did not permit this practice. What's more, soon after *Cardenio* was presented at Whitehall Palace, the Globe burnt to the ground during a performance of *All is True* - that other collaboration of Shakespeare with Fletcher, better known as *Henry VIII*. One stage effect too many - a cannon shot-off - cost the sharers a packet for the rebuild. 1613 was a mixed year for William Shakespeare.

But that's long ago. For the moment all he's really interested in is pumping Cervantes about the art of the novel, which is why Jessop now yawns hugely and falls asleep across Shakespeare's feet.

SHAKESPEARE
Tell me more about unreliable narrators, Don Miguel.
CERVANTES
Well, as I was saying they became fashionable a few years ago but like all fashions they've begun to fade away, or so I believe. But I'm sure they'll turn up again since we all have a soft spot for truly entertaining liars - at least in fiction, don't we?
SHAKESPEARE
(after sipping at a glass of water) Do we? Perhaps. But I've heard it said that you were the very first European writer to invent one to tell your story for you?
CERVANTES
(after sipping at a glass of red wine) Nonsense. All knights-errant had spell-binding biographers prone to exaggeration.
SHAKESPEARE
But Don Quixote's writes in Arabic? You have to get the manuscript translated? And then, on top of that, you appoint yourself its editor?

CERVANTES
  (nod) Mm. That's known as a layered narrative nowadays.
SHAKESPEARE
  And in so doing you pre-date - by several centuries - what
  modern literary theory has termed *the death of the author*, I
  understand?
CERVANTES
  I've never cared for that notion. A Frenchman - what *was* his
  name? - sent me a number of his books which seemed to suggest
  that authors like you or me, William, simply aren't there. Or
  rather weren't there when we did what we did. We were just
  signs of our times apparently. Well, I begged to differ. I still do.
  And what's more I felt so strongly about it I composed a verse -
  ah! His name's come back to me - Barthes - Roland Barthes.

Cervantes' French accent is impeccable - he's rolled the r's, nasalled
the an, dropped the d and sounded the th as a dismissively
explosive t.

SHAKESPEARE
  Was it a rude verse?
CERVANTES
  Childishly so. I never sent it to him, thank Heaven, but it relieved
  my feelings.
SHAKESPEARE
  How did it go?
CERVANTES
  I'm not sure I remember.
SHAKESPEARE
  I'm sure you can. Go on - I love silly verses.
CERVANTES
  "Who gives a fart for Roland Barthes? Given his philosophy
  He could have written more modestly,
  Even anonymously."

Shakespeare laughs.

SHAKESPEARE
  Charming. You should've sent it. Now. Next. Your views on
  magic realism, Don Miguel?
CERVANTES
  Oh, dear. What an embarrassing question.

SHAKESPEARE

(surprised) Is it? Why?

CERVANTES

Because I drank myself to death trying to write the stuff. The result came out with considerable success after I'd gone, but the publisher cheated my widow, poor girl, of the payment he'd promised me on delivery of the manuscript.

SHAKESPEARE

Good Lord. What was it called?

CERVANTES

The Labours of Persiles and Sigismunda. But by the time I was racing death to finish it, I'd already realised - to adapt the title of your favourite play - it was essentially a love's labour lost. Magic realism goes better on stage than on the page. As you must surely know, William. Look at your *Midsummer Night's Dream*, your *Tempest*, your *Winter's Tale*.

SHAKESPEARE

So, you wouldn't recommend it as a path for aspiring novelists to follow?

CERVANTES

Not unless that they happen to be Latin-American - it seems better suited to that part of the world than this.

SHAKESPEARE

You came to realise that reality and fantasy were best kept at odds with each other?

CERVANTES

Yes - mix them together and very soon you become responsible for neither. To say life's a dream is a pretty metaphor but it isn't true. Such writing, blasting the reader's sensibilities into submission with mythology's guided missiles or fairytale flying carpet bombing, mostly succeeds in establishing a self-admiring literary dictatorship over the reader.

SHAKESPEARE

(sly smile) Are you thinking of any comparatively recent, much lauded novelist in particular?

CERVANTES

No. Of me, writing *Persiles*.

They laugh, drink.

SHAKESPEARE

And ventriloquism?

CERVANTES

What?

SHAKESPEARE

It's a term I came across somewhere. Was it in the TLS or the LRB?

CERVANTES

You've lost me now?

SHAKESPEARE

The Times Literary Supplement, The London Review of Books.

CERVANTES

We don't get those where I come from. Could that be a blessing, I wonder? But I did know a superb ventriloquist way back. Had this puppet on his knee called Big Mouth. How he talked! But never once did you see the man's lips move. Street Theatre you'd call it nowadays. But he was always there, day in, day out, getting a bare living, at the Gate of the Sun.

SHAKESPEARE

Where's that? The Gate of the Sun?

CERVANTES

In Madrid. Just up the street from where I used to live.

SHAKESPEARE

(smile) Oh, I see. For a moment I thought you'd succumbed to magic realism after all.

CERVANTES

Well, as I say, reality can have its moments.

SHAKESPEARE

Anyway, ventriloquism seems now to have moved on from the entertainment industry towards a more respectable career in literary criticism.

CERVANTES

How's it managed that?

SHAKESPEARE

By being employed as a term to define a narrative in which the author speaks to the reader through another person. Or several, come to that.

CERVANTES

But we've done that! When haven't we? Told stories in the first person? But in the theatre we tend to do it through dozens of different voices. Surely such a common practice hardly needs definition? As you, of all people, must know?

SHAKESPEARE

Now *that* is where you're mistaken, Don Miguel. Without definitions - the more tendentious the better - our critics would be out of a job and might, of necessity, have to try to survive by writing a novel or play themselves.

CERVANTES

Or take up tax-collecting?

SHAKESPEARE

Quite so. And as for lots of voices in the theatre that's no longer the case either - unless it's a musical. Today would-be playwrights - rather endearingly known as *straight* playwrights - are advised for economy's sake to limit the number of their characters to seven at most, fewer if possible, and ideally none at all.

CERVANTES

This chap tonight seems to have avoided that restriction?

SHAKESPEARE

Only by mixing genres.

CERVANTES

And getting us for free.

SHAKESPEARE

Oh, no, we must demand the Equity minimum, Don Miguel. I certainly shall.

They laugh as Jessop wakes up and barks.

SHAKESPEARE

What is it, Jessop? (looks off) Oh, yes, there's Lily. Sweet girl. Time we moved along.

They get up. Shakespeare slips a ten euro note under his glass.

CERVANTES

I'd have thought Fletcher would've been back with us by now?

Jessop barks again.

SHAKESPEARE

Shush, sir! (to Cervantes) He's only got to hear that name and he barks. But don't worry - Jack'll be back with a copy of that eighteenth century nonsense known as *Double Falsehood*. That's why he got poor Theobald totally squiffy - so he could offer to see him home and rifle his bookshelves. Couldn't wait to get his hands on it to find out if he really did rewrite what we wrote. Heel, Jessop. After you, Don Miguel.

They go. Music to re-establish the scene. Enter a landlord. He sees the empty glasses on the table and the money.

LANDLORD
  (calling back to his wife) Cristina! Did you serve those two gents?

A landlady appears in the doorway.

LANDLADY
  What two gents?
LANDLORD
  They've gone now. (collects the glasses and the ten euro note)
  Still they paid their dues.

Horse whinny off. The landlord looks stage right.

LANDLORD
  Ah, quite a party. If these folks stop and stay we can sing *Praise be to God*, twice over.
LANDLADY
  (peering) Look a bit peculiar to me.
LANDLORD
  Just so their money's good.
LANDLADY
  Best see to the beds.

She goes inside as Father Perez and Dorotea appear followed by Don Quixote supported now by Nicholas on his right and Sancho on his left. Clearly he's almost all in from lack of sleep, lack of food and too much fond imagining. The hobby horse trundles after them on his leading rein that's wound round Sancho's right wrist. They all stop. Don Quixote looks up and registers the Inn of the Four Ways.

QUIXOTE
  (worn out yet ever chivalric) Ah! This castle has a welcome look.
SANCHO
  I should hope so. Seeing how it's that roadhouse we've been aiming for.
QUIXOTE
  (faint but still game) And there before our very eyes is the governor or castellan of this noble fortress.

SANCHO

No, sir, that's the landlord.

QUIXOTE

Doubtless he is indeed lord of much land hereabout, good squire.

Sancho's outbreath of exasperation at Don Quixote's indefatigable fantasizing is shared by the hobby-horse. Another vibrant moment. Meanwhile our attention is directed to Father Perez as he speaks to the landlord.

PRIEST

At present we are five, but we could well become six should another of us decide to appear.

LANDLORD

Another lady or another gent, may I ask?

DOROTHEA

Another gentleman. Very young and rather nervous.

LANDLORD

Well, madam, provided all these gents don't object to sharing a bed - we've got one can take half a dozen at a pinch -

PRIEST

Oh, that will amply suffice -

Sancho butts in fast, indicating Don Quixote who has now sagged once again between him and Nicholas.

SANCHO

Have you got a bed straight off for this one? Look at him. He can't hold up much longer. Nor can I. Nor my friend here. And stabling for his horse. He's in need of a rest, too.

The hobby-horse whinnies agreement.

LANDLORD

We have.

SANCHO

Right. (to Nicholas) Swop you. You stable Paco - I'll see his worship settled. Hold on, sir. Hang on to me. Soon have you tucked down.

Sancho supports Don Quixote while Nicholas leads the hobby horse away.

BARBER

Steady up, old lad.

QUIXOTE

(as he goes in with Sancho) Decent drawbridge, acceptable portcullis -

They've gone.

LANDLORD

Do you wish to eat at our table, father? Or have you brought your own provisions?

PRIEST

None. We shall be happy to eat whatever you can provide. But concerning that exhausted gentleman just now - I think you should know, sir, that he is not always altogether in his mind. He tends, as it were, to exist in the past.

LANDLORD

I must say, father, I did wonder the minute I saw him. We get all sorts here, of course, but not that many in armour with barbers' basins on top.

DOROTEA

I'm sure you don't But this gentleman believes he's a wandering knight out of times gone by.

LANDLORD

(laugh) A knight-errant? Oh, I know all about them! I read their adventures to the wife. And anyone else who'll listen and that means all of us. Very popular they are.

PRIEST

But you don't suppose them to be true, I'm sure?

LANDLORD

Good Lord, no! They're for entertainment, aren't they, after a hard day's work? Everyone knows that.

PRIEST

Except our friend here.

DOROTEA

He thinks all their exploits and adventures are true.

LANDLORD

Oh, dear. (sudden apprehension) Could that mean he's dangerous if roused?

PRIEST

Given correct handling that question won't arise.

LANDLORD

(unconvinced) But is he safe to have in the house?

PRIEST

Oh, yes. After all, he has us, his friends and neighbours, with him. Our purpose is to bring him safely home.

LANDLORD

(still doubtful) Well, so long as you'll vouch for him, father -

PRIEST

I do.

DOROTEA

So will I. He means well. He imagines I'm a princess and that he's my champion. He thinks he's going to kill a giant who's threatening me, pour soul.

PRIEST

He's known at home as Don Alonso the Good.

DOROTEA

But as a knight-errant he calls himself Don Quixote of La Mancha.

LANDLORD

(sudden recall, realisation, alarm) Oh, no! Not that so-and-so! He's a wanted man! A criminal! We've had the law here looking for that one! He's done a lot of damage round here, they say. To property and persons. Oh, no, father, I'm sorry, I can't have that one in the house. No. You'd best get him up and out of here just as soon as you can. Sorry, but - no -

During this speech Father Perez has produced a leather purse from deep within his cassock. He shakes gold and silver coins from it into his palm. Pause in which money speaks louder than words.

PRIEST

(eventually) Think of this as caution money. Against any inconvenience. Of any kind.

LANDLORD

(suitably impressed) Well, father -

PRIEST

You may rest assured I will answer for him at all times and that your love for a fellow man in mental distress will not go unnoticed elsewhere.

Father Perez raises his eyes indicatively to Heaven even as he places the money in the landlord's very open hand.

LANDLORD
    Right, father, right. And that being how it is you'd best take a
    look at what our house can offer in the way of accommodation.
    (to Dorotea) You, too, madam, if you will.
DOROTEA
    Not yet. I'll rest a little out here. The air is so cool now.
LANDLORD
    As you please, madam.

Father Perez and the landlord go in. Dorotea, left alone, catches
her breath, controls the tears starting in her eyes - she's suppressed
so many of her own feelings for so long - and then speaks to us
as best she can, blaming herself, we may note, almost as much as
Fernando, her errant lover.

DOROTEA
    My quest is justice but my need is love;
    Can such a want my wayward husband move?
    How can I say? I hardly know him yet,
    Though to his will I did in troth submit.
    So does love lure us to our own disgrace,
    Our virtue lost in lust's deceitful haste.

She buries her head on her hands. After a moment Cardenio
appears.

CARDENIO
    Good madam, forgive me.

Dorotea looks up.

CARDENIO
    I've dogged your steps.
DOROTEA
    We looked for you.
CARDENIO
    I hid myself. For fear that other self might overcome me. But
    now I hope he may at last be gone. If this is so - I pray it is -
    then tell me, here, at these crossroads, do you intend to turn
    northwards with this so-called Don Quixote and his friends?
    Or will you turn southwards with me to confront our mutual
    enemy at Montoro - Lord Fernando?

DOROTEA
  Never say enemy.
CARDENIO
  He is to me!
DOROTEA
  But not to me! He can't be! Mustn't be! No!
CARDENIO
  But he's betrayed you.
DOROTEA
  I blame his youth. Like you he's young.

Pause.

CARDENIO
  (unmoved) I shall challenge him. Kill him. Your honour
  demands it. So does mine.
DOROTEA
  No! Reflect! Consider! I love him!

Potent pause.

CARDENIO
  Will you turn north or south, madam?

While Dorotea searches for a suitable response to this would-be adult
(and therefore heroic) Cardenio I should like to point out that both
actors here have worked this romantic dilemma with considerable
skill. Playscripts naturally cry out for actors to give them life, so as
texts they can sometimes seem, curiously cryptic or over-emphatic.
Especially as some playwrights offer no stage directions whatsoever
while others put in so many the action is monitored word for word,
second by second. Here I've tried to strike a balance - not too few,
not too many - while also using verse for Dorotea's recapitulation of
her position and then prose for her encounter with Cardenio. Her
emotional upheaval in the face of his new-found resolve needed
Renaissance constraint broken open by modern immediacy. And
what's pleased me most was the way we saw Dorotea surprise
herself as she said *I love him* as a felt truth bursting for the first
time into public speech. Here, too, the relative ages of our quartet
of lovers come into sharper focus. At twenty-six Dorotea is much
older than Cardenio, Lucinda and, crucially for her, Fernando.
In terms of her own time she's almost on the shelf - just as Anne

Hathaway was when she took up with eighteen year old William Shakespeare in 1582; a parallel he may well have noticed when first reading *Don Quixote*. Certainly Dorotea must, for self-respect's sake, make Fernando keep his promise to her, just as Anne did William. But now, before she's found an answer to Cardenio's demand Sancho appears. A welcome interruption that has, in effect, rescued a damsel in distress. Could it be, contrary to received opinion, that once again reality can give a helping hand to romance?

SANCHO
  (seeing Cardenio) Oh no! Not you?
CARDENIO
  Yes. I have returned
SANCHO
  But who as? This time? Eh? Eh?
CARDENIO
  My better self, I hope.
SANCHO
  Me, too. We had enough bother with the other one, didn't we?
  Right? Am I?

Pause. Dorotea changes the subject diplomatically.

DOROTEA
  How is your sad-faced knight, Sancho? Resting quietly?
SANCHO
  Aye. Sleeping like a lamb, bless him. Worn out he was. And if
  you'll pardon me, my lady, I must now see how they've stabled
  old Paco. I promised him I would. He don't trust our Nicholas.
  What do barbers know about horseflesh is what he always says.

Suddenly an equine whinny is heard off. Stage left. It's piercingly loud, vehemently expressive.

SANCHO
  He's heard me! Best get to him - hey up, Paco. I'm with you!
  Hold on!

But as Sancho starts to go off stage left a donkey bray even more raucous - and possibly more alarming to untuned ears - is heard off stage right. A donkey's hee-haw, by the way, can be far more abrasive to human ears than the most macho car horn. Hearing it

Sancho whips round, not once but twice, on the spot. Three times if the actor's up to it. He's as astonished as we are - but much more delighted.

SANCHO
It's *him*! My Dapple! That's his voice! It wasn't me Paco heard! It was *him*! My donk. He knew his trot before I did! Oh, my sakes. All my prayers are answered.

Sancho sinks to his knees dissolved in happy tears. Meanwhile a duet of horse whinnies and donkey brays can ascend to a shattering climax. In fact I'm tempted to offer here a stage direction of what *could* happen rather than what, in fact, *will* happen. Why not? A playwright's thoughts are as free as any novelist's, even if their realisation invariably costs more to produce than the printing of a novel. So now, patient reader, allow me to present my ideal version of this reunion followed by an account of what will in fact get staged - as economically as possible - in a moment or two.

Ideal Version: As the horse and donkey duet crescendoes great shouts are heard off from Nicholas the Barber together with the thunder of hooves pounding at a stable door, followed by a cataclysmic crash as it's knocked down and the hobby-horse rolls furiously on stage, apparently still whinnying, and with nostrils flared. One might almost believe that here is a genuine war-horse. At the same time a hobby-donkey appears from the other side. He's as beautifully crafted as the hobby-horse. His head is an equal marvel. Never did a donkey look more like a donkey. The head is huge; the ears a swivelling delight; the eyes couldn't be more darkly lustrous; his dappled coat's thick as a rug in need of hoovering - especially that elongated mound of it, almost a crest, descending from between the ears to between those eyes - and as for that muzzle of pure white leather soft as a glove, and those yellow teeth like, well, like, well, like description fails me.

But now - impact. Horse and donkey embrace. How? you may ask. Me, too. Well, in this instance of theatrical perfection, they first spin round on their wheels in front of each other, and then freeze, criss-cross, with their stick necks extended one against the other to form a graphic kiss - big heads at one end, small wheels at the other. And now, simultaneously, (plus music and subtly modulated lighting) their whinnies and brays subside into gently reverberative rubber-lipped sighs of delight, which, in their turn,

171

resolve into silent satisfaction. And if this dazzlingly display of the property master's art doesn't get a round of applause I'll give up trying to invent ideal theatre which teases the adult in us, even as it pleases the child that the less solemn among us wish we still were, but can never be again.

How we next involve Sancho, Nicholas (rushing on from the stable yard) and an odd looking stranger we've never seen before (with a green eye patch, gold teeth, gold earrings, gold buttons, black silk sash, sharp boots) in this event I can leave to reality. That's to say the action as it's now getting played out within the modest confines of this presupposed theatre of mine.

Act Four - Scene Four (continued in reality)

As Sancho, still where we left him on his knees, looks up to see Dapple appear, the stranger, described above, enters in pursuit of his runaway mount. Paco, we recall, has not appeared.

SANCHO
(seeing Dapple) Dap! My old beauty!

Hee-haw.

SANCHO
(seeing the stranger) And you! You thieving bastard! Hold on, Dap.

Sancho's on his feet, slapping Dapple on the rump which isn't there, while advancing on the stranger -

SANCHO
(vengeful warrior) Right! Let's have you! You're a gippo, ent you?
STRANGER
(recognising Sancho) Oh, no! Not the fat little sod! Let's get the hell outta here!

The stranger goes, taking his street credibility with him. Sancho charges after him.

SANCHO
Hey! You stop! Stop, thief! Stop!

But Dapple brays just once more and it's Sancho who stops, pushed one way, pulled the other. Rudolf von Laban would be proud of this actor - head in the future, shoulders in the present, bum in the past! If you don't know what I mean - and there's no reason why you should - ask a stage movement historian. Where are we? Oh, yes. Sancho frozen in mid-stage, then following his bottom - swift turnaround - to reunite himself with Dapple, hugging his huge head.

SANCHO
Aye, let him go. You're back, that's all that matters. Never thought to hear or see you again - light of my life.

Hold this poignant pause before Dorotea and Cardenio speak.

DOROTEA
A true reunion.
CARDENIO
Heartfelt.
SANCHO
Aye. Oh, my Dap! (to them) I call him Dapple on account of his sprockly coat. But he's been starved. Where's the belly on you, Dap? We'll soon feed you up again, lad, you see. (to them again) Smartest in our family this one is. Got stole he did. And sold to gippoes from the look of it.

More horse whinnying off as Nicholas appears.

BARBER
There you are, Sancho! Paco's all of a lather. Won't settle.
SANCHO
Here's why. Dapple's back. Paco heard him. We'll take him to him, Nicholas. They ent just stablemates you know, they're soul mates. Come on, Dap, hark who's calling.

Hee-haw answer as Sancho, Nicholas, and Dapple go. Then Father Perez comes out of the inn.

PRIEST
A modest lodging but clean.
DOROTEA
My other champion's returned, father.

PRIEST
  (at Cardenio with reservation) So you have, sir.
CARDENIO
  I think I'm of one mind again.
PRIEST
  I pray so.

Pause before Dorotea voices her heartfelt dilemma.

DOROTEA
  But I am now divided, father. Torn in two by my promise to
  help you bring your deluded neighbour home, and by my need
  to seek my own salvation in Montoro with the help of Don
  Cardenio here? Advise me, father. Should I go north with you,
  or south with him?
PRIEST
  I'm certain God will resolve this question, madam. And so, for
  the moment, let us go in and enjoy the house's hospitality and a
  good night's sleep.

They go. Blackout.

Act Four - Scene Five

Puff of red smoke, then spotlight, and John Fletcher's back, just
as Shakespeare said he would be, waving an old, worm-eaten,
leather-bound book at us. As before he's boiling with resentment,
jealousy and what he feels is unrecognised genius - *his*.

FLETCHER
  Not in the frame at all! Need never have existed - me! (waves
  book at us) I get that old eighteenth century deadbeat home, he
  gives me his play of my play, and what do I fucking find? Jeez!
  (opens book) Title page. *Double Falsehood* "Written originally by
  W. Shakespeare and now Revised and Adapted to the Stage by
  Mr Theobald, 1728." So, like I thought, no credit for me even
  then, let alone now! So sod Theobald for one, and sod whoever
  wrote this fandango for the other! And as for our two resident
  geniuses - or should I say genii? - haven't they made themselves
  at home? Haven't they just? Can't get enough of each other, can
  they? Mutual admiration society. They'll be putting each other

174

up for the Garrick next, but me - I'm only fit for the Groucho, right? If that! Hey! (new tone) Low be it spoken, but I'm coming to the conclusion that this Don Miguel we've got here tonight - who I thought so wonderful - has been seriously, and I *do* mean seriously, over-rated. Right? Both as author and man. Like he's always being cracked-up to be the ultimate officer and gentleman - correct? Always dirt poor but always so brave and charming with it. But what in fact do you really get when you really, really meet him like for real? Well, for starters, you can take that celebrated charm and call it smarm. In spades! Plus loads of ironic put-downs for the likes of me! Plus multiple arselicks for the likes of William! Plus, look at me, aren't I so modestly like out of this world? Jeez! And when I think of all the work I put in condensing his run of the mill romance into a cool, hip psycho-drama - like had it been now, and on the box, I'd have got BAFTA nominated for best adapted screenplay. And as for my kicking the shit out of William's input only to get - what? Good question - open question. Sod all sums it up. No billing, no dosh. I tell you, I'm beginning to wish I'd never alerted Dick Burbage - I can call him that at this distance - to this material in the first place. I'm not saying our show didn't start out well enough. Like I told you it was mega - so much so William comes out of retirement to claim all the credit, doesn't he? Leaving me nowhere,. And so it's gone on ever since, over the years, over the centuries, *Cardenio* - Shakespeare's lost play! - not mine, oh, no. Fletcher, who he? Forget him. Jeezus! Like it's been a nightmare! Still is! A living nightmare!

It would be fun here if theatre could enable such a talented but embittered author as John Fletcher to disappear up his own fixation. But I'm afraid such an effect might well stretch the resources both of an ideal actor, and of any theatrical production, let alone this one. So what we do instead to get rid of him is synchronise a devastating cymbal crash with another puff of red dry ice (Bill the stage manager bang on cue and Lily on the button) followed up by rolling drum rolls and huge, animal-shaped shadows, bloated, headless, stump-legged, hideous, projected all over everywhere. Are we witnessing William Shakespeare's lighting expertise here? I hope so. When he said he'd been helping to *tweak* the lighting design I think it likely he was being his usual, undemonstrative, sociable self. But now this shadow theatre becomes even more surprising, because, here in the middle of it, we discover Don

175

Quixote standing on a makeshift bed in his shirt-tails (yet again) slashing with his sword at full-to-bursting wineskins hanging from the cobwebbed rafters above his head. This, of course, is not a pretty sight but it is a dramatic one. Don Quixote's eyes are shut fast. He's fighting something in his sleep.

QUIXOTE
(as he dreams) Have at thee, rogue! Have at thee, Pandafilando! Giant, usurper, coward! Though thou adopt a thousand shapes I'll slaughter thee! I, Don Quixote of La Mancha, by appointment giant killer to HRH The Princess Micomicona, will have thy guts for garters, thy head on a plate, thy testicles for testament -

More manic swordplay as Sancho rushes in followed by the landlord, Father Perez and Nicholas.

SANCHO
Oh, no, sir! Stop, sir! Them be wineskins you're beheading. Look what's spilt!
QUIXOTE
(eyes still shut) Blood! Giant's blood!
LANDLORD
Our best Valdepeñas!
QUIXOTE
Pandafilando's blood!
LANDLORD
You enemy of God and Man - didn't I - ?
QUIXOTE
(roar) Silence! Let none gainsay me!
SANCHO
But you're asleep, sir! Wake up! Wake up!

Don Quixote falls to his knees in front of Father Perez.

QUIXOTE
Supreme and Royal Highness, thy kingdom is restored.
PRIEST
(gently) You're dreaming, Don Alonso, dreaming. Open your eyes, my son.

Don Quixote wakes up.

QUIXOTE

Father Perez? Master Nicholas?

SANCHO

And me, sir! There wasn't never no giant, sir.

LANDLORD

Ruined, I am! Ruined!

QUIXOTE

And all this blood?

SANCHO

The house red, sir. From them skins.

QUIXOTE

Do you still know nothing of wizardry, Sancho? I tell you Pandafilando was here and I beheaded him. But he with his last necromantic breath has made it seem I have done nothing more than puncture a couple of wineskins. Thus to belittle my victory. But never fear, the rogue is dead. As I shall inform her Royal Highness. Is she below?

SANCHO

Yes, sir, with that other dafty we keep meeting then losing. Only he says he's now more how he ought to be.

QUIXOTE

(still determinedly chivalric) Then let us descend, good squire, that we may report our success to the correct quarter. And rest assured thou shalt also partake of the glory consequent hereunto.

SANCHO

Right, sir, but why don't you talk a bit straighter and put on your breeches while you're at it? Could make you sound and look more like a real champion, right?

LANDLORD

(to Father Perez) Your caution money doesn't cover this, father. It can't come anywhere near.

PRIEST

All in good time, sir. All can be mended - given God's will and commensurate ready cash, of course.

Blackout.

Act Four - Scene Six

As the lights come up we see and hear wine dripping down from above onto the stage as the landlady and a chambermaid

177

(Lily again in very fetching local costume - this girl will go far) hurriedly place three buckets to catch the drips while Dorotea lends a hand vigorously with a mop and Cardenio appears with two more buckets. I'm not sure they need necessarily to be authentic seventeenth century buckets - the point can be just as happily made with modern plastic ones.

LANDLADY
  I don't know what my husband will say!

Enter her husband.

LANDLORD
  God's bollocks! What a thing! Best part of last year's red!
DOROTEA
  I'm sure we can make up your loss, sir.
LANDLORD
  Aye, so your priest says -
CARDENIO
  Isn't his word good enough for you?
LANDLORD
  (retraction into obsequiousness) Oh, it is, sir. Please don't mistake me. It's just the shock of it.

Don Quixote appears, not only fully dressed (thanks to Sancho's insistence) but also breast-plated, as befits a knight-errant whose mission has been successfully accomplished. The look in his eye is now rational enough but he holds up his left hand and arm as if carrying a giant's head by the hair. The fact that it's only an empty wineskin doesn't stop him imagining it weighs heavily. So heavily only a superman such as himself could sustain it in this manner. He comes straight to Dorotea, still with her mop in hand, and addresses her as Sancho, Father Perez and Nicholas arrive behind him.

QUIXOTE
  Behold, Your Highness! Behold the head - the mighty head - of your worst enemy. The giant Pandafilando.

Don Quixote kneels, placing the punctured wineskin at Dorotea's feet with such mimetic artistry we might suppose, despite our better judgment, that it is what it isn't.

178

QUIXOTE

There! I lay this trophy , madam, at your royal feet. May you and your realm now enjoy an eternity of peace and plenitude.

DOROTEA

(playing her part as the Princess Micomicona) Great sir, mirror of chivalry, we thank you. As for this deadly thing it shall be placed upon a spike above our palace gate as a warning to all other ogres who might presume upon us. (to Nicholas) Lord High Steward, remove it from our sight, it is too ghastly to contemplate.

BARBER

(playing his part) It shall be done, Your Highness. (mimes lifting it) Truly it weighs a ton.

Exit Nicholas at a run, bent double by the weight of collusive fantasy. As he goes Dorotea mops the spot as if to cleanse another pool of blood.

DOROTEA

And now, great sir, demand of us what you will.

QUIXOTE

I demand nothing, Your Majesty, save that my loyal squire be recompensed for his service in this venture.

Dorotea turns to Sancho.

DOROTEA

What would you have, great squire?

Sancho, who, like me, has always been enchanted by Dorotea's beauty, blushes.

SANCHO

Oh, ma'am, what wouldn't I have? Well, for a start - ooh. Sorry! Mustn't think like that, must I? Me being me? A married man?

Sancho blushes again. Freud could well have been proud of him at this moment, if Freud had existed at the time of Sancho's creation, that is. But, since he didn't, he made up for it in his own era, and in his own mind, by reading *Don Quixote* with eager attention as a teenager. Might this be why so many of us now find Freud's theories concerning humankind more quixotic than Cervantine?

Possibly . But meanwhile Sancho's got a grip on another part of himself - his brain.

SANCHO
What would I have? Them donks, of course! Why not? The three of 'em! Aye! Go for it! (to Don Quixote) Look, sir. It's like this, sir. While you was knocking off that giant I got my Dapple back. He's with your Rocinante at this minute. Never seen the pair of 'em so happy. But that don't mean you'll go back on your word, sir, does it? About giving me them others, got me? As well? Right?
DOROTEA
Oh, I'm sure not. No knight-errant ever breaks his word, good squire. And certainly not Don Quixote. No.
QUIXOTE
(as his village self - Don Alonso) Dapple's back?
SANCHO
I just said!
QUIXOTE
(still Don Alonso) Then you now have no need of mine. Mine were to make good your loss.
SANCHO
And for me going with your letter to Toboso, remember? There was that, too.
QUIXOTE
The one was not contingent upon the other.
SANCHO
It was on the back of it! Your promise. (turning to Dorotea) Tell him again, ma'am. A promise is a promise. Three donks - three donks. Never mind I got my other one back.
DOROTEA
Great sir, we deem it fit you reward your squire as you have sworn. We, as your liegelord, desire it.

Pause as Don Alonso battles with Don Quixote only to admit defeat with a sigh.

QUIXOTE
At your behest, Most Royal Highness.
SANCHO
(air punch) That's it, sir! Now ask her for her hand! Marry her, sir! Go on! She's worth a dozen of your Dulcineas. Just look at her! She's one of Nature's princesses - what an armful!

QUIXOTE
  Blockhead! How dare you speak thus of either?
PRIEST
  Hush, Sancho! Or you'll spoil our whole endeavour.

Enter the cook who has a word with the landlady before going
with the chambermaid. The landlady addresses her guests.

LANDLADY
  If you please, lady and gentlemen, you may come through to
  dinner.
PRIEST
  With pleasure and appetite, madam.

The landlord and landlady usher Don Quixote, Sancho and
Cardenio out but Father Perez detains Dorotea for a moment.

PRIEST
  At the cost of a couple of cut-up wineskins mistaken for a giant,
  our neighbour believes his quest concluded, so you may, if you
  choose, go south tomorrow, whilst we can take him north - and
  home. I won't say God has spoken but I think He's lent a hand.

They go.

End of Act Four

4th Interlude

Cervantes and Shakespeare with Jessop appear. A subtle
modulation of the lighting might perhaps give them a rather
other-worldly aspect - as if backlit behind gauze.

CERVANTES
  What are these buckets for?
SHAKESPEARE
  Surely you saw the last scene?
CERVANTES
  Perhaps I nodded off? What happened?

SHAKESPEARE

It was simple but effective. All that wine dripping down and everyone bringing on these buckets and mopping up.

CERVANTES

Don't tell me they've just done Don Quixote and the wineskins?

SHAKESPEARE

Yes. Superbly.

CERVANTES

Fancy me missing *that*! Oh, dear. What a shame.

SHAKESPEARE

It was enormous fun. And though I say it myself the lighting was pure poetry.

CERVANTES

I'm sure it was. But fancy missing it. What a thing. I once dreamt something very similar. Except the wineskins were Turks leaping down on me from a mainmast at Lepanto.

SHAKESPEARE

And you killed them?

CERVANTES

Two of them. But by then they'd drenched me in blood. More theirs than mine, thank God. The following day I wrote the scene - from Don Quixote's point of view.

SHAKESPEARE

Jack Fletcher didn't want it in at all but I insisted and it kept its place. The Princess Elizabeth Stuart loved it. So I'm delighted this latest version has done it, too.

CERVANTES

I wonder what they've used for wine?

He dips his finger in one of the buckets and then licks it.

CERVANTES

Coloured water. Seems to taste slightly of blackcurrants. What do you think?

SHAKESPEARE

(dipping, licking) Mm. Ribena.

CERVANTES

What?

SHAKESPEARE

A blackcurrant cordial occasionally drunk by the offspring of health-conscious parents. Full of vitamin C, apparently.

CERVANTES
Are you suggesting the children might prefer something else?
SHAKESPEARE
I am. Most certainly. Alcopops for a start (they laugh). Perhaps
we should lend a hand and clear these buckets?
CERVANTES
Why not? Interactive theatre. Very popular these days, I
understand.

They laugh again, collect two buckets each, and go

Blackout.

Act Five - Scene One

If Bill and Lily have been puzzled to find four buckets already
removed they've been too busy carrying on a laden dinner table to
wonder how or why. At the same time the cast bring their chairs
and stools on with them. Once all are settled the lights come up
to reveal Don Quixote at the head of the table with Dorotea on
his right and Cardenio, now wearing a shirt, on his left. Father
Perez, Nicholas and Sancho are seated on either side of them. The
landlady and landlord serve as required.

Cardenio is questioning Don Quixote with such intensity that
Father Perez and Nicholas are becoming more and more uneasy.

CARDENIO
But can you not, good sir, foretell the fit
As it comes on? Feel every sense unsettle?
I did, that's sure. But since my mind's restored,
Or so I pray, I'll never now
Mistake a barn owl for a hunter's dog,
Nor fear to lose my wits should any choose
To interrupt my discourse whilst I speak.

Prickly pause.

QUIXOTE
Your question is superfluous, young man. You are not me and I
am not you. I am what I am.

CARDENIO

(feeling snubbed) What answer's that?

PRIEST

(at Cardenio - urgent whisper) I beg you, sir, press him no further.

Don Quixote rises to answer Cardenio in full. In verse.

QUIXOTE

I heed no word nor counsel save my own;
An errant knight I am, and so shall die;
My purpose nought but chivalry alone,
In quest of virtues lost in days gone by.
Some the high road of high ambition tread;
Others progress by bold hypocrisy;
Another sort by flattery creep ahead,
But my pursuit is perfect errantry.
So to do good to all and hurt to none;
And by this path achieve a proper end.
If this be foolish then let madness come,
Wealth I despise, while Honour is my friend.

SANCHO

Oh, don't say that, sir! Think of -

DOROTEA

Hush, Sancho.

QUIXOTE

I range the earth to aid the poor and weak,
And by these precepts their salvation seek.

Sancho very nearly disrupted the conclusion of Don Quixote's sonnet but Dorotea hushed him just in time, thus allowing our soldier-poet hero to achieve a moment of respectful silence from everyone on stage. And from us as well, I hope. This pause is broken after twenty seconds or so by the sound of dogs barking furiously off as the chambermaid rushes on.

CHAMBERMAID

(to the landlord) A gent and his lady, sir. In a grand coach with grooms and all.

The landlord goes at once.

LANDLADY
  Did they give any name?
CHAMBERMAID
  No, ma'am. But if you ask me the lady's travelling against her
  will Like a rag doll she is. And I heard her sobbing. Crying like
  the rain.

This has been Lily's third chance to make an impression on us.
Although it's only a 'carriage awaits' or rather a 'carriage arrives'
moment she's taken it well, giving the chambermaid a nicely
modulated country accent with West of Ireland undertones.
Could it be she played Pegeen Mike at drama school? I'll have to
ask her. But back to the plot and the entrance of Fernando with
Lucinda gripped firmly by the wrist. Both wear cloaks and full
face travel masks against the dust of high summer so that even if
we recognise them, or more likely realise who they've got to be if
the plot is to work, we can still happily believe that Dorotea and
Cardenio do not realise who they are until the action demands
that they do. The landlord accompanies them.

LANDLORD
  You're most welcome, sir, madam. But we have only one room
  available and -
FERNANDO
  That'll do.

Lucinda stifles a sob. Fernando flicks a gold coin at the landlord.

FERNANDO
  There! Clean it. Air it. Fresh sheets, lavender.

The landlord catches the coin - it would be in seventeenth century
reality a gold *escudo* - a truly ostentatious gratuity exceeding
anything Father Perez has so far provided. The landlord goes
with his wife and Lily, the chambermaid, leaving the stage free for
romance. Or, as I said earlier, for a display of emotional idealism
at war with social determinism. Dorotea approaches the muffled,
masked figure of Lucinda.

DOROTEA
  What ails you, lady? If I may serve you,
  I will surely help you if I can. Speak.

Fernando counters Dorotea aggressively, melodramatically .

FERNANDO
  Guard yourself, madam! Come not so close!
  Nor try to get an answer from her lips,
  Lest she infect the air with vile deceit.

Outcry from Lucinda.

LUCINDA
  No! Want of deceit has brought me here!
CARDENIO
  That voice!
LUCINDA
  Who's there?
CARDENIO
  I know it like my own!
FERNANDO
  Stay still!
LUCINDA
  I cannot! Let me go!
CARDENIO
  Lucinda!

As Lucinda struggles with Fernando his travel mask gets
dislodged.

DOROTEA
  Fernando!
FERNANDO
  Madam?
DOROTEA
  Do you not know me?

Now Cardenio intervenes to snatch off Lucinda's mask.

CARDENIO
  Let me see that face - there, Lucinda!
LUCINDA
  You! Beyond hope! Cardenio!

Now that all are revealed to each other as convention requires the action can freeze into confrontational silence. Who will break it first? Surely Dorotea? No. Lucinda. To Fernando.

LUCINDA
  Great lord, I conjure you by what you are,
  To be what you should be, and let me cleave
  To him that neither threats, nor lordly gifts,
  Nor importunities, nor promises,
  Could e'er deflect me, such was Heaven's will.
  Regard how Providence by covert ways,
  Unknown to us, has brought my true love here.
  This also know, if yet you rest unsure,
  That Death alone can blot him from my heart.
  Release me to him, sir! Or kill me now!
  This instant! Since I shall be well content
  To lose my life before Cardenio.
  By that he'll live persuaded of the faith
  I've kept towards him, in despite of you.

Here we see Fernando, for the first time in his life, obliged to acknowledge, in public, realities beyond those that rank and money can buy. He doesn't like it. He bites his lip. Dorotea comes and kneels before him. Sancho protests for us.

SANCHO
  Oh, no, madam!
QUIXOTE
  No, Sancho! Say nothing!

Dorotea looks up at Fernando.

DOROTEA
  Sir, if Lucinda's beauty blinds you not,
  Here at your feet kneels she that you betrayed.
  That country girl you swore to wed, to love,
  To honour, and to raise to your estate.
  She that did live an honest simple life,
  Within the bounds of farm and family,
  Till at your seeming heartfelt urgency,
  All set about with earnest vows to Heaven,
  She gave to you in trust her chastity.

A gift so ill-requited I had need
To leave my family in quest of you.
And now by fateful chance I find you here.
It was your will, my lord, I should be yours,
And so I am, since I did will it too;
Despite the gulf of birth between us both;
For you did swear it mattered not a jot.
Love builds the bridge to bring us both across,
You said, and I, believing did consent.
Consider, sir, the love I hold for you
Is as a balance to Lucinda here.
Certain it is she never can be yours,
Because Cardenio's other self she is,
As I am yours, my lord, did you but know.

Pause before Fernando rejects Dorotea's claim upon him with a clumsy but brutal couplet, blushingly delivered.

FERNANDO
No words from you can alter my intent!
This lady's mine in law by Heaven sent!

Another pause. Then, just as Father Perez is about to intervene on Dorotea's behalf Don Quixote strides forward.

QUIXOTE
A word with you, young man.

Fernando - reasonably enough - is astonished at the sight of him. Unlike us he's not yet used to meeting people in bits of rusty armour and unlikely headgear.

FERNANDO
(to all) Who or what is this?
QUIXOTE
A knight as worthy to bear arms as you, sir. And one whose ears are ever open to the complaint of all persons in distress, male or female. How old are you?
FERNANDO
(startled) Seventeen.

And he almost added sir such is Don Quixote's unexpected assumption of authority. He bites his lip again.

QUIXOTE
  Then you have much life to live, Lord Fernando. And great rank to uphold. And even more honour to emulate. Listen to this lady.
FERNANDO
  (teenage sulk) I have! And as for you, whoever you are -
PRIEST
  My lord - I beg you hear this lady as he requests. Her cause is known to me and also to your former friend, Don Cardenio here.
FERNANDO
  Him!
CARDENIO
  Yes, me. Fernando. Let Dorotea speak.

Pause. Fernando, cornered now, tries to save face. He does so by pointedly addressing Father Perez.

FERNANDO
  Only respect for your cloth, father, compels me to comply.

And he turns to Dorotea with as much composure as he can manage. This no longer amounts to much because he's just remembered what he's chosen to forget: that he is in breach of promise. And if Dorotea has kept his affidavit and now has a priest to take her part -?

FERNANDO
  Speak.
DOROTEA
  Good sir - for so you can be - it's better to love one who loves you than one who hates you. You swore to honour our love and I believed you. I am your betrothed, your wife in deed and love. Can you deny it?
FERNANDO
  No, but - (bluster) Yes, I can if choose! Yes!

Father Perez produces Fernando's promise of marriage.

PRIEST
  Here, sir. Here is your sworn word written in your own hand

and sealed by you.
FERNANDO
Let me see it. Give it me.
PRIEST
No. I'm its keeper now.
FERNANDO
But -
PRIEST
Reflect also that the ceremony of matrimony you commanded
between yourself and Lady Lucinda was not, you may thank
God, completed.
FERNANDO
Perhaps not but -
PRIEST
Had that been so you would have condemned yourself to
punishment both here and beyond the grave. A crime against
Heaven's law and ours.

Long pause. Held for as long as is theatrically possible. Then
Fernando releases Lucinda before kneeling in front of her in a
manner more childlike than courtly.

FERNANDO
Lady, to each of us I've been untrue,
Forgive my error, and my blindness too.

Next he addresses Dorotea.

FERNANDO
Oh, Dorotea, you have conquered me
With holy truth, and thus am I set free.

Dorotea takes his hand, he rises. Lucinda comes to Cardenio.

LUCINDA
No words, Cardenio?
CARDENIO
So many, too many.
LUCINDA
What welcome's this?
CARDENIO
A true one. But first comes vengeance.

190

LUCINDA
  No!
CARDENIO
  (at Fernando) Draw, sir.
FERNANDO
  No! My faults I here admit. I do. I have.
CARDENIO
  Not to me! Draw! Justice demands no less!
LUCINDA
  I beg you, there's no longer call for blood.
DOROTEA
  But in its place true blessings from above.
CARDENIO
  (implacable) No! Draw!

Cardenio faces Fernando, sword in hand. Dramatic pause. Dramatic, that is, in the sense that it satisfies the needs of theatre rather than reality because this mind-play of mine can easily provide Cardenio with a sword, and so long as the scene's directed and acted deftly enough we, the audience, won't have time to ask various mundane novelistic questions such as: how has Cardenio suddenly come by a sword? Surely he threw everything away to become the Ragged Knight of the Mountain? And didn't Sancho appropriate all his discarded belongings but there wasn't a sword among them. Money, notebook, shirts, but no sword. So how has he suddenly got this one? Answer: because theatre shoots first and asks questions afterwards. Yes, and can mix metaphors, too. So - back to romance, but Fernando still hasn't drawn *his* sword.

CARDENIO
  No word can answer your offence to me. Nor to my lady here. Nor to your pledged lady there. Draw now, Fernando, or ever live in shame!

Fernando now draws his sword. All protest - *no, no, no!* - but it's too late. They fight. Both boys are fit and expert so their duel can be glamorously exciting. Whether there was a duel in Shakespeare and Fletcher's version we don't know, but Theobald's *Double Falsehood* hasn't got one. This, of course, might only suggest that Theobald lacked a born showman's essential simplicity. As does Don Quixote strangely enough. He steps in and stops the fight just as it's getting truly spectacular. Spoilsport.

QUIXOTE
  (pompous roar) Hold!

And he knocks up both their swords with his.

QUIXOTE
  Enough. Or answer severally to me.
FERNANDO
  (laugh) With pleasure, you old fool!
ALL
  No! Stop! Don't! Please! No!
QUIXOTE
  Yes! Come on, young man!

Fernando lunges straight at Don Quixote who after a pass or two
neatly disarms him, sending his sword flying. Fernando is surprised.

FERNANDO
  How on earth did you do that?
QUIXOTE
  By way of constant practice, sir. Let peace be with you. (to
  Cardenio) And with you, sir. And with your wives. Both have
  spoken and you've not heard them. Yet it's in their love that
  your salvation lies. What's vengeance compared to that? Good
  sirs, give thanks to God your ladies are as full of charity as
  beauty. Injure them no more by injuring yourselves. All wounds
  that you inflict must wound them equally.

Pause.

QUIXOTE
  Let me, if you will, speak for you both. Let me give voice to your
  better selves. Hear what they say. Hear this: we still have many
  years to live. Such faults we have our youth can now excuse but
  age will not. So let us be at peace and learn to love - with honour.

Pause.

QUIXOTE
  Come, sirs, join hands, swear to resume your former friendship,
  and by doing so, endorse your truest selves that shine already
  in your ladies' eyes.

Fernando sheathes his sword, then Cardenio hands his to Sancho, who is surprised and even flattered. Could he be a genuine squire, after all? As Cardenio and Fernando shake hands Don Quixote places his over theirs.

QUIXOTE
  Swear to serve Love and Virtue.
FERNANDO / CARDENIO
  To Love and Virtue we submit.

They embrace then turn to Dorotea and Lucinda. Hugs all round as a guitar chord is heard.

SANCHO
  Look! Our host's brought out his guitar!

Sancho's right. He has. The landlord strikes another chord.

SANCHO
  (to us) Looks like we'll dance and say that - (one finger gesture) - to moaning and groaning.

But no. Sancho's wrong. Lily the chambermaid is clearly about to sing a song which, if logic only applied, ought really to be sung by a boy. But with Lily on stage, it doesn't.

SANCHO
  Oh, no, vocals first, then knees up.

  Song

  What a pretty girl that is,
  Who wouldn't want to have her kiss?
  Tell me, soldier, gone from me,
  Can wars or guns or vain glory be,
  As pretty as she?
  Tell me, sailor, wherever you be,
  Are stars or sails or waves of the sea,
  As pretty as she?
  Tell me, shepherd, with eyes to see,
  Are sheep or grass or leaves on the tree,
  As pretty as she?

What a pretty girl that girl is,
Who wouldn't want to have her kiss?

As everyone applauds Lily I can snatch a moment to assure you
that this tuneful resolution of the romance plot does not signal the
end of the play. We've simply witnessed the classic false climax
before we come to the real wind-up and cathartic wind-down -
or as actors in pantomimes would say, walk-down. Novels tend
to follow the same pattern, of course, but not so quickly. Here,
however, we can have the best of both worlds as even more
vociferous dog-barking is heard off and two officers of the Holy
Brotherhood - the civil guards of the time - stomp in, booted,
spurred, leather-clad, armed, and not especially funny. With
them is a very angry young man. Let's call him Benito. He's the
officers' chief witness and he points at once, in finger-stabbing
fury, at Don Quixote.

BENITO
    That's him! There he is! That one! The thief! And there's my basin
    on his head! What was my dad's before me, and his dad's before
    him. Family heirloom that is. Solid brass. The chins I've shaved
    into it. That loony stole it off me last Wednesday - half-killed me
    to get it - and I haven't earned since. Reckons he can do what
    he likes he does. Thinks he's a knight of old or somesuch, the
    thieving bastard!

The officers approach Don Quixote. Let's not think in Dogberry or
Verger terms. This could be serious.

1ST OFFICER
    Are you Don Alonso Quixano? Also known as Don Quixote of
    La Mancha?
PRIEST
    If I might speak, officer -
1ST OFFICER
    With respect, father, no, this matter is for the law. We have a
    warrant here for this gentleman's arrest.
QUIXOTE
    Arrest? You imagine *you* can arrest *me*?
1ST OFFICER
    We do. Aye. You just listen to the charges, sir.

He nods at the other officer who produces a warrant with a magistrate's seal attached.

2ND OFFICER
(reading it out) "Complaints and denunciations heard this day at the Court of Justice - "
PRIEST
This day? What day?
1ST OFFICER
(heavily) Yesterday, father.
PRIEST
Where?
1ST OFFICER
Valdepeñas. Court seal attached.

He nods again at the other officer.

2ND OFFICER
"Under oath various plaintiffs - see details of same overleaf - state thus against the aforesaid, self-styled Don Quixote - see over for further identification of said gent - thus: one, damaging windmills; two, worrying sheep; three, disrupting traffic; four, robbery with violence, viz stealing one travelling barber's basin - see over for information laid; five, unlawfully releasing thirteen Crown criminals sentenced to serve in our wars against the infidel; six, sedition, in that this said Don Quixote claims publicly that he knows more about justice than the King. Therefore it is decreed he be apprehended, dead or alive, wheresoever he is to be discovered."

The punctilious phrasing of this indictment may have sounded amusing to its hearers at first but by the time the reading's finished any smiles have faded. Consequently Fernando, in addressing Don Quixote, now speaks for all.

FERNANDO
These are serious charges, sir? What do you say to them?

Don Quixote, still seeing himself in his self-flattering mirror of chivalry, answers as only he sees fit.

QUIXOTE

I say that here we have more of shadow than of substance. Opinion instead of truth. What are itemised as windmills were, in point of fact, malignant giants capable of massive destruction. Forty of them - would you believe? - had infiltrated themselves among us in this cunningly commonplace manner. The sheep referred to were, in truth, two opposing armies - unauthorised forces made up of insurgents, terrorists and other undesirables. When I advised them to take their unlawful war elsewhere they attacked *me*, so, in self-defence, I beat the hell out of both sides simultaneously. A singular triumph, though I say it myself, given the odds against me. The piffling charge of traffic disruption I can only assume acknowledges my rescue of an innocent damsel in her coach from abduction for ransom, and possibly worse, by a gang of Basque separatists that our forces of law and order had, as usual, failed to neutralise. The allegation that I gave liberty to a chain-gang destined for the galleys I acknowledge. With pride. For human kind was created free, and not one of us, whomsoever we may be, should enslave another. As for the ludicrous charge that I stole a barber's basin - as if I would stoop so low - when, as you can see -

Don Quixote takes off the basin and shows it solemnly to all.

QUIXOTE

(over this demonstration) - it is nothing of the kind, but rather a stupendous relic, a legendary helmet - of pure gold, I might add - that I have delivered from obscurity. Here it is, revealed for what it is - the fabled helm of King Mambrino, no less, Supreme Lord of the Saracens from the year dot to much later.

BENITO

No! My grandad's basin!

QUIXOTE

This immemorial casque won in battle by Sir Dardinel of Almonte -

BENITO

No! Handed on to me by my dear old dad!

QUIXOTE

(regardless) And thereafter bequeathed to the renowned Rinaldo of Montalbano -

BENITO

Never!

196

QUIXOTE

(relentless) Only to be lost for centuries -

BENITO

No!

This last denial is the start of a wild outburst from Benito who now jumps up and down on the spot, gesturing wildly at the officers and Don Quixote.

BENITO

Didn't I tell you he was out of his head? Look at him! Hark at him! His fancy talk! Telling us - telling me my basin's some old helmet or other! To Hell with that! If I don't know what it is, who does? And he stole it! So take him in! Or I will! Citizen's arrest!

QUIXOTE

Wait! This antiquity may seem merely a brass basin such as any barber might use - our neighbour here, Barber Nicholas, for instance, who has recently elected to appear - for reasons best known to himself - as a Lord High Steward to this lady to my left, who, with equal equinamity has declared herself to be an Ethiopian princess. That neither fully convinced me of their chosen transformations is beside the point except that in such cases a knight-errant is obliged to give doubt the benefit of belief. But be that as it so happened this golden helmet only appears to you in its base metal form -

BENITO

Best Toledo brass!

QUIXOTE

It only appears to you like this because you are culpably ignorant of the transmutatory art and practice of chivalry.

BENITO

But for Christ's sake, it don't even look like a helmet!

QUIXOTE

My point proven. I have eyes to see, you haven't.

The first officer has heard enough. He steps forward, together with the second officer.

1ST OFFICER

Right, sir. You've had your say. You're under arrest. We're taking you in.

197

Most of those present protest, but especially Father Perez, Nicholas, Dorotea and Sancho.

ALMOST ALL
  No! Don't you dare! Hold on! Hardly necessary! Please!
1ST OFFICER
  Stand back! All of you!
PRIEST
  No, sir. You step back if you please.

And Father Perez places himself directly between the law and Don Quixote.

PRIEST
  Don Alonso is our valued neighbour and we, who are fully aware
  of his qualities, and occasional foibles, are here in charge of him.
  We can answer for him, and we will bring him safely home.
1ST OFFICER
  That, with respect, father, is all very well but our warrant states -
PRIEST
  Of course it does but -

Dorotea and Nicholas now intervene.

DOROTEA / BARBER
  We'll vouch for him, too.

Cardenio and Lucinda come forward hand in hand.

CARDENIO
  So will we.
LUCINDA
  He's been such a help to us.
1ST OFFICER
  Even so the law requires -

Fernando, nudged by Dorotea, interrupts him.

FERNANDO
  I suggest you think again, officer.
1ST OFFICER
  Oh? And who may you be when you're at home?

FERNANDO
  Lord Fernando, son of the Grand Duke of Montoro.

Rank has spoken. The law gawps. Such a class-conscious reaction may be regrettable today but it certainly helps us towards a typical Renaissance happy ending.

1ST OFFICER
  (servile) Oh? And this particular gent's a friend of yours, is he, my lord?
FERNANDO
  He is. And of the Grand Duke. Indeed he's one of our family's oldest friends.

Dorotea cannot conceal her delight at Fernando's fictitious support of Don Quixote. Indeed she corroborates it.

DOROTEA
  He's to be guest of honour at our wedding, officer.
1ST OFFICER
  Oh? Right you are, my lady.

The second officer, we now realise has been appalled by his superior's hesitation in the line of duty. He whispers indignantly at the first officer reminding him of his obligations to the law, rather than to rank or sentiment. We don't need to hear what he says - the way he says it is clear enough - and besides here's Sancho barging in and naturally he's already talking.

SANCHO
  And don't forget me neither! You ent having *him*! Oh, no! And me, Sancho Panza, can tell you for why! For a start them windmills. They did him more damage than he did them. One of their sails knocked half his teeth out. We could sue them millers for that. And as for them sheep -
1ST OFFICER
  (his resolve renewed) Duty is duty. We're taking him in. And you too. You're named as his accomplice.
SANCHO
  Bollocks! I'm his squire!

1ST OFFICER

(to the second officer) Let's have the pair of 'em! Take this one first, right?

They advance determinedly on Sancho. But now it is Nicholas who bars their way.

BARBER

Please! Let us go softly and gently as Don Alonso himself so often says.

QUIXOTE

Good point, Nicholas, I do.

BARBER

If these lords and ladies and Father Perez here can vouch for the master, allow me to vouch for the man - a God-fearing old Christian if ever there was one. Most respectable *and* respected. I've shaved him every Saturday for fifteen years or so. What's more I delivered his youngest daughter last September and on top of that, I set his collar bone he broke at wrestling on St John's Day. But beyond all of this I, as a barber, know just as much, if not more, about basins as that young shaver you've brought with you and -

2ND OFFICER

We've dealt with basins!

BARBER

Oh, no, we haven't, sir. Not philosophically speaking. (to Benito) Now you listen to me. Let us agree King Mambrino's helmet is not here -

QUIXOTE

Oh, I can't have that, Nicholas. It *is* here. In my hands. And on my head.

He puts it back on.

BARBER

Please, Don Alonso, I'm not talking to you. I'm talking to this lad on your behalf. I'm introducing him to logic, all right?

QUIXOTE

Oh? If that's all it is - mere logic - fine. Carry on.

BARBER

(to Benito) It's not here - agreed?

BENITO

I've already said! 'Course it isn't!

BARBER

Let us go further - let us say it does not exist.

QUIXOTE

No -

PRIEST

Shush, Don Alonso. Trust Nicholas.

BENITO

(over this action) Jesus! What else have I been saying all along? It isn't what he says it is, is it?

BARBER

Excellent. We've got that clear at last. So next I can ask you - reasonably, nay, logically enough - what is it you are saying it isn't?

BENITO

That gold helmet!

BARBER

Exactly. Well said. But by saying it you have - again in logic - granted its existence.

BENITO

(bewildered) I haven't!

BARBER

You have. Existence only exists thanks to its opposite - non-existence. Now suppose we say your barber's basin only becomes itself when it's being used as a barber's basin -

1ST OFFICER

Right! That's enough chat -

PRIEST

I think not, sir. A little philosophy can resolve a great deal. And enlighten us all. Barber Nicholas here is particularly sound on the Theory of Descriptions.

SANCHO

Aye, folks come from all over to be mystified by him.

The first officer sighs as Nicholas continues.

BARBER

When used to trim a beard this object may be said to be a basin, but when used to protect the head of a knight-errant such as the great Don Quixote of La Mancha - as it is at this very moment - it may be said to be a helmet, and then again, if by chance the cat should choose to have kittens in it, it may be said, with impeccable logic, to be a cat's cradle.

BENITO

But it ent!

BARBER

To say that serves only to demonstrate that you, young man, are as yet unable to read existence as it happens. Your basin now enjoys an alternative reality. What we name we create.

1ST OFFICER

Right, evening class over. By this warrant I hereby -

PRIEST

No, officer, there's yet another kind of truth to be acknowledged and accepted here.

And he jingles another purse of money that he's carried beneath his cassock. Money belts are not a contemporary phenomenon.

PRIEST

Think of this as God's truth expressed in monetary terms. Take these crowns in His Name for a duty performed that nevertheless failed to discover the persons named in your warrant of arrest.

The second officer intervenes earnestly.

2ND OFFICER

Oh, no, father! No. The Holy Brotherhood cannot possibly be a party to financial inducement.

PRIEST

Not in my experience, my son. And most certainly not when that inducement acts in the name of God. As it does here. Why not weigh it in your hand, sir?

Father Perez places the purse in the second officer's hand.

PRIEST

There. Feel how it outweighs merely temporal concerns.

2ND OFFICER

Well, father -

PRIEST

Probity is one thing, over-officiousness another, my son.

1ST OFFICER

He's new to the service, father. Here - allow me -

And the first officer takes the purse and weighs it in his hand rather more complacently.

1ST OFFICER

Mm. Feels just right to me, father. Sort of sacred, really. (to the second officer) Well, it looks like we got it all arse about face, didn't we?

BENITO

(appalled protest) No!

1ST OFFICER

(turning on him) And so did you, sir, from the sound of it.

BENITO

No!

1ST OFFICER

Telling us all sorts.

In the furtherance of a good cause - saving Don Quixote from arrest - Nicholas has, of course, deliberately bamboozled Benito with a display of not entirely scrupulous logic. And now, thanks to Father Perez's manifest bribery here's the law turning on its chief witness. Conscience-stricken, Nicholas comes to Benito and slips a silver coin into his fellow barber's hand.

NICHOLAS

Here, sonny, get yourself another basin.

1ST OFFICER

Right, gents and ladies all, best be moving along -

BENITO

Yes, but I still say -

1ST OFFICER

Oh, no, you don't. Or we'll have you for laying false information - telling us you'd had a valuable antique stolen when it wasn't nothing of the sort. Out! Night, all.

The two officers hustle Benito away but Dorotea, after a quick word with Fernando, follows them. At the same time Sancho comes forward to address us.

SANCHO

Reckon we got off lightly . Never thought we would. Still, money talks louder than talk, they say - least my grandma always did.

Don Quixote comes forward to address us. Sancho retires.

QUIXOTE
There may well be something in what my squire has said but it
is only fair to add that, thanks to our friends here, reason and
reality have now triumphed over falsehood and fusspottery. In
consequence I can now withdraw in good order, retire home,
take a well-earned rest and then prepare for another foray
on the world's behalf. To refashion it as it ought to be but so
unfortunately isn't. Nor shall I omit - meanwhile - to send
that giant's head to my peerless lady, the Princess Dulcinea, at
Toboso, by hand of my indefatigable squire, Sancho Panza.
SANCHO
Oh, no! Give over. I need a rest, too!

While Don Quixote's been talking to us, Lily has brought the
landlady her concertina, and another guitar for Nicholas. Now,
once he's tuned his guitar with the landlord's, all three strike up a
lively dance just as Dorotea returns with a bemused and bashful
Benito.

DOROTEA
Benito's decided he needn't leave us, after all. He'll stay and
in the morning trim every beard and moustache among us.
Starting with my Lord Fernando.
CARDENIO
(laughing, pulling at his wild hair) And me!

He takes Lucinda's hand, Fernando Dorotea's. And they dance
while Lily invites Benito to take hers. He does with alacrity.
Suddenly he's all smiles. Next, Don Quixote, Sancho and Father
Perez (who's somehow acquired a tambourine) join the dance
and now, as the lovers pass closest to us, each one speaks in turn.
Inevitably the lines are formal couplets but they're thrown to
us informally, over the shoulder, by the way, out of a swirl of
happiness.

DOROTEA
Our story ends like an old play;
LUCINDA
True love at last can have his way;

FERNANDO
  Soon tomorrow we'll married be;

Affirmative tambourine clash from Father Perez.

CARDENIO
  And in blest union be always free!

As the dance continues scented rose petals appear to fall gently
from above over everyone. Feelgood blackout.

End.

Except it isn't. Not just yet. Because while the lights are coming
back on, the cast, standing hand in hand to take the first curtain
call - not that this black box has a curtain but the phrase persists - I
can sense several fugitive shadows easing themselves out of their
seats behind me. It seems they can't wait to get away. How many?
Three. Who could they be? They certainly weren't Cervantes
or Shakespeare or Fletcher. Oh, of course! Critics. From the few
newspapers that continue to think theatre might have something
to say, even if it happens in a redundant pumping station - oh, yes,
by the way, I've at last settled on my theatre's name - it's become
The Pump House. Not the *Old Bus Depot*, though that had a certain
sentimental resonance for me, I admit. Ah, we're getting a second
curtain call. So now the question is - will the applause be enough to
justify a third? Three's pretty good for fringe. Will we? Yes. Sounds
like it. Lights down, lights up. Yes, we've just made it, thanks to
ultra quick finger-work on the console keyboard. And now - oh,
no! Someone's shouting out: Author! Author! Not anyone in the
cast - I told them from the start I didn't want any acknowledgement
apart from my name in the programme. So who? Oh, no, wouldn't
you guess? Who else but? It's that master of snide! It's his voice -
Jack Fletcher's. Well, well, I'd best slip out now - I'm not having
him send me up in public. And, besides, I must go backstage to
congratulate everyone, and that means following those critics, then
edging round the side of the Pump House (minding the dustbins)
and re-entering by the rear emergency exit, otherwise known as the
stage door - a notion still of some romance to me. And so, as actors
say when going on stage and leaving others in the wings or in the
dressing room: see you on the green. This is said to refer to the
green cloth spread on the stage in the eighteenth century to indicate

that the play was a tragedy but I prefer to suppose the phrase goes further back - to happier more knockabout performances on village greens by touring companies such as some suppose Shakespeare joined shortly after his forced (or unforced) marriage to Anne Hathaway and the arrival of Susanna and then the twins even if his relationship with Anne remains a mystery. If only he'd seen fit to tell us more about his private life we might have been spared centuries of supposition. To be frank, I had rather hoped he might divulge more during this performance, but no, as ever his instinct for personal discretion has once again proved the better part of valour. Something that cannot be said of Cervantes, who never stops telling us who he is and what he's done. No, on second thoughts, he, too, is discreet about his wife, Catalina, who was half his age. We do know, however, that she, like Anne Hathaway, was a country girl, and brought with her a dowry of a small vineyard, four bee hives, a cockerel and forty-five hens. But I digress. Kindly assume I've gone, leaving this train of thought behind me, and am already embracing the entire company - but especially Dorotea, Lucinda and Lily.

Epilogue

Laughter and chatter from the dressing room off as Shakespeare (with Jessop) and Cervantes appear on the now empty stage. The working light modulates softly (although no one's any longer at the lighting console) to provide a fittingly other-worldly ambience.

CERVANTES
No sign of Fletcher?
SHAKESPEARE
No. He just shouted 'author' a couple of times and then pushed off.
CERVANTES
You don't think he was impressed?
SHAKESPEARE
Jack never is, never was, impressed.
CERVANTES
(grin) Not even by himself?
SHAKESPEARE
(laughing) Trust you to hit the mark. But now, Don Miguel, I'd like to hear your thoughts on this latest version of your story?

Pause.

CERVANTES

Well, as a playgoer, I'm always eager to believe everything on offer while simultaneously doubting it.

SHAKESPEARE

Like Sancho? Facing up to fantasy?

CERVANTES

Exactly. So the first thing I have to admit is that I soon got caught up with my own story. Of course there were various omissions I regretted but on the other hand some clever compressions I was glad of. And the use made of Don Quixote's letter to Dulcinea was a joy - on both sides. In the original, if you recall, Sancho forgets to take it but here, tonight, he didn't and much genuine theatrical fun resulted, I thought.

SHAKESPEARE

I agree. But stage letters were in my time something of a necessary evil. Our plots especially in comedy were forever requiring written confirmation of this or that.

CERVANTES

Such as Fernando's betrothal bond?

SHAKESPEARE

Indeed. And almost invariably they had to be pulled out of the bodices of our boy actors playing the girls. The times I've seen a sponge breast spring out and plop to the floor just as my heroine had to make a romantic plot point.

CERVANTES

Thus getting the wrong sort of laugh?

SHAKESPEARE

(nod) At precisely the wrong moment.

They laugh

CERVANTES

I loved Nicholas the Barber's chop logic about the basin.

SHAKESPEARE

That wasn't you?

CERVANTES

No. Nor was the junior member of the Holy Brotherhood having his doubts about the propriety of ecclesiastical bribery. I wish I'd thought of that. On the whole I'd say this present author - I do tend to wish he'd answered Jack Fletcher's call, despite its ironic intent, I'd have liked to have taken a look a him - I think he's understood my work pretty well - which isn't easy nowadays, or so I'm told. Apparently I'm not quite so timeless as I used to be. I find now some people think rather less of my work than it deserves or else make more of it than they should - which can be equally disconcerting.

SHAKESPEARE

You're far too modest, Don Miguel.

CERVANTES

No, I'm not. If anything pride is my besetting sin. When young and supposedly promising I adopted modesty as a literary pose. It stuck. Became part of my published persona. A venial cover up for a cardinal sin. It continues to cost me every Friday.

Shakespeare laughs.

SHAKESPEARE

You still go to confession?

CERVANTES

Of course. It's the very least one can do in Purgatory these days.

SHAKESPEARE

You've kept faith with the Old Faith?

CERVANTES

Haven't you?

Sharp, circumspect pause.

SHAKESPEARE

My father did. So did my mother.

CERVANTES

And you?

Further circumspection.

SHAKESPEARE

With the greatest respect, Don Miguel, I'd prefer not to reply. I've always taken considerable pains never to answer that particular question. Suffice it to say my bones rest at peace in my local church.

CERVANTES

I wish I knew where mine were.

SHAKESPEARE
You don't? Surely you do?
CERVANTES
Only approximately. They were moved when the convent where
I'm buried got rebuilt. I'm still somewhere in the precincts, they
say, but no one's quite sure where. My more devout admirers
believe my bones lie under the altar in the chapel but, frankly,
I hope not - that would be too heavy a responsibility. And that
isn't me being modest, William, falsely or otherwise.
SHAKESPEARE
Where is this convent? In Madrid?
CERVANTES
Mm. The convent of the Barefoot Sisters of the Holy Trinity.
SHAKESPEARE
Coincidence. My church at Stratford also celebrates the Holy
Trinity.
CERVANTES
I died as a lay brother of the Order.
SHAKESPEARE
Really?
CERVANTES
It was the Trinitarians got me out of Algiers. So at the end I
joined them - out of gratitude.

Both pause to reflect.

SHAKESPEARE
Some people say we died on the same day of the same year.
CERVANTES
Really? When do they suppose that was?
SHAKESPEARE
St George's Day, 1616. The twenty third of April.
CERVANTES
No, not possible. Our calendar was out of step with yours.
SHAKESPEARE
Spain marched to a different drum?
CERVANTES
(nod) Give or take a week or more.

They smile, perhaps laugh a little.

CERVANTES
Towards the end I lost count of days but I do remember it was springtime. And that my wife brought me primroses.

After a moment Cervantes shakes the memory out of his head and speaks more bouyantly.

CERVANTES
But now, William, I want to hear what you really think of this show we've just witnessed? Or, as the French would say so politely, at which we've assisted.

Pause.

SHAKESPEARE
Well, all things considered and given its terms of reference and accepting the only too apparent budgetry constraints, I'd say that on the whole it delivered. Mind you, I do always warm to rough theatre. I love its edge, its attack. And we had plenty of that tonight. Together with trust. The actors clearly trusted each other, they worked as a team even if some parts were a trifle under-cast. But, best of all, they didn't push us away, did they? They drew us, the audience, in.
CERVANTES
I'm sorry, I'm not sure I follow you?
SHAKESPEARE
Oh, surely you've seen actors so blatantly polished and poised they lack all human credibility? So busily bent on proving their professionalism that you simply recoil? Feel pushed away? The West End has plenty of them. Camping and fretting. But not here.
CERVANTES
But what of the play itself?
SHAKESPEARE
Faithful to your story just as you said, Don Miguel. As were all the characters - all were true to their originals.
CERVANTES
Except for that pretty chambermaid.
SHAKESPEARE
Oh? But she was delightful!

CERVANTES

Captivating, I agree. However, if you recall, my maid at the inn was anything but. An ugly, mischievous little sexpot called Maritornes. Put there in pungent contrast to purest Lucinda and abused Dorotea.

SHAKESPEARE

(laughing) Well, call that poetic licence as opposed to prosaic correctness. Precisely your work's point. Tell yourself you've just seen your ugly chambermaid as her ideal self. Not as she was but as she - and your hero - would have wished her to be. Another Dulcinea as it were, who, I seem to remember, was really just a miller's daughter built like a barn door?

CERVANTES

(smiling) Oh, dear, I'm hoist with my own petard, aren't I?

SHAKESPEARE

You've read *Hamlet*, too?

CERVANTES

Twice. But then I read everything. Always have.

SHAKESPEARE

Do I gather you didn't like it?

CERVANTES

(teasingly) I thought it would make a good novel. Provided you'd been prepared to put in a bit more work, William. Over five or six years or so, possibly.

SHAKESPEARE

(amused rather than offended) Oh, no, writing it as a play was bad enough. I was ill at the time - taking sweat-baths, mercury, the lot.

CERVANTES

But you recovered?

SHAKESPEARE

More or less. But it took several years.

CERVANTES

Your put-upon young prince has one thing in common with my silly old knight.

SHAKESPEARE

Has he? What?

CERVANTES

When he says he's only mad north-north-west and that if the wind's southerly he knows the difference between a hawk and a handsaw. That's quixotic. Don Alonso was entirely rational except on the subject and practice of chivalry. But back to this show. What's your final verdict on the script?

211

SHAKESPEARE

Well, naturally I can't help comparing it with my version and Jack's. And, as has been said, he made the most of the romance action while cutting back on the comedy. Here it's the other way round. I can see why. Your knight and squire's presumptions can still find comic parallels today whereas the niceties of betrothal contracts or interrupted wedding ceremonies are more difficult to dramatise however central they may be to the action. Especially if verse is called for. Which it was and while what we got here wasn't up to Jack's standard it served its purpose. Nor was the prose anything like mine either - but again it did its job. After all, in the theatre the words are there, whether in verse or prose, not on their own account but at the actors' disposal. They are there for them to play with. I found one unit particularly apposite -

CERVANTES

Unit?

SHAKESPEARE

Don't you know the phrase?

CERVANTES

No.

SHAKESPEARE

A useful term. Just as an act is made up of scenes, so scenes are made up of units. That's to say passages - long or short - in which a single objective is paramount.

CERVANTES

Objective?

SHAKESPEARE

Point to be made, action to be achieved.

CERVANTES

It all sounds very technical.

SHAKESPEARE

It is.

CERVANTES

But what was it you found particularly apposite?

SHAKESPEARE

Don Quixote's sonnet.

CERVANTES

His nonsense verses up in the mountains?

SHAKESPEARE

No. His defence of himself as a latter-day knight-errant to everyone at the inn. That sudden change from overblown prose into modest verse matched his aspirations. He still looked absurd, of course, but suddenly he sounded like a perfect, gentle knight. It was a genuine transformation and I was thrilled - goose-pimpled all down my back, always a good sign. The Sancho, inevitably, went too far occasionally, but then what comic doesn't? In that he reminded me not so much of Bob Armin as of Will Kemp who could never, ever, resist an ad lib. The trouble we had with him. To be honest I was glad when he finally left the company.

CERVANTES

The Cardenio did well, I thought?

SHAKESPEARE

A clever actor, yes. And as for the Dorotea, well, we agreed about her from the start, didn't we?

CERVANTES

We did.

SHAKESPEARE

Mm. Thanks to her handling of the denouement - together with the clever casting of Fernando - they got round the Bertram problem. Something I singularly failed to resolve -

CERVANTES

In *All's Well, that Ends Well*?

SHAKESPEARE

Oh, no, don't tell me you've read *that*, too?

CERVANTES

I quite liked it. Though I agree your hero Bertram was a pain in the neck.

SHAKESPEARE

Frankly, I wish I'd never written the play. Do you have works you'd willingly forego? Suppress? Disinherit?

CERVANTES

No, I've never had to bother. Posterity's done that for me. These days I'm only really remembered for *Don Quixote* whereas the world can't stop reviving everything of yours. Why, even your lost scripts get ghost-written - look at this one. And if that sounds jealous, William, I am. But then I've told you about me and the theatre. As for your Bertram - he struck me as a thoroughly Mediterranean young man. If anything even more unthinkingly macho than my Fernando.

SHAKESPEARE

Yes. And that's the problem - dramatically. How - within the conventions of what we used to call comedy - do you pair off selfish, arrogant young men with unselfish, modest young women? And convince an audience they'll live happily ever after? At least tonight your Fernando looked young enough to be forgivable. And your Dorotea was beautiful enough - spiritually, physically - to make me believe for that crucial instant that is the heartfelt climax of any proper play - that given Dorotea that predictable young stud could and would grow up. But in *All's Well, that Ends Well* I'd written myself into so many corners I just couldn't bring it off. Hence the title.

CERVANTES

I like the comma in it. It casts a nice doubt on the proverb's complacency.

SHAKESPEARE

Thank you. I wish I had more readers like you, Don Miguel.

CERVANTES

I must say I did wonder whether the dormant novelist in you was stirring in his sleep as you wrote the play. The settings - the Roussillon, Paris, Florence - cry out to be realised as part and parcel of the story. Do you know the Roussillon, by the way?

SHAKESPEARE

No. Nor Paris. Nor Florence. I simply took the story and its settings from a book of translations from the Italian. It had a good title - *The Palace of Pleasure*.

CERVANTES

I once walked through the Roussillon.

SHAKESPEARE

Why?

CERVANTES

To get to Italy. You follow the Roman road.

SHAKESPEARE

That must've been a long walk?

CERVANTES

It was. But I was young and the law was after me.

SHAKESPEARE

Really? What had you done?

CERVANTES

Killed a man in a duel. And the penalty for that was to have your right hand chopped off.

SHAKESPEARE

So you fled the country?

CERVANTES

And joined the army. And a couple of years later lost this hand instead.

He laughs, indicating his maimed left hand.

SHAKESPEARE

I'm sure the irony wasn't lost on you, Don Miguel?

CERVANTES

No, nor the pain of it.

SHAKESPEARE

What was the duel about? A woman?

CERVANTES

Yes. My sister. My opponent had called her a whore. And that's an insult you can't let pass, can you? Even if it happens to be true which in Andrea's case it was, I regret to say now - though I couldn't then. But there you are that's life and honour for you - or should I say for us? In our time?

SHAKESPEARE

For some it was, certainly.

CERVANTES

Not for you?

SHAKESPEARE

No. I managed to steer clear of that sort of trouble.

CERVANTES

Clever of you.

SHAKESPEARE

So I thought. But now I wonder. The more you tell me of yourself, Don Miguel, the more I think I should perhaps have lived more and written less.

CERVANTES

Rubbish! Leave action to young idiots like I was. And your Bertram.

They laugh.

CERVANTES

Perhaps we should be going?

SHAKESPEARE

I suppose we should. I could offer you a drink at the Garrick? May I?

CERVANTES

Thank you. I'd like that.

SHAKESPEARE

I'm what they call an honorary member. The porters turn a blind eye to Jessop - that's to say they feed him potato crisps and brown ale - shamelessly.

Jessop wags everything in happy anticipation.

CERVANTES
  Who was Garrick?
SHAKESPEARE
  A great actor and founder of the Shakespeare tourist industry.
  He organised a jubilee for me at Stratford in 1769. All London
  came. He didn't put on any of my plays there but he did recite
  an ode in praise of me to great effect. And the firework display
  at the end was splendid, despite the rain.
CERVANTES
  Do I hear voices?

He has. They are Bill's and Lily's off.

SHAKESPEARE
  Time to go. Once and for all.
CERVANTES
  Indeed. So it would seem.

They go off - opposite prompt side. That is to say stage right, but,
from our point of view, stage left.

SHAKESPEARE
  (off) Heel, Jessop. After you, Don Miguel.
CERVANTES
  (off) No, after you, William.

At their jointly courteous departure the lighting's changed - from
warm other-worldliness to off-peak economy mode. Enter Lily.
She carries a bedding roll, a sleeping bag and a thermos flask of
tea.

LILY
  There's no one here, Bill.
BILL
  (off) I'm sure there was. I heard voices.
LILY
  You can't have. (looks round again) No. Nothing. No one.

Enter Bill, also with a bedding roll and sleeping bag.

BILL
  It wasn't just voices I heard. There was a dog. It barked.

He too looks around. Lily doesn't any more. Instead she puts
down the thermos and then spreads out her bedding roll and
sleeping bag.

LILY
  Bill?
BILL
  (turning back to her) Yes?
LILY
  Let's get real, shall we? (grin) Your bag or mine?

Bill laughs, drops his stuff beside hers.

BILL
  Yours - for a start. It's bigger.

Lily laughs, kicks off her trainers.

LILY
  Right.

She slips out of her jeans.

LILY
  No more imagining. Us now. You and me.

Bill agrees. Pulls off his sweatshirt.

This time I think it best if I now dim the working light to black so
that Lily and Bill can enjoy their improvised pleasures in private.
After all, they've made this black box their home - at least for the
three week run of the play - while they look for a new bed-sit.
They couldn't keep up with the rent on their old one just off the
Mile End Road gone posh. They're now hoping against hope that
Shakespeare's Don Quixote will transfer, at least for a limited season,
somewhere more central than the Pump House. Perhaps even -
you never know - to the West End? If that happened - Heaven!
They'd get two Equity minimum wages between them (Bill, with
luck, might even qualify for a bit above) and they'd be able to put

down a month's rent in advance, and the same again as caution money, on another place to call their own. At Acton North, say, or Dagenham East - anywhere with a Tube line handy. Fantasy may be their chosen career but, as we've seen, they are a practical young couple. So let's wish them - and the play - all the luck in the world - the real world - and make our own ways home. To somewhere I hope more comfortable than the stage floor of The Pump House.

Postscript

I sneaked back the other day - just to see how things were going. The front of the building's been transformed. The company's hung out a big flag - bright yellow with Picasso's iconic sketch of Quixote and Sancho under a childlike sun on it. Plus a huge banner with the title, red on white, all along it. It looks great, brave, hopeful. And they've put out masses of photos from the show - the one of Don Quixote with the Stuffed Vulture on the plastic rock has been blown up to a metre square! The others are more modest - roughly A2 or A3, I'd say. As for quotes from the reviews - well - we got three from the dailies, but only one from the sundays, and whoever that reviewer was came on the second night - so, let me put it like this: Bill and Lily have done some expert promotion, selecting the best bits from the reviews, omitting the worst - editing most creatively. For example, they've splashed the Guardian twice: first it says: *an ingenious evening* but they've missed out: *that ultimately raises more questions than it answers*. And then they've achieved: - *lively even brilliant* from the same review by losing the preceding qualification: *Intermittently*. From the Telegraph they high-light: *Full of infectious fun, knockabout energy ... ingeniously staged on a shoestring ... surprisingly versatile lighting design...* only to suppress what follows: *...but not exactly Shakespeare, alas*. As for the Times they've only managed to extract *...effective reconstruction of lost Jacabean crowd pleaser* from a litany of nit-pickings. Clearly, unlike William Shakespeare, this reviewer is no lover of rough theatre. Or perhaps of theatre at all?

But Bill and Lily's craftiest efforts have been applied to the Independent on Sunday. Here they present an ideal notice with a vengeance; unmissably placed slam-bang to your right as you enter the theatre. First to catch your eye is a photo (inset) of Dorotea as first seen with her hair down, bathing her bare feet in the mirror pool. What a looker! Then, your unregenerate heart having missed at least two beats, you can read this: *...an astonishing evening... the finest adaptation of Don Quixote I've ever seen... a revelation... breath-taking... a theatrical experience to treasure... I laughed till I cried, cried till I laughed.*

I won't spell out word for word what all the dot, dot, dots stand in place of, except to say that the critic in question was, in fact, comparing our show - not at all to our advantage - with another stage version of *Don Quixote* she'd seen recently in French-speaking Canada. A spectacular five hour epic apparently, entitled *A bas Quichotte!* Reading her review at breakfast last Sunday I must admit I choked with rage on my toast and marmalade. Her comparisons weren't just odious they were otiose. Even so, I'm afraid it could be argued that here, Bill and Lily have gone too far. Let's hope the Independent's lawyers advise against action on the grounds that fringe outfits like ours aren't worth the hassle.

Oh! Stop press! Breaking news! Here's Bill coming out with a new blow-up. And this one - from the look of it - is a straight quote. No disingenuous dots, just honest commas. Yes! It's a rave from Time Out. Hey! It says: *Knockout classic fun, this show's your genuine don't miss, make tracks, go see, like it's the real, real thing! An event!*

And now, by happy coincidence, people are beginning to arrive. On foot, by bike, by car, by taxi. And they're crowding into the Pump House - no, they're not! - they're spilling out as a queue. They've got to queue for tickets at the box office! Which isn't your usual glass-fronted cubby hole but a wobbly trestle table from which it's Fernando's turn to sell tickets. Cash only. We don't do plastic. He's as amazed as I am. And now the phone's ringing non-stop. At this rate we'll soon have to put out the *House Full* sign. Have we got one? Hey, no sooner hoped for than done! By Lily, who's propping it up outside. Only it doesn't say House Full; it prefers the exploitative romance of *Returns Only Tonight.* And she's so full of smiles, I really do think she must have heard something that seems to suggest the show may have a future after its run here. Mind you, back-stage rumours are often wishful thinking but then again, who knows? Who knows?